A GUIDED TOUR OF HELL . . .

Below them in the dungeon, behind thick iron bars set into stone, were scores of creatures bearing only a passing resemblance to men and women. Their clothes were torn and filthy, stained with blood. Some were completely covered with hair, looking like rabid, snarling beasts. They hurled themselves against the iron bars and howled like wolves. Some attacked each other, jaws snapping, claws slashing, and a few had fallen and were being greedily devoured by others in their cells. Still others looked almost normal, except for their emaciated appearance, their hollow, staring eyes devoid of any sanity, and their abnormally long and pointed canine teeth, visible as they opened their mouths to emit throat-rending screams and thrust their hands out through the bars.

"Here is the solution to your case, gentlemen!" Dracula shouted over the uproar. "The dawn of a new race! The new breed brought forth by my creator!"

"Enjoyable action adventure." —*Fantasy Review*

8 TIMEWARS

THE DRACULA CAPER

SIMON HAWKE

ACE BOOKS, NEW YORK

For Adele Leone and Richard Monaco

This book is an Ace
original edition, and has never
been previously published.

THE DRACULA CAPER

An Ace Book / published by arrangement with
the author

PRINTING HISTORY
Ace edition / October 1988

ISBN: 0-441-16616-4

Ace Books are published by
The Berkley Publishing Group,
200 Madison Avenue, New York, New York 10016
The name ''ACE'' and the ''A'' logo
are trademarks belonging to Charter Communications, Inc.
PRINTED IN THE UNITED STATES OF AMERICA

10 9 8 7 6 5 4 3 2 1

A CHRONOLOGICAL HISTORY OF THE TIME WARS

April 1, 2425:   Dr. Wolfgang Mensinger invents the chronoplate at the age of 115, discovering time travel. Later he would construct a small-scale working prototype for use in laboratory experiments specially designed to avoid any possible creation of a temporal paradox. He is hailed as the "Father of Temporal Physics."

July 14, 2430:   Mensinger publishes "There is No Future," in which he redefines relativity, proving that there is no such thing as *the* future, but an infinite number of potential future scenarios which are absolute relative only to their present. He also announces the discovery of "non-specific time" or temporal limbo, later known as "the dead zone."

October 21, 2440:   Wolfgang Mensinger dies. His son, Albrecht, perfects the chronoplate and carries on the work, but loses control of the discovery to political interests.

June 15, 2460:   Formation of the international Committee for Temporal Intelligence, with Albrecht Mensinger as director. Specially trained and conditioned "agents" of the committee begin to travel back through time in order to conduct research and field test the chronoplate apparatus. Many become lost in transition, trapped in the limbo of nonspecific time known as "the dead zone." Those who return from successful temporal voyages often bring back startling information necessitating the revision of historical records.

March 22, 2461:	*The Consorti Affair*—Cardinal Lodovico Consorti is excommunicated from the Roman Catholic Church for proposing that agents travel back through time to obtain empirical evidence that Christ arose following His crucifixion. The Consorti Affair sparks extensive international negotiations amidst a volatile climate of public opinion concerning the proper uses for the new technology. Temporal excursions are severely curtailed. Concurrently, espionage operatives of several nations infiltrate the Committee for Temporal Intelligence.
May 1, 2461:	Dr. Albrecht Mensinger appears before a special international conference in Geneva, composed of political leaders and members of the scientific community. He attempts to alleviate fears about the possible misuses of time travel. He further refuses to cooperate with any attempts at militarizing his father's discovery.
February 3, 2485:	The research facilities of the Committee for Temporal Intelligence are seized by troops of the TransAtlantic Treaty Organization.
January 25, 2492:	The Council of Nations meets in Buenos Aires, capital of the United Socialist States of South America, to discuss increasing international tensions and economic instability. A proposal for "an end to war in our time" is put forth by the chairman of the Nippon Conglomerate Empire. Dr. Albrecht Mensinger, appearing before the body as nominal director of the Committee for Temporal Intelligence, argues pas-

sionately against using temporal technology to resolve international conflicts, but cannot present proof that the past can be affected by temporal voyagers. Prevailing scientific testimony reinforces the conventional wisdom that the past is an immutable absolute.

December 24, 2492: Formation of the Referee Corps, brought into being by the Council of Nations as an extranational arbitrating body with sole control over temporal technology and authority to stage temporal conflicts as "limited warfare" to resolve international disputes.

April 21, 2493: On the recommendation of the Referee Corps, a subordinate body named the Observer Corps is formed, taking over most of the functions of the Committee for Temporal Intelligence, which is redesignated as the Temporal Intelligence Agency. Under the aegis of the Council of Nations and the Referee Corps, the TIA absorbs the intelligence agencies of the world's governments and is made solely answerable to the Referee Corps. Dr. Mensinger resigns his post to found the Temporal Preservation League, a group dedicated to the abolition of temporal conflict.

June, 2497–
March, 2502: Referee Corps presides over initial temporal confrontation campaigns, accepting "grievances" from disputing nations, selecting historical conflicts of the past as "staging grounds" and supervising the infiltration of modern troops into the so-called "cannon fodder" ranks of ancient warring armies. Initial numbers of temporal combatants are kept small, with infiltration facili-

tated by cosmetic surgery and implant conditioning of soldiers. The results are calculated based upon successful return rate and a complicated "point spread." Soldiers are monitored via cerebral implants, enabling Search & Retrieve teams to follow their movements and monitor mortality rate. The media dubs temporal conflicts the "Time Wars."

2500–2510: Extremely rapid growth of massive support industry catering to the exacting art and science of temporal conflict. Rapid improvements in international economic climate follows, with significant growth in productivity and rapid decline in unemployment and inflation rate. There is a gradual escalation of the Time Wars with the majority of the world's armed services converting to temporal duty status.

Growth of the Temporal Preservation League as a peace movement with an intensive lobby effort and mass demonstrations against the Time Wars. Mensinger cautions against an imbalance in temporal continuity due to the increasing activity of the Time Wars.

September 2, 2514: Mensinger publishes his "Theories of Temporal Relativity," incorporating his solution to the Grandfather Paradox and calling once again for a cease-fire in the Time Wars. The result is an upheaval in the scientific community and a hastily reconvened Council of Nations to discuss his findings, leading to the Temporal Strategic Arms Limitations Talks of 2515.

March 15, 2515– *June 1, 2515:*	T-SALT held in New York City. Mensinger appears before the representatives at the sessions and petitions for an end to the Time Wars. A cease-fire resolution is framed, but tabled due to lack of agreement among the members of the Council of Nations. Mensinger leaves the T-SALT a broken man.
November 18, 2516:	Dr. Albrecht Mensinger experiences total nervous collapse shortly after being awarded the Benford Prize.
December 25, 2516:	Dr. Albrecht Mensinger commits suicide. Violent demonstrations by members of the Temporal Preservation League.
January 1, 2517:	Militant members of the Temporal Preservation League band together to form the Timekeepers, a terrorist offshoot of the League, dedicated to the complete destruction of the war machine. They announce their presence to the world by assassinating three members of the Referee Corps and bombing the Council of Nations meeting in Buenos Aires, killing several heads of state and injuring many others.
September 17, 2613:	Formation of the First Division of the U.S. Army Temporal Corps as a crack commando unit following the successful completion of a "temporal adjustment" involving the first serious threat of a timestream split. The First Division, assigned exclusively to deal with threats to temporal continuity, is designated as "the Time Commandos."

October 10, 2615: Temporal physicist Dr. Robert Darkness disappears without a trace shortly after turning over to the army his new invention, the "warp grenade," a combination time machine and nuclear device. Establishing a secret research installation somewhere off Earth, Darkness experiments with temporal translocation based on the transmutation principle. He experiments upon himself and succeeds in translating his own body into tachyons, but an error in his calculations causes an irreversible change in his sub-atomic structure, rendering it unstable. Darkness becomes "the man who is faster than light."

•

November 3, 2620: The chronoplate is superceded by the temporal transponder. Dubbed the "warp disc," the temporal transponder was developed from work begun by Dr. Darkness and it drew on power tapped by Einstein-Rosen Generators (developed by Bell Laboratories in 2545) bridging to neutron stars.

March 15, 2625: *The Temporal Crisis:* The discovery of an alternate universe following an unsuccessful invasion by troops of the Special Operations Group, counterparts of the Time Commandos. Whether as a result of chronophysical instability caused by clocking tremendous amounts of energy through Einstein-Rosen Bridges or the cumulative effect of temporal disruptions, an alternate universe comes into congruence with our own, causing an instability in the timeflow of both universes and resulting in a "confluence effect," wherein the timestreams of both universes ripple and occasionally intersect, creating "confluence points" where a crossover from one universe to another becomes possible.

Massive amounts of energy clocked through Einstein-Rosen Bridges has resulted in unintentional "warp bombardment" of the alternate universe, causing untold destruction. The Time Wars escalate into a temporal war between two universes.

PROLOGUE ─────────

> *His is the House of pain.*
> *His is the Hand that makes.*
> *His is the Hand that wounds.*
> *His is the Hand that heals.*
> —H. G. Wells, *The Island of Dr. Moreau*

Janos Volkov was curled up, shivering, on one of the benches in Whitechapel Station, waiting for the change. He always knew when it was about to come; he always dreaded it. There was no cure short of death and he could no more kill himself than he could disregard the programmed imperatives locked within the cybernetic implant in his brain.

The East London Railway platforms were deserted at this late hour in this far from the best of neighborhoods. The platform was built around an open cutting, between strong retaining walls of cool, damp stone. The roof was high, to allow for the dispersion of the fumes given off by the steam engines. Covered gaps at the top allowed the steam to escape. Giant cast-iron ribs supported the roof and large stone archways spanning the tracks served to brace the walls. The underground was still relatively new, not quite twenty years old, but like most of the soot-blackened city, the stations and the tunnels had already taken on the appearance of great age, resembling catacombs with tracks running through them.

As Volkov huddled on the platform bench in foetal position, sweating and racked with fever spasms alternating with chills, the train pulled into the station, making its last scheduled run of the day. A few passengers got off. Several of them glanced at Volkov with disgust as they passed and quickly looked away. A tall and well-dressed gentleman in a black inverness and top hat made a brief comment to his companion about how something should be done about the drunken derelicts cluttering up the city, though in this neighborhood, such a sight was not at all unusual. Neither gentleman seemed to have any objection to the derelict women walking the streets of Whitechapel, whose favors they had come seeking. Volkov ignored them. He barely even heard them. There was a roaring in his ears and he hugged himself tightly, his teeth chattering. His teeth were unusually long and sharp, especially the canines. He was not a tall man, but he was powerfully built, not at all the sort of physical development one would expect to accompany the dissipation of advanced alcoholism. But then, Janos Volkov was not an alcoholic.

As the last of the passengers left the platform, the measured footsteps of a police constable echoed throughout the once again deserted station as he approached the huddled figure on the bench. Constable Jones was on his way home to his wife after a long day of walking his beat. He had missed the train and he was irritated. He stood over the shivering form for a moment, his hands clasped behind his back, clutching a small truncheon as he rocked back on his heels.

"'Ello, 'ello," he said in a strong Cockney accent. "Wot's this then, eh? Go on with ya, old sod, ya can't sleep 'ere."

There was no reaction from the shivering man curled up on the bench.

"'Ere, move along now," said Constable Jones, tapping Volkov lightly on the soles of his boots with his truncheon. The touch of the truncheon seemed to send a galvanizing charge through Volkov. He jerked and thrashed on the bench, as if in the throes of an epileptic fit. A low growl escaped his throat.

"'Ere, none o' that, now," said the policeman, raising his voice. "Get on with ya. Move along, I said."

He prodded Volkov in the side.

Volkov jerked around with a snarl. The policeman's eyes grew wide and his jaw dropped as he backed away involuntarily, staring at the wild, yellowish eyes, the snarling mouth flecked with foam, the face all covered with hair, the long, protruding teeth. . . .

Volkov crouched on the edge of the bench, growling low in his throat, his clawed hands digging into the wood, his eyes staring at the policeman with a baleful glare. His unruly grey hair hung down to his shoulders, which were hunched as he crouched upon the bench, his legs bent under him, prepared to spring.

"'Ere you," said Jones, swallowing hard and backing away from him fearfully, "you stop that, now, understand?"

Volkov leaped.

Constable Jones had enough presence of mind to drop down to the ground, ducking beneath the leap, which carried Volkov several yards past him. He grabbed for the whistle on the end of his lanyard, brought it to his lips, and blew three shrill blasts in rapid succession. Volkov crouched several yards away from him, growling like a beast, his teeth bared in a snarl, saliva dribbling down onto his chest. The policeman turned and ran.

Moving with astonishing speed, Volkov sprang after him and caught him before Jones had run ten feet. He leaped and brought him down hard to the stone floor of the platform, his claws digging deep into the policeman's shoulders. Constable Jones cried out and rolled over beneath him, fighting for his life. He made a fist and struck Volkov in the face with all his might, but the blow had almost no effect. With a roar, Volkov raised his right hand, fingers hooked like talons, and brought it down in a slashing motion across the constable's face.

Jones screamed as the long claws opened up his face from his left temple to the right side of his jawbone. And then the snarling mouth plunged down. Sharp teeth fastened in his throat, ripping it open, severing the jugular and sending a fountain of arterial blood spurting out into Volkov's savage face. The policeman's frenzied screams became a horrible gurgle and then there was no sound at all except for the sounds of Volkov feeding.

Inspector Grayson pulled back the bloody sheet, allowing his companion to inspect the body lying on the table in the morgue. Unlike the sallow, thin-featured and clean-shaven Grayson, he was robust, thirty-five years old, six feet tall and broad-shouldered, with a tanned complexion, thinning dark hair and a thick, bushy, dark moustache. He examined the wounds in a professional manner.

"The constable's name was Jones," said Grayson. "Allan Jones. Worked out of Bishop's Gate Station. He was a good lad, according to his sergeant, strong, alert, not one to dawdle about. The body was discovered on the Whitechapel platform by a . . ." He paused to consult his notebook. ". . . a Mr. Randall Jarvis, track maintenance engineer for the East London Railway. The time of discovery was approximately four a.m. Apparently, there were no witnesses. What do you make of the wounds, Doctor?"

"Interesting," said the large man in the tweed suit. He reached into the pocket of his jacket and removed a large bowled briar. He took out a rolled leather pouch filled with shag tobacco and started to pack his pipe.

"Those slash marks across his face," said Grayson, "and the way the throat's been torn open, suggest to me some sort of sharp, pronged instrument. Like one of those garden tools, you know, what the devil do you call it?"

"A garden fork?" the doctor said, puffing his pipe alight. "No, I shouldn't think so. Something like that would tear the flesh a great deal more than this and the force with which the assailant would have had to strike should have left a bruise at the initial point of entry. Unless the instrument was filed to the sharpness of a razor. Still, that would seem unlikely, especially given the manner in which the throat was torn out. The same instrument clearly did not create both wounds."

"What the devil would have done it, then?" said Grayson.

"Unlikely as it may seem," his companion said, staring at the body and puffing out a cloud of strong Turkish tobacco smoke, "the character of the wounds would seem to indicate an animal of some sort. Those seem to be claw marks across the face of the deceased and the throat appears to have been torn open by teeth. Observe also the markings on the shoulders."

"An animal!" said Grayson. "The devil you say! What sort of animal? A rabid hound, perhaps?"

"Unlikely. If it was a hound, then it would need to be a very large one indeed. Note the spacing of the marks upon the deceased's face. Imagine the size of the paw that would have made those wounds. However, you'll notice that there are *five* slash marks. A dog has only four claws on its forepaw and they are hardly sharp enough to create wounds such as these.''

"What then?" Grayson said. "A jungle cat? Some animal escaped from a circus or the zoo?"

"Again, not very likely, for the same reason I've just mentioned. The number of claws would be insufficient. Besides, there have been no recent reports of any such animals escaping from the zoological gardens and at present, there are no circuses in town. Look here."

He made a claw of his right hand and positioned it over the wounds.

"Good Lord!" said Grayson. "Surely you're not suggesting that a *human* hand could have done that!"

"A hand not unlike a human's, at the very least. You see, Grayson? An opposed thumb is called for. It is possible that a great ape might have done it, one of the larger primates, such as an orangutan. I believe there is such a creature at the Zoological Gardens. However, there have been no reports of its escaping, though it would be simple enough to make an inquiry. Even so, it would seem highly unlikely that such a creature could manage to make its way from Regent's Park to Whitechapel unobserved by anyone. It is a curious matter, indeed."

"A bloody headache, is what it is," said Grayson. "Something like this could get entirely out of hand. What would your Mr. Sherlock Holmes have made of this?"

Conan Doyle smiled. "I was waiting for you to ask me that," he said. "Somehow, I did not think that it was only my medical expertise that you were seeking. Those damned stories have become something of a nuisance for me."

"Come now, Doctor," Grayson said, "surely you can employ some of this art of deduction that you write of so convincingly to cast some light upon this case. After all, the creator of a detective as brilliant as Sherlock Holmes must surely possess some of his abilities."

"You flatter me, Inspector," said Conan Doyle. "However, Sherlock Holmes is dead and dead he shall remain. I have had such an overdose of him that I feel towards him as I do towards *pâté de foie gras,* of which I once ate too much, so that the name of it gives me a sickly feeling to this day. I tossed him over the falls at Reichenbach and there's an end to him. And although I must admit that assisting Scotland Yard in an actual case intrigues me, it would do much to increase the already intolerable clamor for more of my stories about Holmes if word of this were to get out."

Grayson cleared his throat uncomfortably. "Yes, well, with all due respect, Dr. Doyle," he said, "perhaps in that case you will understand why I would very much appreciate it if this consultation were to remain strictly unofficial. Soliciting your opinion as a medical man is one thing, however—"

"Consulting a writer of popular fiction would be quite another," Conan Doyle said. "I quite understand. The slant the newspapers would give to such a consultation could prove somewhat embarrassing to Scotland Yard. And it would be no less embarrassing to me, come to think of it, if I proved unable to assist you in any way." He chuckled and clapped the man on the shoulder. "You can set your mind at ease, Grayson. We shall keep this matter strictly between ourselves."

Grayson sighed gratefully. "I'm so glad you understand, Doctor. Frankly, I must admit that I am baffled by this case. And if, as you suggest, we are indeed faced with some wild animal running about loose in the East End, there could be widespread panic. Something must be done and quickly."

"Well, let us see what Constable Jones has to tell us about his assailant," Conan Doyle said, bending down over the body. "Hold my pipe a moment, will you, Grayson? Thank you. Now, it would seem reasonable to assume that a stout young man like Jones would not surrender his life meekly. He would certainly have struggled. Therefore, it is entirely possible that if we were to examine underneath his fingernails . . . ah, what have we here?"

"What is it?" Grayson said, leaning forward intently.

"If you would be so kind," said Conan Doyle, pointing, "I noticed a small wooden box beside that microscope there on the counter, undoubtedly it holds some glass slides. No, no, bring the entire box, please. The slide must be quite clean. Thank you. Ah, yes, perfect. Now, we shall place our find upon this slide here . . ."

"What is it," said Grayson, bending over and squinting at the slide. "Hair?"

"So it would appear," said Conan Doyle. "Now, the question is, what *sort* of hair?"

"Can you tell just by looking at it through the microscope?" said Grayson.

"To some extent," said Conan Doyle. "I have studied zoology and there are certain differences to be observed between human and animal hair, coarseness of the fibre, for example, the thickness of the shaft . . . let's see now, ah, there we have it." He peered into the microscope. "It has been some time since I have observed various samples of animal hair through a microscope while at Edinburgh University, but I am fortunate in that I possess an excellent memory. I had given some thought to writing a monograph upon the subject, but . . . well! That *is* curious!"

"What is it, Doctor?" Grayson said. "What do you see?"

"See for yourself," said Conan Doyle.

Grayson squinted through the eyepiece, then straightened up with an apologetic shrug. "I never studied zoology," he said. "I couldn't tell that bit of hair from one plucked out of my own head."

"If that sample *had* been obtained from your own head," said Conan Doyle, "I would be tempted to make a most unorthodox diagnosis of your condition, Grayson. In that event, I would suspect that you were suffering from a disease generally regarded as a form of insanity."

"And what disease would that be, Doctor?"

"Lycanthropy, Inspector Grayson. The belief that one is capable of becoming a wolf or, more specifically, a legendary creature known in folklore as a werewolf."

1 ————————————————

The man who came to the door of 7 Mornington Place in northwest London was of medium build, with blue eyes, light brown hair parted neatly on the side and a large, full and slightly drooping moustache that somehow did not quite seem to fit his boyish face. His eyes were expressive and alert as he gazed past Amy Robbins at the three strangers on his doorstep. They were well dressed, two men and a young woman. One man was clean-shaven, with angular features, blond hair and a hooked nose. The other was heavyset, muscular, with dark red hair and a full beard. The woman was very blond, statuesque, with an erect carriage and a very striking face.

"These people insist on speaking with you," Amy Robbins said. "I have told them you were very busy—"

"That's all right, Jane," he said, using her pet name. "How may I help you?"

"Mr. Wells?" said Finn Delaney.

"I am H. G. Wells. We have not met before?"

"No, sir, we haven't. My name is Finn Delaney. This is Mr. Creed Steiger and this is Miss Andre Cross. We have come a long way to speak with you on a matter of some importance. It concerns your writing. We understand that you are a busy man and we are quite prepared to compensate you for your time."

"Well, I must say, your offer is appreciated, but quite unnecessary. Do come in."

8

They entered the modest, but comfortable rooms. "May I offer you some tea?" said Wells.

"Please don't trouble yourself, Mr. Wells," said Steiger. "We won't take up much of your time."

"No trouble at all. Please, come this way."

He led them to a small and tidy study, filled with bookshelves and a writing desk. The desk had some papers spread out on it and a wastebasket beside the desk was filled with crumpled paper. Several of the crumpled sheets had missed the wastebasket.

"I have been busy writing articles for the *Pall Mall Gazette*," said Wells, picking up the errant litter. "Merely some light sketches, dialogues and essays, an occasional book review . . . excuse me, you are American, are you not?"

"Yes, Mr. Delaney and I are from the States," said Steiger. "Miss Cross is originally from southwest France."

"I see. Again, how may I help you? You mentioned something about my writing. I am astonished that anyone in America could be familiar with it. I have only recently begun my journalistic career."

"We were not quite so much interested in your articles for the *Gazette*," said Andre, "as in a story you once wrote called 'The Chronic Argonauts.'"

"Good God!" said Wells, sitting back with surprise. "That was some seven years ago! It was printed in the *Science Schools Journal*. I was only twenty-one at the time and woefully incompetent at writing fiction. I abandoned it after only three installments because I realized that it was hopeless and that I could not go on with it." He shook his head. "The story was clumsily invented and loaded with irrelevant sham significance, an entirely inept romance with the most absurd, rococo title. What possible interest could you have in it?"

Steiger spoke carefully. "Well, actually, Mr. Wells, it was not the story itself so much as the idea that intrigued us. The idea of traveling through time, that is. We are academicians of a sort, specializing in the sciences, and as such, our reading tends to be quite diversified. We were struck by the fascinating combination of ingredients in your story, philosophy, science, fiction. . . ."

"Science fiction," said Wells, pursing his lips thoughtfully. He smiled. "Something of a contradiction in terms, is it not?

You know, it's interesting that you should say that, because lately I have been giving a good deal of thought to writing some short fictional pieces with a sort of scientific slant. My editor, Harry Cust, mentioned that Lewis Hind, the literary editor of the *Gazette*'s supplement, the *Budget,* might be interested in just that sort of thing. Short pieces that can be read in one sitting, you know. I had even given some thought to resurrecting that old story you just mentioned, rewriting it perhaps, with an entirely different slant.''

"How did you happen to come by it?" said Andre. "I mean, what suggested it to you?"

Wells frowned. "I honestly don't recall, Miss Cross. You see, for years, I had been seeking rare and precious topics, 'Rediscovery of the Unique!' 'The Universe Rigid!' The more I was rejected, the higher my shots had flown. All the time, as it turned out, I had been shooting over the target. All I had to do was lower my aim—and hit. To be quite honest, I found the secret only recently in a book by J. M. Barrie, called *When a Man's Single.* One of the characters in Barrie's book spoke of a friend of his who managed to sell articles based upon the most insignificant and everyday occurrences—the repairing of a pipe, the selling of a pair of old flower pots to a hawker, that sort of thing—and I realized that here was the formula for my salvation. I had been quite ill, you see, and my incapacity forced me into giving up my teaching and looking elsewhere for my livelihood. Writing seemed to be the only recourse for a man in my condition. Thankfully, I am much improved now, but things have come to such a pass that I am presently earning more money with my articles than I ever did in my class-teaching days. It all started with a simple little piece on staying at the seaside and I've been dashing them off ever since. Apparently, people like to read that sort of nonsense. Frankly, I am both amused and astonished that my work should have attracted some scholarly interest . . . but 'The Chronic Argonauts,' of all things! How on earth did you manage to stumble upon it?''

"Our library collects a wide variety of periodicals, Mr. Wells," Delaney said. "We were quite intrigued by what you might call some of the metaphysical implications in your story, unfinished though it was. We were anxious to discuss some of your ideas with you and, when circumstances brought us to

England, we thought we would try to look you up.''

Wells shook his head and chuckled. ''Metaphysics? I am afraid that I cannot be of much help to you people in your . . . uh, researches. I have some slight scientific training, true, but the idea of traveling through time is ludicrous, of course. Only a crank would take such a thing seriously.''

He paused for a moment and cleared his throat uneasily. ''Of course, I am not suggesting for a moment that you are cranks, you understand. Who is to say what strange courses will not lead to scientific knowledge? Science is a match that man has just got alight. And it is a curious sensation, now that the preliminary sputter is over and the flame burns up clear, for us to see only our hands illuminated and just a glimpse of ourselves and the patch we stand on visible, and all around us . . . darkness still.'' Wells smiled. ''A slight paraphrase from my own 'Rediscovery of the Unique.' ''

''Has anyone else, that is, besides Mr. Cust at the *Gazette*, spoken to you of such matters?'' said Andre. ''Glimpses into the future of scientific endeavor such as traveling through time or biological experimentation?''

''What manner of biological experimentation?'' Wells said, frowning faintly.

''Well, purely fictional, of course,'' said Andre. ''The sort of thing one might make a story of. Examining the social implications of scientific discoveries, for example.''

''Ah, I see. How very fascinating that a woman should be interested in such things. You are, I perceive, one of these progressive women. Mind you, I entirely approve. Above all, I respect intelligence in women. Especially the intelligence to strive for social reform. I regard the idea of women in the work force, treated equally, as absolutely essential to our progress. But then I perceive that I am straying from your question. No, I do not recall discussing such ideas with anyone in particular. Such things as traveling through time I regard as useful fictional devices, tricks whereby one might pretend to look ahead and see where our present course may lead, as you suggest. However, I must confess that I am still somewhat at a loss as to what your specific interest in all of this may be.''

''Well, there is a . . . colleague of ours,'' said Steiger, ''a Mr. Nikolai Drakov, who has been pursuing some rather, well, I suppose you would think them farfetched experiments in the physical sciences. We thought perhaps you might have met him."

"Drakov. A Russian gentleman?"

Delaney leaned forward intently. "You *have* met him?"

"No, no, I was merely commenting upon the name," said Wells. "No, it is entirely unfamiliar to me. Do you mean to tell me that I have inadvertently touched upon an actual topic of scientific research? With a story such as 'The Chronic Argonauts'? It seems truly difficult to believe."

"Well, not specifically, Mr. Wells," said Delaney. "Let us say that you have strayed close to a somewhat peripheral field of study that our colleague is engaged in. However, it seems to have been purely coincidental."

"Indeed! How very odd! And how very intriguing. Tell me, is it possible that I might meet this Mr. Drakov?"

"Regrettably," said Delaney, "we have no idea of his current whereabouts. You see, Mr. Wells, it is a somewhat delicate matter and, well, if we may speak quite confidentially . . ."

"By all means," said Wells, puzzled.

"Professor Drakov has been pursuing research that is quite esoteric and frankly, more than a little dangerous. It has not been very well received and it has caused him some difficulties that resulted in his disappearance. He had been working very hard, you see, and we have some reason to suspect that he has suffered some distress, a lapse, if you will, which caused him to feel persecuted and, well—"

"You are concerned about your missing colleague, about his health, and you are seeking information as to his whereabouts," said Wells. "And something in what I have written led you to believe that I may have discussed certain ideas with him?"

"Apparently, we were wrong," said Steiger. "We're sorry to have taken up so much of your time, Mr. Wells."

"Think nothing of it," Wells said. "I regret that I could not be of assistance to you, but I have never met the gentleman and this is the first time that I have ever heard his name. You have reason to believe that he may seek me out?"

"We think it's possible that he may come here," said Andre. "And we are quite concerned for him. I suppose it is an unlikely possibility, but if by chance he should contact you, Mr. Wells, he may seem quite lucid, but if you were to humor him, and perhaps inform us confidentially—''

"Without letting him know that I have spoken with you?'' Wells said.

"We merely wish to see that he receives the proper attention,'' Steiger said. "Or to satisfy ourselves that he has fully recovered from his collapse.''

"I see. Well, I suppose there is no harm in it. How long will you remain in London?''

"Until we have completed our inquiries,'' said Steiger. "In any event, we will leave word where we can be reached at the Hotel Metropole, where we are staying.''

"Well, if I should hear from your friend, I will certainly let you know,'' said Wells.

"Thank you,'' said Andre. "And now we really should leave you to your work.''

Wells escorted them out.

"What was that about?'' said Jane, after they had left.

"Most peculiar,'' he said. "Something about a crank professor involved in some sort of mysterious research and disappearing after suffering a breakdown. They thought I might have knowledge of him because of something they had read in one of my stories. Something which apparently by coincidence touched upon the nature of his research. I can't imagine what that might be; they were quite reticent about it. Very strange, indeed.'' He shook his head. "It seems that one of the hazards of the writing profession is that one attracts all manner of disquieting individuals. I must be sure to speak to Cust and instruct him not to give out my address.''

"Well, that was a waste of time,'' said Steiger as they rode in their coach back to the hotel. It would be another year before Frederick Lanchester produced the first English four-wheeled car and Herbert Austin began to build his design in Birmingham. The traffic in London was still predominantly horse-driven, although there were quite a few bicycles and many chose to travel by rail in the underground. The Industrial Revolution was still relatively young.

Finn Delaney took off his top hat, loosened his tie and unbuttoned the bottom of his waistcoat. He looked at Steiger with amazement. "You call having an opportunity to meet *H. G. Wells* a waste of time?''

"I'm not as overwhelmed by literary celebrities as you seem to be," said Steiger wryly, "especially when they're teatime socialists. Besides, I was referring to the fact that we're no closer to finding Drakov than we were when we started this wild goose chase. If you ask me, we're really reaching this time."

"You didn't seem to think so when General Forrester suggested the idea," said Andre. Of the three, she was clearly the most uncomfortable. She did not appreciate the tightly constricted waists of late Victorian female fashions, so necessary to the highly desired "hourglass look." She preferred clothes that provided greater freedom of movement and she found the fashions of the Victorian era too tight in some places and too long and loose in others. She also did not care for the style which called for her to wear her hair up and she absolutely loathed the hats.

"Okay," said Steiger, "I'll admit I thought it was an interesting coincidence that he wrote about time travel in *The Time Machine* and biological experimentation that sounded a bit like genetic engineering in *The Island of Dr. Moreau,* but that doesn't mean Wells had contact with people from the future."

"It's a rather uncomfortable coincidence that the scientist Drakov abducted from the Special Operations Group's genetics project is also named Moreau," said Delaney. "And that the beast-men Wells wrote about happen to resemble some of Moreau's genetically engineered creations. The point is that Wells hasn't yet rewritten 'The Chronic Argonauts.' *The Time Machine* will not be published for another year and *The Island of Dr. Moreau* did not appear until 1896. I think the Old Man was right. We need to satisfy ourselves that there was no temporal contamination involved in Wells' writing those stories."

"And by doing that, temporal contamination is exactly what we risk," said Steiger. He sighed. "Look, don't get me wrong, I respect Forrester and I thought this was a good idea at first, but I think Drakov has become an obsession with him. He once had a chance to kill him and he didn't do it, because he couldn't kill his own son. I'm not blaming him for that; he couldn't have known what it would lead to, but the trouble is he's blaming himself and he won't let up. Something like that has to affect a man's judgment. I don't think contacting Wells was very smart. For all we know, Wells had forgotten all about that story. How do we know he didn't start thinking about it again as a result of our having brought it up? Okay, if that's the case, then no real harm's been done. After all, *The Time Machine* was written and we didn't actually change anything. Maybe all we did was provide some reinforcement. But unnecessary contact with people who are influential in their time periods is risky. Very risky. I think it's better just to have him watched discreetly.''

''We can do that,'' said Delaney, ''but I think it's also important to establish contact. We need to be in a position of maximum effectiveness if Drakov shows up and causes a temporal disruption. Wells is going to become a pivotal figure in this time period. He's going to have contact with people like Einstein, Churchill, Roosevelt and Stalin—''

''As I recall, he found a lot to admire in Stalin,'' Steiger said dryly. ''Only one of history's greatest butchers.''

''We know that,'' Delaney said, ''but Wells didn't. Don't forget, Roosevelt also found a lot to admire in Stalin at first. At the time, a lot of people thought he represented real hope for Russia. Dismissing Wells as a 'teatime socialist' is doing the man a real injustice, Creed. He was against Fascism and he was the first to warn the world of the dangers of atomic warfare. And he also had the nerve to warn Stalin, to his face, that stifling dissent and instituting class warfare would do Russia a great deal of harm. He realized that the United States and the Soviet Union would become the superpowers of the 20th century and he was concerned about the effect of Stalin's policies not only on his own people, but also on world opinion. As Wells saw it, the United States and the Soviet Union had the same long-term goals—social progress—and their means of reaching those goals were also the same—industrialization. It made sense to him that the two nations should work together, only he saw that what Stalin was doing was pushing them further and further apart.''

''He was hopelessly naive,'' said Steiger patiently. ''He was one of those socialists who had this great dream of a world state, a utopia where everybody pulled together in the name of the common good. It always worries me when people start talking about 'the common good.' Once they start talking about it, they haven't got very far to go before they start passing laws for 'the common good.' Unfortunately, no one ever seems to agree on what 'the common good' is. The Council of Nations is a perfect example. A thousand years later and they're still trying to figure it out. That's how the Time Wars came about, remember? Preserve the present, fight your battles in the past; it's for 'the common good.' Notice how well that worked out? Seems to me somebody else in the 20th century had a great idea for a 'world state.' It was what Hitler called the Third Reich, wasn't it?"

"Oh, come on," Delaney said. "Wells wasn't talking about that kind of world state. He dreamed about a race of supermen, a sort of modern Samurai, but he wasn't talking about anything like Hitler's master race. His modern Samurai was an analogy for the type of people *we* are, educated and technologically sophisticated citizens of a democratic society. He foresaw a great deal of what actually did happen, a shrinking world, growing interdependence based on technology. He wrote about it in *When the Sleeper Awakes,* imagining a world in which everything was bigger and more crowded, there was more air transportation, more diversified and bigger economic speculation. He wrote about the future in *A Story of Days to Come* and *A Dream of Armageddon* and *Anticipations.* That 'teatime socialist,' as you call him, that young man who seems so happy right now to have found the secret of writing hack journalism successfully, later saw the future almost as clearly as if he had traveled there himself. Doesn't that make you wonder?"

"Maybe it would if he was a bit more accurate in his predictions," Steiger said. "That socialist 'world state' he was dreaming of, for example. It never did happen."

"Didn't it?" Delaney said. "To someone from this time period, our society might look a great deal like a socialist world state. In his autobiography, Wells wrote that one of the things he wanted most was to see a new form of education, particularly new ways of teaching old subjects. He was the first to envision something he called the subject of Human Ecology, where history wasn't taught from a perspective of memorizing useless facts and dates, but from an analytical standpoint, making it relevant to social movement. As he put it, "the end of all intelligent analysis is to clear the way for synthesis." He felt that only a sound analysis of history could bring it into context with current affairs and enable the forecasting of probable developments. As he put it, looking at life not as a system of consequences, but as a system of constructive effort. He was talking about Futurism, Creed, a field that didn't even begin to come into its own until the late 20th century! He was one of the first writers to recognize that there would be a change brought about in human relationships and human endeavors by increased facilities of communication. When McLuhan said the same thing in the 1960s, everybody thought it was an incredibly original insight. Because he called himself a socialist, Wells has been misjudged by history, criticized as being naive. In fact, he was among the first of the so-called socialists to attack Marxism, because he believed that it was based on a medieval approach, ignoring the use of scientific imagination.

"Look at the world he came from," Delaney said, gesturing outside the coach window. "A society built around a rigid class structure, the beginnings of industrialization in a world where illiteracy was the rule rather than the exception. People in this society were criticized when they tried to rise above their class, their 'station' in life. Wells realized that an industrial society built on a class system would have to wind up exploiting an uneducated working class. In this time period, the only visible alternative to that was socialism. This was a time of labor demonstrations and riots. Wells was responding to the temper of the times. He didn't see how the system of weekly wages employment could change into a method of salary and pension without some sort of national plan of social development. Socialism seemed to offer an answer."

"Share the wealth," said Steiger sarcastically. "From each according to his ability, to each according to his need, is that it? Christ, Finn, don't tell me you're seriously defending that kind of thinking!"

"I'm not. That was the Marxist line. But strictly speaking, labor unions are a socialist concept. Forget the word 'socialist' for a moment. Wells said, 'So long as you suffer any man to call himself your shepherd, sooner or later you will find a crook around your ankle.' Wells looked at America and said, 'The problem of personal freedom is not to be solved by economic fragmentation; the Western farmer lost his independence long since and became the grower of a single special crop, the small shopkeeper either a chain-store minder or a dealer in branded goods, and the small entrepreneur a gambler with his savings and a certain bankrupt in the end.' Are those the words of a Communist or are they the words of someone who already saw the trend towards multinationals?"

"I hadn't realized you were such an authority on Wells," said

Steiger. "You're quoting stuff that wasn't in the mission programming tapes. You couldn't have had time to bone up on his writings just to prepare for this assignment. Why the intense interest?"

"Because it all started with temporal physics. I've never fully understood 'zen physics' and anything that I can't understand tends to drive me crazy," said Delaney.

"Hell, temporal physics drives everybody crazy," Steiger said. "There can't be more than a handful of people who've even got a grip on it. But what does that have to do with H. G. Wells?"

"The idea of temporal physics first appeared in science fiction," said Delaney, "and Wells was one of the first to write what we now know as science fiction. He admitted that he didn't really understand physics, yet in some of his early essays, he was grasping at the same ideas scientists such as Planck and Bohr and Einstein grappled with. In that essay he mentioned to us so casually, 'The Universe Rigid,' he tried to explore the idea of a four-dimensional frame for physical phenomena. He tried to sell it to Frank Harris at the *Fortnightly Review*, but Harris rejected it because he found it incomprehensible and Wells wasn't able to explain it to him because he didn't fully understand it himself. He was reaching, trying to come up with something he called a 'Universal Diagram.' It took a genius like Einstein to formulate those ideas and revolutionize scientific thought, but Wells was already intuitively heading in that direction. He couldn't really see it, but he *knew* something was there.

"Once I realized how far ahead of his time Wells was," Delaney continued, "I became interested and started studying his writings. People tend to think of him as merely a writer of imaginative fiction, but he was much more than that. He was an uncanny forecaster. He predicted Feminism, sexual liberation, Futurism and multinational economy. What Wells called 'socialism' wasn't really all that different from the democratic ideals of America from the late 20th century onward. Women in the work force. Sexual equality. Public education. Labor unions. National health plans. Social Security. What Wells did not realize was that these so-called 'socialist' ideas could exist within the framework of a capitalist society. But imagine how he would have perceived the society *we* came from, where governments don't behave like independent nations so much as like interdependent corporations. Would he have understood the subtle distinctions? I don't think so. The Council of Nations would have seemed like the governing body of a world state to him and, in a way, it almost is. Technological development created a world structured like a spiderweb—touch one strand of the web and you create movement in all the other strands as well. To someone from this time period, it would look like a single entity, a 'world state.' You're focusing on the socialist label, but remember that the socialist of the late 19th century became the liberal of the 20th century. Wells wrote about the unfeasibility of economic fragmentation, but political fragmentation also proved unfeasible. We never did develop exclusively along the lines of socialism or capitalism or libertarianism. What eventually happened was a sort of natural synthesis brought about by technological development and a shrinking economic world. It began in the 20th century, when America started to adopt certain so-called 'socialist' ideas to put them into practice in a democratic society and the Soviet Union began to adopt certain 'capitalist' ideas and put them to work in the framework of a totalitarian, communist society. They were still paying lip service to different ideologies and they were still antagonistic, but the techno-economic matrix was already placing them on a course that would eventually intersect. Not even war could stop it. And that was precisely what Wells predicted, except he didn't use the same terms. Instead of a world state, what we wound up with is a sort of 'world confederation,' because the techno-economic matrix became a more powerful motivating force than any political ideology. It became a political ideology in itself and if you read him carefully, you'll realize that Wells knew it would happen!"

Steiger pursed his lips thoughtfully and sat in silence for a moment, thinking.

"You still think it was a waste of time?" said Andre.

"Maybe not," said Steiger. "And you're right, Finn, it does make me wonder. But the question is, did Wells arrive at his conclusions on his own or did they come about as a result of temporal contamination? And if they did . . . what can we do about it?"

From the outside, the Lyceum Theatre resembled a small Greek temple, with its six tall columns supporting the roof over the entrance. Originally a concert hall, it later housed a circus and Madame Tussaud's first London wax museum. It was the meeting place of the Beefsteak Society and renamed the Theatre Royal Opera House in 1815. After being destroyed by a fire, it was rebuilt and reopened as the Royal Lyceum and English Opera House. In 1871, an unknown actor named Henry Irving was hired to take the leading roles in the productions staged by Col. Hezekiah Bateman. Within a few short years, Irving had taken over the management of the Lyceum and he had become the rage of London, acclaimed as *the* Hamlet, the actor's actor. As he rehearsed the company in his own adaptation of Lord Tennyson's *Becket,* Henry Irving had no idea that he would soon reach the peak of his career by becoming the first actor to receive a knighthood.

"No, no, *no!*" he shouted, storming across the stage and running his hands through his long hair, his long, thin-featured face distraught. "For God's sake, Angeline, you must *project!*"

He said the word "project" as if it were two words, rolling the "r" for emphasis. His strong, mellifluous voice filled the empty theatre.

"You are understudying Miss Ellen Terry! Consider the burden, the *responsibility* that is upon your shoulders! You are *whispering!* No one shall hear you beyond the second row!"

The young blond actress covered her face with her hands. "I'm sorry, Mr. Irving," she said in a small voice. "I . . . I am not feeling very well. I . . ."

She swayed and almost fell. Irving caught her, a sudden expression of concern upon his face. He lifted her chin and looked into her face intently. "Good Lord, Angeline, you're white as a corpse!"

"I am sorry, Mr. Irving," she said, her voice fading. "I fell . . . cold . . . so very cold . . ." She sagged in his arms.

"Angeline!" said Irving, holding her up. "Angeline? Heavens, she's fainted. Stoker! *Stoker!*"

Irving's manager, a large, red-headed man with a pointed beard, came hurrying from the wings.

"Help me with her," Irving said. They gently lowered her to the stage.

"Angeline?" said Stoker. He picked up her hand and patted her wrist. There was no response. He placed his hand upon her forehead, then felt her pulse. "Dear God," he said. "She's dead!"

Irving gazed at him, thunderstruck. *"Dead!"* He shook his head. "No, that's not possible. She merely swooned."

"There is no pulse, I tell you!" said Stoker. He bent down and put his ear close to her mouth and nose. "Nothing. Not a whisper of a breath."

"Mother of God," said Irving. "And I said she was as white as a corpse!" He put his hand to his mouth.

Stoker felt for a pulse in her throat. He shook his head with resignation. "Her heart's stopped beating," he said. "Hello? What's this?"

He pulled aside the lace at her throat. There were two small marks over her jugular vein.

"What is it, Bram?" said Irving.

"Take a look," said Stoker.

"Pinpricks?"

"More like bite marks," Stoker said.

"What?"

"Look how pale she is," said Stoker softly. "White as a corpse," he murmured, repeating Irving's words.

"What are you talking about?" said Irving.

"I am almost afraid to say it," Stoker said. "Perhaps my imagination is merely overactive. But those marks are not imaginary."

"Bram, for God's sake! What is it?"

"Have you read *Carmilla,* by Le Fanu?" Stoker said.

Irving stared at him uncomprehendingly. "What? Sheridan Le Fanu, the novelist? What are you . . ." His voice trailed off as he stared at the marks on Angeline's throat. "You mean that story about a countess who was a—" He caught himself and lowered his voice so that only Stoker could hear him. "—a *vampire?"* He swallowed hard and shook his head. "No, no, that is absurd, a fantasy. Such creatures don't exist."

"How can we say for certain?" Stoker said. "I admit it sounds incredible, Henry, but how else can you explain those marks upon her throat?"

"She must have accidentally stabbed herself with something, a brooch, perhaps."

"Twice? Both times, directly over the jugular vein?"

"No, I have heard enough," said Irving. "I am sending everyone home before you have the entire cast in a panic."

"I do not think that would be wise," said Stoker. "The police will probably want to question everyone."

"The police! Must we have the police?"

"I see no avoiding it," said Stoker. "We have a dead young woman on our hands and no explanation for her demise. The police will have to be called in. An investigation must be made."

Irving passed his hand over his eyes. "Oh, dear Heaven! Very well, Bram, you handle everything. But for God's sake, be careful what you tell them! Please, make no . . . fanciful suggestions. As for myself, I am quite done in by all of this. God, she died in my very arms! If the police wish to speak with me, they can find me at home, but if there is any way it can be avoided—"

"I will handle things, Henry," said Stoker.

"Yes, yes, you'll see to everything, won't you?"

"I always do," said Stoker.

"And for Heaven's sake, no wild theories about . . . you know."

Stoker glanced up at him and then looked back down at the dead girl. "Yes," he said. "I know."

2 ────────────────────────────────

Electricity had come to London, but it had not yet arrived in Limehouse. Westminster Bridge was the first place to receive electric lighting in 1858, but it was not until 1887 that the first station of the Kensington and Knightsbridge Electric Lighting Company was opened. The first large power station started operation in Deptford in 1889; the London Electricity Supply Company was formed and the city was lit electrically from Fleet Street to Aldgate, but it took a long time for electricity to completely replace gas and in 1894, much of London was still illuminated by gaslight. The gas companies were consuming over six million tons of coal per year and the resulting effects could be seen in London's famous fogs. An atmosphere permeated by soot particles had blackened the city's buildings and it was frequently so thick that coach traffic was forced to move at a snail's pace and pedestrian travelers often became lost in their own neighborhoods due to lack of visibility.

The lime kilns around the docks which gave Limehouse its name dated back to the 14th century. It was a center of shipbuilding, a part of the industrial East End. Most of the area's residents were employed in the shipyards and on the docks and most of them were poor. There was a large population of immigrant Chinese, especially around the Limehouse Causeway, where gambling houses and opium dens could be found by those in search of London's more decadent diversions. It was in Limehouse that Sax Rohmer's evil Oriental mastermind, Fu Manchu, made his London headquarters.

Just off the Limehouse Causeway, in a tiny side street that was little more than an alleyway, there was a small apothecary shop owned and operated by an elderly Chinese named Lin Tao. The old man was bowed and wrinkled, with a stringy white beard that reached halfway down his chest and a white braid that hung down his back to his waist. His forehead was high and he always wore a small, embroidered cap, not unlike a Jewish yarmulke. His slanted eyes, rather than giving him the so-called "cruel" aspect stereotypically attributed to his people, were soft and kind. He spoke English excellently, in a quiet, musical voice with a Chinese accent, and he lived in the back rooms of his establishment with his young orphaned granddaughter, Ming Li, whom he was educating in the trade.

Ming Li preferred to go by the name Jasmine, which had been bestowed upon her by an old ship's captain who frequently came to Lin Tao's apothecary shop for a preparation to ease the pain of his arthritis. Jasmine was the scent she wore and most of Lin Tao's non-Chinese customers called her by that name. She was nineteen years old and very beautiful, with thick, jet black hair that hung down to her hips and a narrow, oval face. She was as slender as a bamboo stalk and her legs were long and exquisitely formed. She had long since learned what most men wanted from her, but she was not as vulnerable as she looked. Although few people knew it, her grandfather, for all his withered appearance, was a master of an ancient Oriental form of combat and he had taught it to his granddaughter. In China, he had once been an important man. It was for that reason they had left, booking passage on a freighter of the Blue Funnel Line. Lin Tao had become too important and too well known. And his age had made him vulnerable to ambitious younger men. He had started anew in London and in Limehouse; he had become a respected man in the Chinese community. A man of authority. A man whose granddaughter no one in the know would touch, because an insult to Ming Li would have meant death. Besides, Jasmine knew how to protect herself. And Jasmine was in love.

The man Jasmine was in love with lived upstairs in a small room above the apothecary shop. He helped her grandfather in the shop and he seemed to know a great deal about the apothecary's art, though his knowledge was of a different sort than Lin Tao's. They often spent long evenings in discussion over tea, sharing their respective knowledge. The man was secretive about his past, but Lin Tao understood that and he had instructed Jasmine not to bother him with questions. He respected his boarder's privacy. He also respected his wisdom. This man had come into the shop two months ago, looking for work. He had been penniless. At first, her grandfather meant to turn away this bearded stranger with the shabby clothes, but it quickly became apparent to him that this man had culture. He also possessed a great deal of unusual knowledge, though he would not say how he came by it. He had proper manners, unusual in an occidental, and he spoke the language of the mandarins as if he had been born in China. He also spoke a number of other languages with equal fluency, a definite advantage in a community of Chinese and Lascars and numerous other foreigners, many from the ships that called at the West India Docks. He said he was a doctor. When Jasmine was alone, she sometimes said his name out loud to herself, enjoying the sound of it. Morro. Dr. Morro.

In her imagination, she had created a romantic past for him, knowing nothing of his real history. He had once been an important man, a man of position, but something terrible had happened, some tragedy which had hurt him deeply, making him turn his back on everything he knew. He kept this secret hurt close to his heart, punishing himself for whatever it was that he had done. He was an older man, old enough to be her father, but Jasmine did not see him in that light. She wondered what it would be like to ease his hurt, to take it from him with her love, to help him find his way to a place of position in the English society as a respected physician, a surgeon perhaps, in one of London's better hospitals with an office of his own in Harley Street and a fine home in Grosvenor Square which she would share with him as his wife.

But, although Dr. Morro was always kind to her, his manner towards her was more that of an uncle than a potential lover. He did not look at her as other men did, with desire clearly written in his eyes. And he was often preoccupied, so that sometimes he did not hear her when she spoke to him and she had to raise her voice slightly to break through his train of thought. There were times when he would be sitting with her grandfather, drinking tea and talking quietly, and they would abruptly stop their conversation the moment she came in. Then they would resume it once again, as if casually, but Jasmine knew that they were no longer talking about the same thing. Her curiosity got the best of her and she started to eavesdrop on their conversations. She learned that Dr. Morro was looking for a man, a man he was certain had to be somewhere in London. An evil man. And Jasmine knew that this evil man had somehow been the cause of Dr. Morro's troubles. His name was Drakov. It was not an easy name for her to say. Nikolai Drakov.

The Hotel Metropole on Northumberland Avenue was one of London's newer and more luxurious establishments. The soldiers of the Temporal Corps were gathered in the suite occupied by "Prof." Finn Delaney and his colleague, "Dr." Steiger, under their cover as visiting academic researchers from the States. Their "secretary," Miss Andre Cross, occupied an adjoining suite, since an unmarried woman sharing rooms with two single men would have been considered a highly improper arrangement in this time period. The adjoining suites had become a temporal command post and the frequent comings and goings by the Temporal Corps soldiers stationed at various points in the city were structured to maintain the fiction of an ongoing research project funded by an American foundation, ostensibly the writing of a series of textbooks concerning the social history of England.

Members of the cleaning and maintenance staff had brought in several writing tables and they regularly found the suites cluttered with piles of books and papers which they had been specifically instructed not to disturb. The "student assistants" and "copyists" who supported the research made a point of frequenting several of the local pubs, where they could be observed in animated discussion over pints of bitters, engrossed in arguments about the history of the city and its people. Often, other patrons of the pub would be consulted for their "local expertise" and the word was that these young researchers and their professors were not bad sorts, for Americans; they were polite and enthusiastic about their subject, attentive listeners, full of questions.

No one suspected that these eager young academicians were anything other than what they seemed. In fact, the five young men and two young women were all soldiers from the 27th century, trained by the Temporal Observer Corps and programmed through their cerebral implants with more information about Victorian England than the average citizen could ever hope to possess. They each maintained two separate cover identities, one as members of an academic research team from America and another as British subjects. It was a complicated temporal stake-out which had taken months to set up, but for soldiers of the Temporal Corps, time was a flexible commodity.

Pvt. Scott Neilson had secured a position as a laboratory assistant at the Metropolitan Police crime lab in New Scotland Yard. Cpl. Thomas Davis had found work with *The Daily Telegraph* as a reporter. Pvt. Richard Larson had obtained employment with *The Police Gazette*. Pvt. Paul Ransome was a clerk with the Bank of England. Sgt. Anthony Rizzo was at the Public Record Office in Chancery Lane. Sgt. Christine Brant had found a job as a barmaid at the Cafe Royal, a hotbed of society gossip, and Pvt. Linda Craven was employed at the Haymarket Theatre, where she was an assistant to the wardrobe mistress and in excellent position to monitor the theatre district. They were temporal agents on the trail of a cross-time terrorist, a man named Nikolai Drakov.

"The interview of H. G. Wells did not produce any leads to the whereabouts of Drakov," Steiger was saying as he paced slowly in the sitting room of the suite. The support team was seated all around him, listening attentively. "I am of the opinion that maintaining contact with Wells is too risky. Captain Delaney does not agree. Lieutenant Cross is inclined to support Captain Delaney, but she is in favor of only the most limited contact for the present. Before we go any further with this briefing, I want to hear some feedback on that question. Opinions?"

"Is there any reason why we can't use our cover to legitimize further contact with Wells?" said Corporal Davis. "Since he's currently engaged in writing newspaper articles about everyday aspects of British life, wouldn't that support our consulting him in that capacity, as if we were asking him to help in our research?"

"No, that's definitely out," said Delaney. "Talking to people in pubs is one thing, but consulting Wells in that capacity would involve creating an episode in his life that never happened. We couldn't risk having him be involved in an academic project that never existed. We're supposed to be writing textbooks, remember? If he was to mention it in his own writings at any point, it would create the problem of having to alter any historical records he might leave. A bigger problem is that it might also affect the direction his own writing may take, since he did write historical works, and that would involve a risk of temporal contamination. Besides, he's completely dependent on his writing for his survival at this point and he's not going to be eager to have people pestering him for help in some sort of nebulous research project."

"I agree," said Sergeant Brant. She glanced at Davis and shook her head. "I don't think we can take the risk of getting close to Wells ourselves. The more contact we have with him, the more chance there is of our influencing him in some way. I'm in favor of covert surveillance. If Drakov contacts him, that may change everything, but why take unnecessary chances? We still haven't found any evidence of his presence here."

"I'm not so sure of that," said Private Neilson. "I was going to wait with this, but I think it may be important. Something unusual came up this morning at the crime lab. Late last night, a policeman was murdered at Whitechapel Station. His throat was torn open and his face was ripped to shreds. No one saw anything, but the man in charge of the case, Chief Inspector William Grayson, has issued specific orders to keep it quiet. And he's also brought in Dr. Conan Doyle to assist in the investigation in an unofficial capacity."

"Arthur Conan Doyle?" said Delaney.

"Yes, the same man who wrote the Sherlock Holmes stories," said Neilson, nodding. "He's very sharp. He examined the body and concluded that the wounds on the face were inflicted by a clawed hand, with four fingers and an opposed thumb, and that the wounds on the throat were probably made by animal teeth. He also checked the fingernails of the deceased and found several small hairs, which he examined under a microscope. He said the hair apparently came from a wolf. I couldn't confirm that, because Doyle took the samples with him for further study, but I was able to examine the body. There was a significant loss of blood, which could be accounted for by the severed jugular, but there were also traces of human saliva around the wound. I couldn't find any more hair samples, but I managed to obtain some skin scrapings from under the deceased's fingernails. There's a limit to what I can do given the primitive equipment at the crime lab, so I brought the samples with me. I'll admit it's a long shot, sir, but I think there's a chance we may be looking at some custom-tailored DNA here. I'd like permission to clock back to base and see if there are any lupine chromosomes in this sample.''

"Wait a minute," said Steiger, *"lupine* chromosomes? Are you telling me you think this policeman was killed by a *werewolf?"*

"Well, you did say not to overlook any possibilities, sir, no matter how farfetched or remote," said Neilson. "Since we know Drakov's been creating humanoid lifeforms through genetic engineering, I considered the various possibilities. Conan Doyle could be wrong, in which case we've got somebody running around in the East End who apparently likes to drink human blood and needs one hell of a manicure. Or else Doyle is right and those hairs he found *were* wolf hairs, in which case it could be that we've got a psycho with a blood fetish who's also got a trained wolf. Or maybe he puts some sort of metal claw tips on the ends of his fingers and wears a mask made out of real wolf hair, to make people think he's a werewolf. Or . . . he's really a werewolf. Chromosome mapping of the skin scrapings should tell us if we're dealing with a normal human or one that's been genetically designed."

Private Larson glanced from Neilson to Steiger. "A *werewolf?* Jesus, Fleet Street would have a field day with that. Especially after the Whitechapel murders."

"That was six years ago," said Corporal Davis, who was assigned to *The Daily Telegraph*. "There weren't any newspaper records of killings in London at this time that would fit that sort of pattern. Either it was completely hushed up or we've got a possible temporal anomaly on our hands."

"I think this may be the break we've been looking for, sir," said Neilson. "We know Drakov had Moreau design hominoids patterned after characters out of mythology, such as those creatures you encountered on your last mission. Well, why *not* a werewolf?"

"It's wild, but it sounds like just the sort of thing he might do," Delaney said, glancing at Steiger. "I say we check it out. It shouldn't take long."

"Do it," Steiger said to Neilson. "Set your warp disc for a thirty-second clockback. I want that chromosome analysis now."

"Yes, sir," said Neilson. He programmed his warp disc and disappeared, clocking ahead to TAC headquarters in the 27th century.

He reappeared exactly thirty seconds later, looking tired and needing a shave. He looked slightly ill. Temporal transition often produced nausea and dizziness and some soldiers never became accustomed to it.

"Well?" said Steiger.

"There's no doubt about it, sir," said Neilson, for whom hours had passed. "I've been up all night, going over the results. I had them run the samples three times to verify the results. They came out the same each time. The chromosome maps of the samples show definite hybridization with lupine genetic material, probably virally fixated. It's got our genetics people tremendously excited. They say it's extremely sophisticated engineering, very trick. They're guessing that there's a hormonal trigger, which would make the change cyclical. Most of the time, the infected person probably looks completely normal, but once the hormonal cycle triggers expression of the lupine genes, a definite physical change would occur. It looks like we've got a real live werewolf on our hands, sir."

"*Damn,*" said Steiger. "We've hit pay dirt. Good work, Neilson. You've earned some rest. Go next door and get some sleep."

Neilson grimaced wryly. "Are you kidding? Who could think of sleeping at a time like this?"

"I want you to get some rest," said Steiger. "I'm going to need everybody at a hundred percent from now on. We can't afford any mistakes. A genetically engineered werewolf is bad enough. Conan Doyle's involvement raises the stakes. This could get real tricky."

"What about Wells?" said Delaney. "All things considered, we'd better keep tabs on him, too."

"Right," said Steiger. "It's not a wild goose chase anymore. Neilson, you follow Conan Doyle's involvement in the case down at the police lab. Keep me informed of Inspector Grayson's progress. I want to be notified the minute any similar killings occur. Rizzo, I want a report from the Public Record

Office on all recent real estate leasehold transactions within the last six months. Ransome, ditto with recent depositors at the Bank of England, anyone who opened accounts containing significantly large sums. Drakov likes to highroll. If he's here, you can be sure he's got a pile of money with him. I want those two lists compared as soon as possible. Brant, you're assigned to H. G. Wells. I want him under twenty-four-hour surveillance as of now. Private Craven will relieve you. You'll work in shifts. Quit your cover jobs, I'll want you completely mobile from now on. Andre, you take Conan Doyle when he's not down at the police lab. Be careful, we know he's highly observant, so don't get spotted. Finn, you relieve Andre. Davis and Larson, I want you two to continue covering Fleet Street. You know what to look for. If any of this breaks, try to get assigned to the stories. I want to be kept up to date on anything the newspapers get a hold of, *before* they get the information.''

"Sir, if the story does break in the papers," said Davis, "we'll be expected to write something. How do you want us to handle the coverage?"

"Keep it reasonably straight," said Steiger. "Above all else, I want to avoid any sensational coverage that comes too close to the truth. Cooperate with the police. They'll appreciate reporters working with them for a change. That should give you an inside track. I don't want *anybody* writing stories about werewolves. Play the other reporters off against each other. Do whatever you can to keep a lid on this."

"Yes, sir."

"All right. Drakov is here, probably somewhere in London. I want him nailed this time. The command post will be manned around the clock. I want that creature found and neutralized, but Drakov is the first priority. If you find the creature, don't kill it unless you absolutely have to. It could lead us to Drakov."

Neilson cleared his throat. "I'm sorry, sir, but with all due respect, I think we'd better concentrate on taking out the creature first. As soon as possible."

"I understand your concern, Neilson," said Steiger, "but Drakov has to be stopped and we're not going to be getting any reinforcements. Considering the crisis, we were lucky to get you people. We can try to minimize the loss of life, but there's no avoiding the fact that we're going to have casualties."

"I don't think you understood me, sir," said Neilson. "I'm

sorry, I'm a little tired; I guess I didn't make it clear. Loss of life is not the only problem. There was just enough of the viral genome left in the lupine hybrid to render it infectious. This creature is contagious, sir. If any of its victims should happen to survive, there's a good chance they'll come down with a serious case of lycanthropy."

Steiger stared at him. *"Infectious DNA?"*

Delaney gave a low whistle. "Trust Drakov to come up with a real nightmare. Anybody know where we can get a good supply of silver bullets?"

"Why do you even *bother* to ask me for my opinion?" said Ian Holcombe, the Yard's chief of forensics. "Why not simply trot down to Baker Street and ask Mr. Sherlock Holmes? He'll look at the soil markings on the dead girl's petticoats and tell you in which cow pasture she had her last assignation. He'll smell her handkerchief and trace down her lover through the chemist's where he bought her perfume. And then he'll examine the callosities on the lover's hands and prove beyond a shadow of a doubt that the blackguard strangled her and there you'll have your case solved, neat as a pin. What do you need with me?"

"Steady on, Holcombe," Grayson said wearily. "I merely asked Dr. Doyle for his opinion on the case. Don't get your back up. I should think you'd be glad for the help. It's not as if you lack for things to do."

"Wolf hairs, indeed!" said Holcombe. "Wolves in London! Next I expect he'll be telling us that Westminster Abbey is infested with vampire bats!"

"Ian, just tell me what caused this young woman's death and I'll cease troubling you," said Grayson. "I've had a long night and I am very tired. I haven't even had an opportunity to eat breakfast this morning."

"Well, I *beg* your pardon," Holcombe said with exaggerated courtesy, snorting through his thick moustache. "You're not the only one who's overworked, you know. My assistant hasn't shown up yet and I'm trying to do twenty things at once. Tell me, do you think you could manage to bring me a corpse that expired in some *ordinary* manner, shot or stabbed or hacked to pieces with an axe, perhaps? Why do you insist on finding people who have been torn to pieces by wild animals or drained of all their blood?"

"Holcombe, what in Heaven's name are you talking about?" said Grayson.

"This girl," said Holcombe, gesturing at the sheet-shrouded body on the table. "She died from shock brought about by a profound loss of blood. Insult to the system, you know. It's astonishing that she had the strength to move about at all."

"What caused it?" Grayson said.

"Undoubtedly, she was bled by Sweeny Todd, the demon barber of Fleet Street," Holcombe said sarcastically. "Perhaps it happened when she went in for her shave. Or some Styrian countess gave her a love bite, how should I know? Why not call Le Fanu and ask him? Better yet, call Robert Louis Stevenson. Maybe Mr. Hyde was in need of a transfusion."

"Ian, *please* . . .," said Grayson, shutting his eyes.

"Well, look for yourself," said Holcombe, throwing back the sheet. "All I could find were those two marks on her throat there. See? It's obvious. Varney the Vampire has claimed another victim. Call Thomas Prest, he wrote the book, ask him what old Varney has been up to lately. Scribblers of penny dreadfuls in the crime lab! I've never heard of such a thing! This isn't Scotland Yard anymore, it's a bloody literary society. Ah, Neilson, there you are! Where the devil have you been? You look as if you have been up all night. Do you think I could manage to distract you from your carousing long enough to get some work done?"

"I'm sorry, Dr. Holcombe," said Neilson, putting on his apron. "I'm afraid I overslept this morning. I—"

"I don't wish to hear any excuses. I'd simply be tremendously flattered if you managed to show up on time. This place is a veritable madhouse. People coming and going, why already this morning you have missed Miss Mary Shelley. She was here with Inspector Grayson, looking for the odd spare part or two."

"Ian, is it even remotely possible that I might get a straight answer from you this morning?" Grayson said, exasperated.

"I don't *know* how she managed to lose such a great deal of blood," said Holcombe. "There, are you satisfied? I've proven my ineptitude. Perhaps she was a hemophile. Perhaps young Neilson did it, he was obviously out all night, stalking unwary actresses. Open your mouth, Neilson, let's see your teeth."

"Sir?" said Neilson, frowning.

"We seem to be infested with wolves and vampires this

week," said Holcombe. "Do try to keep up, Neilson. Inspector Grayson has promised us a surprise later in the afternoon. He's going to bring us someone who's been turned to stone by one of the Gorgon sisters. Oh, and while you're at it, after you've finished cleaning up, see if you can find me a large mallet and a wooden stake. It wouldn't do to have this young lady stumbling about the lab and knocking things over after we have closed up for the night."

There was a knock at the laboratory door. Neilson opened it to admit Conan Doyle. "I was told that I could find Inspector Grayson here," said Doyle.

"Ah, there you are, Watson!" said Holcombe. "Come in, come in, the game's afoot! Professor Moriarty has bitten an actress in the neck and we're all terribly concerned! Do let me know how it all comes out. I'm off to down a few pints myself, at the pub across the street. I'm obviously only in the way here!"

He stormed past an astonished Conan Doyle and slammed the door on his way out.

"Has that man gone mad?" said Doyle.

Grayson sighed. "Please accept my apologies, Dr. Doyle. I'm afraid that Holcombe's not himself today. Apparently, his professional pride's been stung a bit over—"

"Say no more, I quite understand," said Conan Doyle. "In point of fact, I *am* something of an interloper here. I think I can understand his irritation."

"Ian Holcombe's a good man," said Grayson. "I suspect his irritation is directed more at himself than at you. It seems I've brought him another body to confound him."

"What? Not another one?" said Doyle, coming closer.

"No, not a 'werewolf' this time," Grayson said, smiling wryly. "This time, we apparently have the victim of a vampire."

"A *what?*"

"See for yourself," said Grayson. "Miss Angeline Crewe, an actress with Mr. Irving's company at the Lyceum. She collapsed on stage during a rehearsal and apparently died within moments of her collapse. Notice the marks upon her throat."

"Hmmm, yes, I see," said Conan Doyle. "Definitely teeth marks. And cause of death was a significant loss of blood?"

"Yes, that is what Holcombe said. An insult to the system, as he put it. Surely you're not suggesting that she *was* killed by a vampire?''

"Rubbish, Grayson," said Conan Doyle. "That's utter nonsense. What have we to do with walking corpses who can only be held in their graves by stakes driven through their hearts? It's pure lunacy. However, the vampire of legend was not necessarily a dead man. A living person might have the habit. I have read, for example, of the old sucking the blood of the young in order to retain their youth. We must seek our answers among the natural, rather than the supernatural phenomena."

"What do you mean?" said Grayson.

"There are any number of contributing factors that could combine to sustain the legend of an undead vampire," Conan Doyle said. "For example, did you know that teeth appear longer in an exhumed corpse because the tissue of the gums shrinks after death?"

"I didn't know that," Grayson said.

Conan Doyle nodded as he examined the body. "It's quite true. In the past, there were few, if any, truly reliable tests for death, you see, and this gave rise to an uncommon number of premature burials. You will, no doubt, be familiar with the practice once followed by many of the coffin makers, who had devised various sorts of bellfries to stand atop the graves, with ropes leading down through tubes into the coffins so that someone buried prematurely could pull upon the rope and ring the bell as a signal for rescue. It never proved to be a very practical solution. Exhumed corpses found with blood upon their mouths were sometimes thought by the more imaginatively inclined to have left their graves and fed upon the flesh of the living. The actual explanation was a great deal less dramatic, though no less tragic. They were not really dead at the time of their burial and when they awoke in their coffins, they often bit themselves in their frenzy to escape. Also, for a long time, there was ignorance of the fact that hair and nails continue to grow for some time after death. This also contributed to the erroneous belief that the corpse was still 'living.' Unusual soil conditions in various parts of the world, particularly in volcanic regions, can result in an antiseptic environment that delays decomposition, which would account for reports of unusual preservation of dead bodies. Again, people often seized upon the more melodramatic explanations rather than the actual truth. Incomplete observation is worse than no observation at all, Grayson, and under properly observed conditions, all such things can be logically explained. Someone happens to see a so-called body leave a mausoleum and we have a report of walking dead, when a more careful investigation would undoubtedly have unearthed —you will excuse the pun—the explanation that a derelict had broken into a tomb to find shelter from the cold.''

''But you spoke of living persons having the habit of vampirism,'' said Grayson.

''Quite so,'' said Conan Doyle. ''There was, for example, the famous case of the notorious Gilles de Rais of France, tried in the year 1440 for the murder of over two hundred children. He stabbed them in their jugular veins and allowed their blood to spurt upon him so that he could drink it while he abused himself. At approximately the same period, there was also a Wallachian prince named Vlad Dracula, who built the citadel of Bucharest in 1456 and was so fond of impaling people upon spikes that he became known as Vlad Tepes, from the word *tzepa* in his native language, meaning 'spike.' He impaled over twenty thousand Turkish prisoners after one battle alone. From there, perhaps, stems your folklore concerning impaling vampires with wooden stakes. And then there was the case of the Hungarian countess, Elizabeth Bathory, brought to justice in the year 1611 for the killing of over six hundred young girls. She tortured them in her dungeons, bled them and then bathed in their blood, supposedly to benefit her complexion.''

''Good God,'' said Grayson.

''Yes, shocking examples of human brutality at its worst,'' said Conan Doyle, ''but nevertheless, brutality practiced by living humans, not dead ones. This sort of vampirism, Grayson, is a grotesque aberration, an insanity which I suspect may have its roots in a twisted sexual depravity. However, it is a disease of the living, not the dead. As for this poor girl, there is no question but that she was bitten in the neck by another human. A human with sharp teeth, however, quite possibly filed, in the manner of the cannibal tribesmen of New Guinea. As to the massive loss of blood, there could be any number of explanations. Possibly, she was a bleeder, a hemophiliac, or perhaps she was profoundly anemic. She may have lost a great deal of blood in some other manner upon which I would not care to speculate given so little evidence, but I would venture to suggest, if I may, a careful investigation of her co-workers and associates. There is a strong possibility that practices of perversion may have been involved here. In such a case, it will be difficult to ferret out the truth, as such secrets are darkly kept. But in any case, I would not recommend that you trade in your truncheon for a string of garlic bulbs.''

"You have missed your calling, Dr. Doyle," said Grayson. "You would have made a brilliant detective."

"Nonsense," said Doyle. "I am merely well informed on a wide variety of peculiar subjects, of little use to the average man, but of some value to one who writes romances. Besides, I have not the temperament for police work."

"Well, the literary world's gain is Scotland Yard's loss," said Grayson. "And I will conduct a thorough investigation of Miss Crewe's fellow actors and her friends, as well. I am most grateful for your assistance. Speaking of which—"

"Ah, yes, of course," said Conan Doyle. "The hair samples." He frowned. "Most unusual. They are extremely like a wolf's, but then again, they do not quite compare. You may be seeking a man with unusually coarse hair of a steel gray or silver color. In such a case, I would expect this coarseness to extend to his features, as well. He would be very hirsute, a primitive looking sort of individual, possibly of Mediterranean blood."

"You can tell all this from some samples of his hair?" said Grayson, amazed.

"Simple inference and deduction, Grayson, based upon what we know of physical types. In any case, you would be looking for an unusually powerful man. It would have taken one to bring down a strong man such as Constable Jones. Some savage derelict, perhaps, but undoubtedly a madman. As for the nature of the wounds, I have a theory about the weapon which might have been used, but I would like to consider it some more." He looked down at the body of Angeline Crewe and frowned. "It may even be possible that this poor girl's death is connected with the murder of Constable Jones. Savagery is the common factor, Grayson. Savagery and bloodlust."

3 ──────────────

The Cafe Royal, at 68 Regent Street, was not the sort of place Inspector William Grayson frequented. It was a bit too rich for his blood and he had never cared much for French food. He preferred a public house and the congenial company of the working classes. The Cafe Royal was more a gathering place for writers and artists, not really his sort at all, in spite of what Ian Holcombe might think. On the ground floor of the Royal was a cafe, a grill room and a luncheon bar. The basement held a wine cellar and a billiard room and the upper floors were private rooms.

The manager conducted Grayson to the Domino Room. The decor was fashionably elegant. Grayson thought it was a bit much. The seats were all upholstered in red velvet and the tables topped with marble. The corners of Grayson's mouth turned down slightly as he saw the people at the table they were heading for. They were all poufs. Their postures and affected gestures were unmistakable. But then, he had expected this. He had, after all, come to the court of the so-called "Apostle of the Utterly Utter."

Oscar Wilde was at the height of his success. The leader of the Aesthete movement, Wilde's belief was that art had no real use and existed only for its own sake. As such, claimed Wilde, art knew no morality. "A book," he said, "is either written well or badly, it is not moral or immoral." Grayson did not consider himself particularly competent to judge whether or not Wilde's books and plays were written well or not, he was content to leave that to the reviewers, but he had read Wilde's controversial novel, *The Picture of Dorian Gray,* and while he did not quite agree with the reports in the press that called it "filthy," it certainly addressed the question of morality. The character portrayed in it was completely immoral.

Grayson had no difficulty recognizing Oscar Wilde in the group. The man had been caricatured extensively in the press. He was the oldest one among the young men at the table. Grayson guessed his age at about forty. The author, poet, dramatist and lecturer was a large man, on the plump side, though Grayson thought he was a good deal slimmer than the newspapers portrayed him. He was not a bad-looking man, though his manner and the softness of his features were decidedly effeminate. Grayson knew he had a wife and two children, but his preferences seemed to lie in a less family-oriented direction. His manner of dress was elegant. He wore a dark, well-tailored coat and striped trousers, his silk cravat was tied perfectly, his hair was neatly combed and parted in the middle and he wore a fresh buttonhole. He looked every inch the gentleman, albeit an elaborately flamboyant one.

"Mr. Wilde," Grayson said.

Wilde held up Grayson's card, which the manager of the cafe had given him, and glanced at it insouciantly. "Inspector Grayson," he said in an appealing, almost musical voice. "It is not often that I receive a calling card from Scotland Yard. So tell me, Inspector, am I to be inspected?"

The young man at his side tittered, setting off a small chorus of birdlike noises from the others. Grayson recognized Lord Alfred Douglas, the twenty-four year old son of the Marquess of Queensberry. The son was not much like his sporting father. He was a pretty, spoiled-looking boy; in fact, he could easily have been Dorian Gray himself.

"I would like to ask you a few questions, Mr. Wilde, if I may," said Grayson.

"Goodness, a police interrogation," Wilde said. "I trust that I am not about to be arrested?"

"Why, Mr. Wilde," Grayson said, affecting an innocent tone, "have you done anything to be arrested for?"

The playwright smiled. "I suppose that would depend upon

what one considers criminal," he said. "I can think of any number of reviewers who believe that I should be arrested for my work and others who feel that I should be arrested for my manner. Tell me, Inspector, in which class would you fall?"

"The working class, Mr. Wilde," said Grayson.

"Oh, well done, Inspector!" Wilde said. "I hardly expected to find wit in Scotland Yard."

"It takes wit to do what we do, Mr. Wilde," Grayson said. "Perhaps not your sort of wit, but wit nonetheless."

"I see. I take it you do not approve of me, Inspector Grayson," Wilde said.

"I do not know enough about you personally to approve or disapprove," said Grayson. "I could conjecture, but then the law does not deal with conjecture. The law is concerned with proof, which may be very fortunate for you. On the other hand, if you were speaking of my disapproval as concerns your work, I am afraid that I must disappoint you. I quite enjoyed your play, *Lady Windermere's Fan*, and I found *Dorian Gray* quite interesting."

"Indeed?" said Wilde. "Interesting is a rather ambiguous word. You did not find it 'filthy' or 'immoral,' a 'dangerous novel,' as the newspapers called it?"

Grayson saw that Wilde's young cohorts were hanging on his every word, expecting to see him poignard the policeman with his wit. Perversely, Grayson decided to play out the game, if for no other reason than to deny them the pleasure of seeing him flustered.

"Didn't you yourself say that art was neither moral nor immoral?" Grayson said.

"I did, indeed," said Wilde, a slight smile on his face, "but then I was asking *your* opinion."

"My opinion, since you ask," said Grayson, "is that with *Dorian Gray*, you seem to have contradicted yourself."

"The well bred contradict other people," Wilde said. "The wise contradict themselves. But what an unusual reaction! Tell me, Inspector, just *how* did I manage to contradict myself?"

"Well, you've stated that art is neither moral nor immoral," Grayson said, "but in *Dorian Gray*, you have presented a young man who is utterly immoral, devoted only to his own pleasures and perverse desires, and in the portrait which ages in his stead, you clearly imply that it is not only age which results in the portrait's growing ugliness, but the immoral deeds committed by the ever youthful Gray; evil, as it were, having an obvious malforming effect upon the soul. A very Catholic idea, Mr. Wilde, even a very moral one. And in the end of the story, Dorian Gray's sins finally catch up with him and he receives his just desserts. One might well ask, how can a story be neither moral nor immoral, and yet still have a moral?''

"Grayson, you positively overwhelm me!" Wilde said, beaming. "I refuse to even try to trump such a refreshingly original review! There is clearly more to you than meets the eye. Would you care to join us?"

"No, thank you, Mr. Wilde," Grayson said, "I am afraid I have a number of inquiries yet to make."

"Well, then, I shall not waste any more of your time. How may I help you?"

"I understand you are familiar with the company currently playing the Lyceum," Grayson said.

"Henry Irving's production of *Becket*?" Wilde said. "Indeed, I am. Has there been some sort of trouble?"

"One of the young actresses has died," said Grayson. "A Miss Angeline Crewe. She collapsed on stage last night during a rehearsal. It seems she had not been well. The cause of death has not yet officially been determined and we are merely making some inquiries of her friends and co-workers, purely a routine matter."

"How tragic," Wilde said, "but I fear I did not know that young woman. That is to say, I did not know her very well. She was an understudy, I believe. Rather too prim and proper for an actress. We exchanged greetings on occasion, but that is all."

"Did she seem unwell to you at the time?" said Grayson.

"No, I would not say so," Wilde said. "A bit pale, perhaps, but then she was very fair complected."

"Yes, that would follow," Grayson said. "It seems that she was quite anemic. You would not, by any chance, happen to know if she was a bleeder?"

"Not to my knowledge," Wilde said.

"Apparently she was keeping company with a certain young man," Grayson said. He consulted his notepad. "A Mr. Hesketh."

"Tony Hesketh?" Lord Douglas said, surprised.

"Yes, that is the name," said Grayson. "You know the young man?"

"Well, yes, as a matter of fact, I do," said Douglas. Grayson noticed Wilde give Douglas a sidelong look. "I am surprised to hear that he was keeping company with . . . an actress."

"Friend of yours, Bosie?" said Wilde, a touch too casually.

"I haven't seen him for some time," said Douglas.

"It seems that no one has," said Grayson. "Any idea where I might find him, Lord Douglas?"

Douglas gave an elaborate shrug. "The last time I saw Tony, he was otherwise engaged. Not with an *actress*, I mean." He said "actress" as if it were a distasteful word. "He was with a dark, Mediterranean looking gentleman."

"Mediterranean?" said Grayson. "Could you describe him?"

"Tall, slim, black hair, swarthy, but in an elegant sort of way," said Douglas. "Well mannered and well dressed. A man of obvious means. He was foreign, a titled gentleman. He was a very striking looking man. I remember he wore a top hat and an opera cape. I do not recall his name."

"When exactly was this, Lord Douglas?" Grayson said.

"Oh, I can't be sure," said Douglas. "Two weeks ago, perhaps? Maybe three."

"And where was this?"

"Why, at the Lyceum," Douglas said.

"You would not, by any chance, happen to know where I could reach this gentleman?" Grayson said.

"Haven't the faintest," Douglas said.

"Well, if you should happen to see him again, or Mr. Hesketh, perhaps you'd be kind enough to let me know," Grayson said.

Douglas shrugged.

"Something tells me, Inspector Grayson, that this matter is not entirely routine, as you put it," said Wilde. "Do you suspect some sort of foul play in this young woman's death?"

"I am merely making inquiries, Mr. Wilde."

"I see. Well, Bram Stoker would be your man, then. He manages all of Henry Irving's affairs and he is the Lyceum Theatre's mother hen."

"I see. Well, thank you for your help," said Grayson. "And

if you see either of those gentlemen again, I should very much like to speak with them.''

"So would I, Inspector," Wilde said, glancing curiously at Douglas.

Grayson was glad to leave. Wilde seemed likeable enough, despite his nature, but he did not care much for the coterie surrounding him, particularly the young Lord Douglas. It was, felt Grayson, a dangerous association, especially given the character of the boy's father.

His thoughts would prove prophetic. Within a year, the Marquess of Queensberry, outraged by his son's relationship with the notorious Wilde, would accuse Wilde of being a sodomite. And Wilde, urged on by the irresponsible Douglas, would ignore the entreaties of his friends and commit the greatest mistake of his life by suing Queensberry for libel, thereby placing the burden of proof for the accusation upon Queensberry's counsel, who would come to trial prepared to bring forward a number of young men to testify that Wilde had committed ''indecencies'' with them. Wilde would drop the suit on the third day of the trial on the advice of his counsel, but by then it would be too late. Like many artists who were ignorant of the subtler realities of life, Wilde never understood the importance of the distinction between what was widely known and more or less ignored in certain social circles and what was legally proven in a courtroom, where it could not be ignored. On the same day he dropped the suit, Wilde would be arrested and eventually sentenced to two years of hard labor. He would serve the full sentence and upon his release, would be shunned by the society that had once lionized him. He would spend the remaining three years of his life in exile and die in Paris, yet in spite of everything, he would retain his spirit to the end. On his deathbed in the Hotel d'Alsace, while suffering from the acute pain of cerebral meningitis, he would jokingly complain about the aesthetically unappealing wallpaper in his bedroom. "It is killing me," he would say with his last breath. "One of us *has* to go." As for Lord Alfred Douglas, the instigator of it all, he would emerge from the affair unscathed and go on to write a book about his relationship with Wilde. So much for the ironies of life.

But as Grayson left the Cafe Royal, his thoughts were not concerned with Oscar Wilde and his flirtations with disaster so much as with the missing Tony Hesketh and his unidentified foreign companion. "A primitive looking sort of individual," Conan Doyle had said, "possibly of Mediterranean blood." And Doyle had also hinted at the possibility of perversion being involved, secrets darkly kept. Some not kept so darkly or so well, thought Grayson, wryly. Douglas had not left much doubt as to the character of Tony Hesketh. Links were forming. A swarthy, foreign gentleman linked to Tony Hesketh. Hesketh linked to Angeline Crewe. Angeline Crewe was dead and Tony Hesketh was missing. And the last place any of them had been seen was the Lyceum Theatre. It was time to have another talk with Mr. Bram Stoker.

Tony Hesketh's sanity was hanging by a thread. He did not know where he was. He knew only that he was in a dark, damp cell, barely illuminated by a single torch set into a sconce in the stone wall. It was like a dungeon in a medieval castle; what little he had seen of it when he was brought here was in ruins. He heard the distant drip of water. He could not move to explore his surroundings because he was manacled to the wall, his arms chained to an iron ring above him. He could barely remain standing to support his weight and when he sagged down from exhaustion, the chains sent a wrenching pain through his shoulders. His coat had been removed and his white shirt had been ripped open, exposing his throat and chest. He was cold, but there was a burning pain in his neck, at a spot on his throat directly over the jugular vein.

He did not remember how he came here. The last thing he could recall was going down to Whitechapel with his new friend, his rich, exotic and exciting friend, and they had walked through the thick fog together, fog so thick that Hesketh couldn't even see where he was going, but his friend had taken him by the hand and led him, promising a wild, new experience . . . and then somehow they were here, in this ruined castle—how could there possibly be a castle in Whitechapel!—and he was led down to the dungeon as his friend walked ahead of him, carrying a torch, and it looked as if no one had disturbed the dust of centuries, as if they had somehow stepped out of London and into another place in another, long forgotten time. And then the nightmare had begun.

The sun was going down. Tony Hesketh could not see outside,

but he knew the sun was going down as surely as if there were a window in the dungeon cell. After three weeks in this horrifying place, three weeks of the same, mind-numbing, terrifying routine, he knew. His eyes had grown accustomed to the dim light and on the far side of the cell, he could see the large black coffin carved from ebony and worked with intricate designs and silver filigree, resting on a marble pedestal. He remembered the chilling words that had been spoken to him the night he had been brought here and chained to the stone wall.

"I will sleep close to you now. I will remain with you until the change has taken place."

He had not known what those words meant then, but he knew now and it frightened him beyond all measure. He could feel it happening. After the first time, he had been sick, retching uncontrollably, his stomach cramping, his vision blurring. Then he became racked with fever and then chills. Sweat poured from every pore. He soiled himself repeatedly, but the chains were never taken off and now he stank, encrusted with his own filth. And he was starving. He wasn't given any food. From time to time, he was allowed a drink of water, but lately it no longer satisfied his thirst. His thirst now was for another kind of drink. It filled him with loathing, but he could not resist the urge.

The sun was down. Tony Hesketh hung from his chains and whimpered. The lid of the coffin opened slowly, with a creaking sound. Like a wild animal, Tony strained against the chains. The manacles bit deeply into the soft flesh of his wrists and blood began to flow. In spite of himself, the sight of it excited him.

"It is almost finished, Tony," said the man standing before him, dressed in elegant black evening clothes and a long, silk-lined opera cape. "Soon now, very soon, your new life will begin."

"Oh, God," moaned Tony. "It hurts. It hurts so much, please, can't you make it stop?"

"Are you hungry, Tony?"

"No, no, please, no more, not again—"

"You are hungry, aren't you?"

"No!"

"Aren't you?"

"Yes!" Tony whispered savagely. "Yes, let me, please . . ."

"Then give me what I need."

"Yes, *do it*," Tony whispered, "*do it now!*"

He bent his head back, exposing his throat. Warm lips caressed his neck and then he felt the fire of sharp fangs penetrating the soft skin of his throat and he moaned, then shuddered as he exploded in a violent climax. His mouth was opened wide in ecstasy, revealing long, protruding teeth.

It was getting very late and Goodtime Gordy still hadn't found a customer. The night was chilly and her shawl was threadbare, but she could not seek refuge from the cold or even buy herself a nip of gin to warm up her insides. She had run out of money and there'd be no crib for her tonight unless she found a means of paying for it. The trouble was, it was a buyer's market and with every passing day, Gordy had less and less to sell.

It was the young ones, she thought miserably. More of them every day, younger and prettier, still with all their teeth, where did they all come from? All that was left for her to do was to sell herself more cheaply. At this rate, soon she'd be giving it away. She didn't know what she was going to do. She was getting old and ugly and she looked worn out. The few teeth she had left were loose, her back was hurting her, her eyes were sunken and bloodshot and her nose was veined with ruptured capillaries from a steady diet of gin. She was twenty-eight years old.

A hunched over figure shambled towards her through the mist and she quickly prepared to make a desperate pitch. She loosened her shawl and opened up her blouse, pushing up her breasts. She had to remember to smile with her mouth closed, so as not to reveal her missing teeth.

"'Ello, Ducks," she said, striking a saucy pose. "'Ow's about a bit o'—"

Two hairy hands shot out and grabbed her by her shoulders with incredible strength. She felt claws sinking deep into her flesh. She heard an animal growl and saw a face more horrible than anything that she had ever seen in her worst nightmares. She had time for one, brief, piercing scream.

Steiger poured himself a shot of straight Scotch whiskey and tossed it down, then refilled the glass. There had been two more killings. First the actress, Angeline Crewe, drained of almost all her blood, and then a Whitechapel streetwalker named Glynnis Gordon, "Goodtime Gordy" to her friends, found in an alley with her throat torn out. They had been unable to keep that one out of the papers. Her body had been discovered by two of her neighbors and they had spoken to reporters. One paper had run the story under the headline, "Return of the Ripper?" Another proclaimed, "Whitechapel Murder in the Style of Springheel Jack!" And there were no leads. Nobody had seen a thing.

It was maddening. The file search of recent depositors at the Bank of England and recent real estate leaseholds had produced a large number of correlations which Rizzo and Ransome were busy checking out, but it was taking too much time. Brant and Craven were now on full-time surveillance duty, watching H. G. Wells, but he was going on about his normal routine and nothing unusual had happened. For all they knew, nothing would. It could be simple coincidence that Wells had foreseen so many future developments, coincidence that he had written about a scientist named Moreau who was engaged in biological experimentation, coincidence that he had written about time travel. And there had been nothing unusual in Conan Doyle's behavior, either. He kept consulting with Inspector Grayson, but otherwise, he did not seem to be involved in any temporally anomalous events. Only Neilson had come up with any significant information as a result of his cover position at the crime lab. What he had come up with wasn't much, but it was cause for worry.

"I think we've got at least two of them," Neilson was saying. "The Crewe murder was different from the other two. She fits the classic profile of a vampire's victim in fiction. Whatever happened to her, she apparently went along with it willingly, or at least willingly in the sense that she wasn't assaulted with the same physical force as the other victims. There may have been some other form of duress, perhaps psychological, maybe even biochemical, because she apparently never complained about what happened to her."

"What do we know about her?" Steiger said.

"From what Grayson told Conan Doyle in my presence," Neilson said, "all I know is that she had recently arrived in London from Richmond Hill. Her family is very well off. They weren't very pleased about her wanting to become an actress. She was seeing a young man named Tony Hesketh, who has apparently disappeared. Hesketh may have been bisexual. He was close to some of the young men in Oscar Wilde's circle and he was last seen at the Lyceum Theatre in the company of a dark, foreign looking man dressed in elegant evening clothes and an opera cape, described as a Mediterranean type, a gentleman, elegant and striking looking, with a title.''

"Sounds like Count Dracula," said Finn Delaney.

Steiger gave him a sharp look. "You don't think . . ."

"I was only kidding," said Delaney. An anxious expression crossed his face. "I think."

"Let me see those lists," said Andre. She grabbed the lists of recent bank depositors and real estate leasehold transactions and started scanning them.

"Oh, come on," said Steiger. "Drakov would never be that obvious."

"I don't know," said Delaney. "It could be just the sort of thing that would amuse him, throwing down the gauntlet that way. Jesus, a genetically engineered vampire. And if such a creature's genetic makeup was also contagious—"

"It would be, knowing Drakov," Steiger said.

"How about that for temporal terrorism?" said Delaney. "Unleashing a plague of vampires and werewolves on Victorian London. And the timing is positively macabre. Just one year before Bram Stoker started work on *Dracula*. One year before *The Time Machine* was published."

"And it was always believed that Stoker based his character on the historical Dracula from the 15th century," said Andre, still scanning the lists. "Drakov might just have decided to make the character *truly* historical. And the similarity of their names, that would only be one more thing that would make the idea appeal to him."

"Anything?" said Steiger, watching her scan the lists.

She shook her head.

"You know, we may be overlooking something, sir," said Neilson. "What about rentals?"

"Jesus, rentals!" Steiger said. "How the hell would we ever track down rentals? There's just no way!"

"Possibly not, sir," Neilson said, "but on the other hand, would Drakov really go in for a bed-and-breakfast sort of deal? I mean, it doesn't seem very likely that he'd rent ordinary rooms like your average London boarder. He'd want something bigger, probably, more private. An unused estate, maybe, or a warehouse—"

"A warehouse!" said Delaney. "And all the killings so far occurred within the same general area, the East End of London, within easy access of the docks on the Thames."

"Neilson, you seem to be the only one who's doing any thinking around here," Steiger said. "Start checking the warehouse district on the docks during your off-duty hours from the crime lab. I'll try to get you some help. There can't be that many warehouses standing empty, so you can automatically eliminate the ones in active use. Maybe we're finally getting somewhere. Christ, it's like looking for a goddamn needle in a haystack. Somehow, we've got to get a break on this."

"What about the newspaper reports?" said Andre.

"Not much we can do about them now," said Steiger. "I'd rather have them writing about a new series of Ripper murders than vampires and werewolves loose in London."

"There's one more thing, sir," Neilson said. "The man who's missing, Tony Hesketh. It may not be a bad idea to stake out his apartments. If he returns, he may no longer be the same, if you know what I mean. He's been missing for about three weeks. I don't know how long it would take for the viral genome to bring about a mutation, but if he's not dead, he may provide us with our first real lead."

"Good idea," said Steiger. "I'll pull Rizzo off the estate search and assign him to watch Hesketh's rooms. Have we got an address on him?"

"Not yet, sir," Neilson said, "but I might be able to sneak a look at Grayson's files and get it."

"All right, do it. But be careful. Don't get caught. We can't afford to have you sacked from your job at the lab. It's been our only source of information so far."

"I'll be careful, sir."

"Okay, get going." Steiger checked his watch. "Who's watching Conan Doyle now? Craven?"

"Yes, I had her relieve me for about an hour so I could make the briefing," Andre said.

"All right, get back there. She'll have to relieve Brant at Wells' house in several hours and I want her to be fresh."

"How are you holding up?" said Delaney.

"I'm not getting much sleep, if that's what you mean," said Steiger. "But then holding down the fort has never been my style. I'll be glad when something breaks and we can stop stretching ourselves so thin. But until then, it's got to be a waiting game." He tossed back another drink. "I only hope we won't have to wait too long."

The small, slightly built man with the prematurely grey hair and beard stood in the entrance to the offices of the *Pall Mall Gazette,* holding a folded copy of the paper in his hand and glancing around nervously.

"Excuse me," he said, stopping a young man walking past him, "are you on the staff here at the newspaper?"

"Well, after a fashion, I suppose," said the young man. "How may I help you, sir?"

"My name is Moreau. Dr. Phillipe Moreau. The gentleman who wrote this story, about the killing in Whitechapel—"

"The murder of the prostitute, you mean?"

"Yes, I was wondering if I could speak with him."

"Well, I am afraid he is not in the office at the moment, Dr. Moreau, and I have no idea when he will return. I was just leaving myself. I am not actually on staff here; I write occasional articles, but perhaps I can assist you?"

"Oh, I see. Well, I don't know, Mr.—"

"Wells."

"Thank you, Mr. Wells, but I don't think that will be necessary," said Moreau. "Perhaps I should not even have come. I just thought, perhaps—"

"Why don't we sit down?" said Wells. "There is obviously something troubling you. If there is anything that I can do to help, I will certainly try."

"Yes, all right," said Moreau, taking the seat Wells indicated. They sat down at a desk.

"Now then," said Wells, "what about this murder?"

"Well, I have a daughter, you see," Moreau said hesitantly. "That is, I had a daughter. I have not seen her for quite some time. She came to London and, well, I have been searching for her—"

"And you thought perhaps this dead girl could be your daughter?" said Wells. "You wanted to satisfy yourself as to her identity?"

"Yes, precisely," said Moreau. "The newspaper gave her name as Gordon, I know, but it is possible that she had taken another name. . . ."

"I understand," said Wells. "However, if that had been the case, we would really have no way of knowing, you understand. You realize that the odds of this poor murdered girl being your missing daughter are really quite small."

"Yes, yes, highly unlikely, I know," said Moreau, "but something told me—I just simply had to know, you see. Perhaps if I could speak to someone who had an opportunity to view the remains . . ."

"I do not know if that would help you, Doctor," Wells said. "As I understand it, the body was . . . well, the poor girl's face was damaged beyond all recognition. Her neighbors identified her mainly by her clothing and a few personal possessions. The murder was quite savage. Considering the odds, why subject yourself needlessly to such an ordeal?"

"You don't understand," said Moreau, "I *must* know. The nature of the wounds, the manner in which—" He suddenly caught himself and stopped.

"What about the nature of the wounds, Doctor?" Wells said, watching him carefully. "Why should that happen to interest you?"

"Nothing, you misunderstood me," said Moreau. "I am merely distraught. I should not have come here. Forgive me for taking up your valuable time . . ."

"One moment, Doctor," Wells said, catching him by the arm.

"Please," said Moreau. "Let me go."

"Not just yet, Doctor," said Wells. "I do not think that I misunderstood you. And something tells me that you are not being entirely truthful with me. Why come to the newspaper? Why not go to the police?"

"Yes, undoubtedly that is what I should have done," Moreau said. "I merely thought that—"

"Why don't we go see the police together?" Wells said. "We can go right now."

"No, really, thank you, but there is no need for you to trouble yourself. It's really quite—"

"You really do not want to go to the police, do you?" said Wells. "Why is that? What are you afraid of?"

Moreau looked at him with alarm. "I see what you are thinking," he said. "You think perhaps I may have had something to do with this crime."

"I am merely wondering why you seem reluctant to go to the police," Wells said. "Why are you so interested in this murder? What is it about the nature of the wounds? What do you mean? You are not really seeking a missing daughter, are you?"

"Yes, of course I am," Moreau said. "Why else would I be so concerned?"

"That is what I would like to know, Dr. Moreau," Wells said. "You are obviously an educated man, and yet the newspaper reports clearly stated that the dead girl was a Cockney, strictly working class. Moreover, your accent is slight, but definitely French, I think, as is your name. I suppose it is possible that an educated French gentleman could have a daughter by a Cockney mother, but then if that were so, why would you be reluctant to go to the police? That would be the natural avenue of inquiry for a man seeking a missing daughter, would it not?"

A number of the people in the office had become interested in the conversation. "What is it?" one of them said. "Some sort of problem?"

"Please," said Moreau in a low voice. "I cannot discuss this here."

"I think we had best get to the bottom of this, Dr. Moreau," Wells said.

"No, let me go," Moreau said, pulling away, but Wells would not let go. Moreau's sleeve was pulled back, exposing a strange-looking bracelet. It caught Wells' attention. It was made from an unusual black material, with small, numbered studs arranged upon it in a pattern.

"What's this?" said Wells, looking down at it.

"Don't touch it!" Moreau said, jerking his arm back violently.

"I think perhaps we had better speak with the police," said Wells.

Moreau looked around frantically, seeing himself being hemmed in. "Please," he said, "I beg you, no police. They would not understand. I swear to you, I am no criminal."

"Who is this chap, Bertie?" one of the other reporters said. "What's he on about?"

"Have we got some kind of trouble here?" another said.

"Please," Moreau said softly. And then his eyes grew wide. "Bertie?" he said. "Herbert Wells?"

"Yes," said Wells, looking at him strangely.

"Herbert *George* Wells?"

"How is it that you happen to know my full name, Doctor?" Wells said. "I did not give it to you and I do not use it professionally. I am certain we have never met."

"Please, Mr. Wells," Moreau said, "I promise to answer all your questions, but we must speak somewhere in private. I assure you that I have no personal involvement in this killing, but I believe I know who was responsible."

"Very well," said Wells, "but I promise you that if you do not adequately explain yourself, I will summon the police."

Moreau nodded. "Very well, I shall accept that. But please, let us speak in private."

"There is a small teashop just down the street," said Wells. "Come, we can talk there. Give me your arm."

"You think I will try to run away?" Moreau said.

"I think you are a desperate man, Dr. Moreau," said Wells. "There is an edge of hysteria in your voice and panic in your eyes. Very well, we shall simply walk together, but if you run off, rest assured that I am quite capable of giving the police a completely accurate and detailed description of you."

Moreau nodded. They left the building together and started walking down the street, towards one of the teashops operated by the Aerated Bread Company.

"What is that curious bracelet on your wrist?" said Wells.

"If I told you the truth," Moreau said, "you would not believe me. You would think me mad."

"I never leap to uninformed conclusions, Doctor," Wells said.

"No, you wouldn't," said Moreau, smiling. "Not you."

Wells frowned. "I find your remarks most puzzling. You behave as if you knew me."

"In a manner of speaking, I do," Moreau said. "Shall I tell you what I know? You are at the moment living with a woman whom you introduce to your neighbors as your wife, although she is not your wife. At least, not yet. Her name is Amy Catherine Robbins and you call her Jane. She was a student of yours. You left your wife, Isabel, for her. You were not always a journalist. You used to teach once under Professor Huxley at the Normal School of Science in South Kensington. You have two brothers, Frank and Freddy; you have been astigmatic from an early age and your health was always poor. You almost died of appendicitis in your youth and you broke your leg when you were seven years old—''

''Good God!'' said Wells. ''How is possible that you know so much about me?''

''I will tell you the complete truth, Mr. Wells,'' Moreau said, ''because I am in desperate need of help and I believe that you can give it to me, but I must tell it to you slowly, otherwise you will surely think me mad. I must convince you that I am not. More than you could possibly realize depends upon it.''

''What manner of doctor are you?'' Wells said. ''Are you a physician or one of these mystics who claims the ability to read minds and such?''

''I would have an easier time convincing you that I am capable of reading your thoughts than of who and what I really am,'' Moreau said. ''I am a professor and I am also a scientist, specializing in the biological sciences.''

''Biological experimentation?'' Wells said suddenly.

''Yes,'' Moreau said, glancing at him sharply. ''What made you ask that?''

''Scientists engage in experimentation, do they not?''

''Yes, I suppose they do,'' Moreau said. ''Still, it was curious that you should say that.''

''Let us return, for the moment, to the topic at hand,'' said Wells. ''This murder. You claim you know who was responsible? A patient of yours, perhaps?''

''No,'' said Moreau, ''I do not see patients. But the man I am seeking, the one who I believe may be responsible for this, is without question insane. He was once a sort of colleague of mine. His name is Drakov.''

''Nikolai Drakov?'' Wells said.

Moreau stopped, frozen in his tracks, staring at him wildly. *''How did you know that?''*

Wells took his arm. ''It appears that we both have some surprises for each other,'' he said. ''I will answer your questions just as soon as you have answered mine.''

They reached the ABC teashop and went inside. There were several couples in the shop, mostly young, lingering over tea and biscuits. The advent of the teashops was a blessing to young couples in a time where a ''proper'' young woman couldn't think of going alone to a young man's apartment. To young people without a lot of money, a teashop was the perfect place to meet. Nothing could be considered improper about taking a walk together, then spending some time enjoying a "cuppa" and a biscuit or two. It was a date that any young man could afford.

They took their seats at a small table and ordered a pot of tea. Wells saw that Moreau had been staggered by his knowing Drakov's name. Strange, he thought, he had never been much good with names, but he had remembered that one because of the peculiar circumstances under which he had heard it. He wondered what connection there might be between those three Americans who had come to call on him and this curiously intense Frenchman.

Wells scrutinized him closely. Moreau was a small man, perhaps five foot five or six, slightly built, sharp featured, foxlike. He was younger than he seemed to be. Wells guessed he was in his early forties, but he looked older. It wasn't only the grey hair. There were crow's-feet around his eyes, which were red from lack of sleep. He was pale and there were worry lines around his mouth and above the bridge of his nose, between his eyebrows. He was clearly a man under a great strain.

"Before we discuss this any further," said Moreau, "you have to tell me how you know Drakov's name. You've seen him? You know where he is? You *must* tell me!"

"Calm yourself, Dr. Moreau," said Wells. "In point of fact, I do not have to tell you anything. What I should be doing is taking you to the police. If you have knowledge about a crime that has taken place, it is your duty to give that information to the authorities. I agreed to speak with you in private because you promised you would explain yourself. Well then, explain."

Moreau stared at Wells for a moment, then briefly closed his eyes and took a deep breath. "What if I were to tell you that I have come here from the future?"

"From the future," Wells said, watching him uneasily. He chose his words with care. "If you were to tell me that, Dr. Moreau, if that is indeed your name, I would have a great deal of difficulty believing you. I doubt that anyone could substantiate such a fantastic claim."

"Nevertheless, it is true," Moreau said. "I am a time traveler, Mr. Wells. And what is more, I can prove it to you."

4 ─────────────

The frenzied screams woke Stanley Turner and he leaped out of bed and rushed to the window. He threw it open and looked down into the courtyard. The woman lying on the cobblestones below wasn't screaming anymore. She was lying on her back and a man was bending over her. In the fog and the dim light from the streetlamp at the entrance to the courtyard, Turner couldn't see much more than their shapes. He shouted, but there was no reaction from the killer. Across the courtyard, several of the neighbors had thrown open their windows as well, but the killer seemed oblivious to his audience.

"Wot is it?" Turner's wife said, sitting up in bed and clutching the covers to herself, frightened by the screams which had awakened them. "Stan, wot's 'appened?"

"Stay 'ere," Turner said, moving from the window. He rushed out of the small apartment, pausing only long enough to grab a large carving knife, and ran down the stairs. He encountered one of his neighbors in the hall, Joe Tully, a brawny man who worked in the slaughterhouse and picked up beer money as a bareknuckle boxer.

"There's a murder—," Tully started.

"I know, I saw!" said Turner. "Quick, let's get the bloody bastard!"

They ran out into the courtyard, along with three other men who came out in various states of undress from the other

uildings. Shouting to each other, they ran towards the murder-
r, still bent over the body in the narrow courtyard of the
ul-de-sac. They were almost on him when he suddenly turned
ɔ face them, growling like a wild animal. The five men were
rought up short, staring with shock at the face all covered with
air, blood dripping from the snarling mouth.

Before any of them could move, the werewolf leaped and
rought down one of the men. A vicious swipe with a clawed
and cut off his scream. The remaining four men were galva-
ized into action. One of them brought a club down hard upon
he creature's back, but it had no effect. Turner leaped in with
is knife. He felt a hairy hand grabbing his own with an iron
rip and yanking hard and the next thing he knew, Stanley
urner was sailing through the air. He struck the building wall
ɔn the opposite side, hitting with his back and shoulders. He
eard a crunching sound and he dropped down to the cobble-
tones, stunned. He heard another scream as the man with the
lub was lifted high overhead and flung down upon the wrought
ron fence so hard that his body was impaled by the iron spears
t the top. They entered his back and penetrated his chest. The
nassive Joe Tully was flung aside as if he didn't weigh a thing
ind then another vicious swipe of the claws blinded the other
nife-wielding man. As he screamed, slashing about him
ɔlindly with his blade, the werewolf plunged a hand deep into
is stomach and ripped out his intestines.

The courtyard became filled with screams as people from the
ooms above watched the figures struggling in the fog. Joe Tully
came at the creature with his fists up in a boxing stance, the
corded muscles in his shoulders standing out, his barrel chest
hrown out, his left arm held out in front and his right cocked
ɔefore his chest. He took a swing with his left fist and the
creature caught it in its right hand. Tully swung his right and the
creature caught it with its left. Holding Tully's clenched fists
tightly in its hands, the werewolf began to squeeze. Tully
struggled, kicking at the creature, then howled with pain as the
bones in his fingers shattered. He was forced down to his knees
and then the creature let go of his ruined hands and grabbed his
hair, jerking his head back violently, exposing the throat. The
claws descended with a whoosh and Tully's throat was slashed
so deeply that his head was almost completely severed from his
body. Then the creature came towards Turner.

Turner sat with his back against the wall, holding the knife before him in both hands. His hands were shaking. He couldn't move. His back was broken. He saw the horrifying apparition approaching, heard the screams from above, felt the creature's fetid breath and then—

"Janos," a deep voice said from somewhere behind the creature.

The werewolf turned.

Turner heard the shrill blasts of a police whistle somewhere close by, in the fog.

"Come, Janos. Enough."

The werewolf turned back to Turner, snarling, eager to finish him off.

"I said *enough*, Janos! Come!"

Turner was amazed to hear the creature whimper like a dog.

"Come, Janos!"

It shambled off away from him and through the mist, Turner could barely make out the figure of a very large man dressed in a long dark cloak, a high silk hat, and carrying a walking stick. He turned and walked away quickly through the fog, with the creature hunched over, shambling along behind him. Stanley Turner was still holding the knife out in front of him with trembling hands when the police arrived.

"Lord, what a bloody awful mess," said Grayson, looking around the courtyard.

"Bloody's the word, all right," said Constable Wilkes shaking his head. "I've never seen anything like this in all my life."

It was still late and the fog was thick, but with the aid of their lanterns, they could see the bodies scattered all around the small courtyard. Blood was everywhere. They could hear the wailing of the women upstairs in their rooms, where members of the Metropolitan police force were trying to take statements from them. Grayson had instructed his men to keep the courtyard clear, not to allow anyone to come down until all the bodies had been removed and to keep everyone away from their windows. He also had a couple of men block off the entrance to the cul-de-sac. Wilkes had been the first to arrive on the scene, within moments after it had happened, and his whistle had summoned several other men on patrol, whom he had immediately directed to keep the neighbors inside.

"You've done well here, Wilkes," said Grayson, nodding. "You've got the situation well under control. The last thing we needed was to have everyone tramping around down here, acting hysterical."

"Thank you, sir," said Wilkes. "But just the same, I'm glad you're here, sir. I was about at my wit's end. Near as I could make out, one man did all of this. One man! Makes Jack the Ripper look like a bleeding amateur."

"That's enough of that!" said Grayson. "I want no talk about the Ripper, understood? That happened years ago. It's over. Over and done with."

"Right," said Wilkes, indicating the bodies. "Tell them."

"Get a hold of yourself, man," said Grayson. "Snap to. There's work to be done."

"Yes, sir. I'm sorry, sir."

"Right. Now where's the bloke who survived?"

"Right over there, sir," Wilkes said, pointing. "Wouldn't let us move him, thinks his back is broken. He's in shock, I think. Keeps saying that a—"

"Who's that with him?" Grayson said suddenly.

A man was crouching down on one knee beside Turner, talking to him.

"Here, you!" shouted Wilkes, rushing forward. He grabbed the man and yanked him to his feet, spinning him around. "Who are you?" he said. "How'd you get in here?"

"Dick Larson, *The Police Gazette*."

"Oh, bloody hell!" said Grayson. "Who let him through? I'll have his guts for garters! That's all we need, reporters!"

"Come on, you, out!" said Wilkes, grabbing Larson by his coat.

"Just a moment," Grayson said. "How did you get here so fast?"

"I've been investigating the other killing, Inspector," Larson said, "asking questions of people in the pubs hereabouts. I heard all the commotion and I ran to see what was going on."

"Well, we don't need any reporters getting in our way," said Grayson. "Those damn stories you people have been writing are going to have the entire city in hysterics. I've got a responsibility—"

"In that case, I suggest you listen to me, Inspector," Larson said. "That is, unless you want it to get about that there's some sort of werewolf on the loose."

Grayson grabbed him by the shirtfront. *"What* did you say?"

"Steady, Inspector," Larson said, gently prying his fingers loose. "I don't want to frighten people needlessly any more than you do. This man's still in shock, but he's starting to come out of it. I managed to get a few words out of him about what happened here tonight. I don't think I'll print what he told me he saw. In fact, I've been trying to convince him that he saw something else, not only for the public good, but for his own good, as well. The poor sod's been through enough without being thrown into a madhouse."

"I think you and I had better have a little talk, Mr. Larson," Grayson said. "Stick around until I get this mess cleaned up. Wilkes, make sure he doesn't go off anywhere."

"Right, sir," said Wilkes. Grayson went to supervise the removal of the bodies and interview some of the neighbors. "You had to go and blunder in here, didn't you?" Wilkes said to Larson. "And here I'd just been complimented on how well I had things under control."

Larson held out a cigarette case to Wilkes. "Cigarette?" he said.

Wilkes looked around. "Thanks," he said, taking one.

"You're welcome, Constable—?"

"Wilkes. Brian Wilkes."

"Take it easy, Brian," Larson said. "I'm not going to cause you any trouble. Believe me, something like this is bigger than just getting a good story. The maniac who did this must be stopped and it won't help you stopping him if we all start writing lurid stories about ghastly creatures lurking in the shadows of Whitechapel. Any idiot can write that sort of nonsense. I'd much rather write a story about how the police brought a deranged killer to justice than print stories criticizing you chaps and making your job that much more difficult."

Wilkes raised his eyebrows. "You having me on, mate?"

"Not in the least," said Larson, puffing on his cigarette. "Look at it this way, Brian, I could hand you all sorts of rubbish about social responsibility and the like, and it wouldn't be entirely rubbish, mind you, but the simple fact of the matter is that I intend to make something of a name for myself as a police reporter, covering crime in the city, and I've a few ideas as to how to go about that.''

"You don't say," said Wilkes. "How's that?"

"Well, there are places a reporter can go where a policeman would be too highly visible and there are people who would speak to a reporter, but would never be seen talking to police. A clever man could develop his own sources of information, information that the police might not otherwise have access to. Such a situation could benefit both that reporter and the police, if they were to work together.''

"Yes, I suppose I can see that," said Wilkes. "What you're proposing is a sort of cooperation. Each scratching the other's back a bit, as it were. You let us in on a tidbit now and then and don't write anything we wouldn't like you to and in exchange, we let you in on things other reporters wouldn't have, is that it?''

"I see you grasp the concept," Larson said, smiling. "And if it would help your situation, I could sort of mislead other reporters and then I'd have all the proper details when the whole thing was wrapped up. I'd have the best story then, you see.''

Wilkes grinned. "I shouldn't think that would make you very popular with your fellow members of the press.''

"I'm not out to win any popularity contests, Brian. We're all competitors, after all. Except for myself and Tom Davis of *The Daily Telegraph*. We've made sort of an arrangement to get the lion's share for ourselves, a silent partnership, as it were. I'm going to speak to Grayson about it. What sort of chap is he, by the way?''

"Chief Inspector Grayson? Blade straight and steel true, that one. I wouldn't try putting anything over on him, if I were you. I'd present it to him straight up, like you've just done with me. If you deal straight with him, he'll deal straight with you, but Lord help you if you cross him. He's like a ratting terrier. Once he's got his teeth into you, he never lets go until you're done.''

"I'll keep that in mind," said Larson.

"You do that, mate," said Wilkes. He clapped him on the shoulder. "Thanks for the smoke.''

"Don't mention it," said Larson. He smiled. It was a good beginning. Now to see if he could win Inspector William Grayson's trust.

• • •

"They did what?" said Steiger.

"They clocked out," said Linda Craven. "Right there in the teashop. One minute they were sitting at the table, drinking tea, and then the next, they simply disappeared. There were several couples in the shop, but nobody noticed them clock out except me. I came in after them, as if I was waiting to meet someone, and I was pretending to read a magazine, but I was watching them out of the corner of my eye. I saw the man Wells was with look around quickly, to see if anyone was watching, and then suddenly they were gone. I'm sorry, sir, the man didn't match Drakov's description and it just never occurred to me that he might have a warp disc."

"Christ," said Steiger. "What did this man look like? Describe him, carefully."

Craven bit her lower lip. "A small man, about five foot five or six, thin, grey hair and beard, very animated. Maybe late forties to mid-fifties, hard to tell his age exactly. His face was thin, sharp-featured, sort of delicate—"

"Moreau!" said Steiger.

Her eyes grew wide. "The head of S.O.G.'s Project Infiltrator?" she said.

"That's the one," said Steiger. "The description matches."

"Oh, God," she said. "I should have put it together, but I just didn't think—"

"Never mind," said Steiger. "Nothing we can do about it now. Get back to Wells' house. If he shows up again, contact me immediately."

"Yes, sir."

"And Craven? One more thing. If you spot Moreau again, even if it's in broad daylight with a dozen witnesses around, *waste* him. Understand?"

She swallowed hard. "Yes, sir."

Wells stood motionless in the small apartment above the apothecary shop, his face pale, his breath caught in his throat. A moment ago, he had been sitting in a teashop in Fleet Street and now, suddenly, inexplicably, he was . . . somewhere else. He blinked several times, looking around. Moreau stood before him, watching him anxiously.

"Where are we?" Wells said.

"In my rented room in Limehouse," said Moreau.

Wells shook his head. "Limehouse? No, that isn't possible."

"Look for yourself," said Moreau, moving to the window and opening the drapes.

Wells looked out the window. He could see soot-begrimed buildings, factories and warehouses and the river just beyond them. "Limehouse," he said softly. "This cannot be. I must be dreaming."

"I assure you, Mr. Wells," Moreau said, "you are not dreaming. If further proof is required, I can supply it."

"No, no, wait," said Wells. "I must take this in. This is incredible. I have to think."

"May I offer you a drink?" Moreau said.

"Yes, I think I'd better have a drink," said Wells. "A strong one, if you please."

Moreau poured him a whiskey and added just a dash of soda from the gasogene on the sideboard. Wells tossed it down.

"How is this possible?" said Wells. "How did we get here?"

"This bracelet you were so curious about," Moreau said, pulling up his sleeve and showing it to him. "It is called a warp disc. Simply put, it is a sort of time machine."

"A time machine!" said Wells.

"It is capable of broadcasting a sort of field," said Moreau, "by tapping into—well, it would be far too complicated to explain to a man of your time. However, as you can see, it does work."

"I think I had better sit down," said Wells. He slowly eased himself into an armchair and let out a long breath. "Dear God," he said. "Are you telling me that we have actually traveled through *time?*"

"Only in a manner of speaking," said Moreau. "No more than a moment or two have passed since we left the teashop. However, I could just as easily have programmed—that is, instructed the disc to take us back several centuries if I had wished to. Or ahead. The method of travel is called temporal transition. A sort of teleportation, if you will. We can go from one place to another within the same time period, or from one time period to another with equal ease."

Wells shook his head. "And all this is accomplished by a device so small that it can be contained within that bracelet? Amazing! It is beyond belief!"

"And yet you have experienced it, Mr. Wells," Moreau said.

"How can you *not* believe it?"

"Indeed," said Wells, "unless you have somehow mesmerized me and brought me here without my knowing it . . ."

"Would a more conclusive demonstration satisfy you?" said Moreau.

"I . . . I do not know," said Wells. "That is, I—"

Suddenly, Moreau was gone.

He had simply vanished, right before his eyes. Wells blinked, then shook his head, then slowly took a deep breath and let it out.

"Steady on, Bertie," he told himself. "You're not going mad. You're only dreaming. This cannot possibly be happening. There is a rational explanation for all this, there has to be—"

Moreau suddenly reappeared before him and Wells jumped about a foot. Moreau was sweating heavily and his shirt clung to him, as if he had been in intense heat for some time. He was holding his coat in his hands. Something was wrapped inside it. And it was moving.

"I have brought you something," said Moreau. "A present."

He placed his coat in Wells' lap. There was something wriggling around inside it. Wells sat perfectly still, afraid to move.

"What is it?" he said. "Not a snake? Moreau, you wouldn't—"

"Open it and see."

Wells slowly untied the coat sleeves and unwrapped what was inside the coat. He stared, bug-eyed, at the small, ungainly, reptilian-looking creature cradled inside Moreau's coat on his lap. It was a baby dinosaur.

"You have studied the biological sciences, Mr. Wells," said Moreau. "Perhaps you will recognize the creature as a baby sauropod. A Camarasaurus of the Upper Jurassic, to be exact. Have no fear, it cannot harm you. It is an herbivore. Its teeth and claws cannot injure you. I regret to say that you will not be able to watch it grow to its full size of 19.8 meters in length, with a weight that could reach as high as twenty-five tons. It will not live very long in this climate. It is far too cold for its constitution."

Wells stared with disbelief at the shivering little great lizard in his lap. He touched it hesitantly. It looked somehow pathetic.

"Take it back," he said. "Please."

"As you wish," Moreau said. He picked up the coat, wrapped it around the little dinosaur, and disappeared again, to reappear a moment later, even wetter with perspiration than before. "Convinced?" he said.

Wells leaned forward and put his head in his hands. "I think I would like another whiskey, please," he said.

Moreau poured him another glass and then changed into a fresh shirt. Wells held the drink in a trembling hand. He sipped it slowly this time, trying to calm himself.

"So it's true, then," he said finally. "My God. One *can* travel through time!"

"Indeed, one can," Moreau said. "I have come from hundreds of years in the future, Mr. Wells. A future you shall write about one day."

"So *that* is what it was all about then," Wells said. "Those other three who came to see me—"

"What other three?" Moreau said sharply.

"The ones who told me about Nikolai Drakov," Wells said. "They said something about my story, 'The Chronic Argonauts' . . . they wanted to know if I had met him, if I had discussed the subject of future scientific developments such as biological experimentation—"

"What were their names?" said Moreau.

Wells sighed. "I have never been very good with names," he said. "It is surprising that I recalled this Professor Drakov's name. They were Americans. One of the three was a young woman, blond, quite fit and very striking looking, and the other two were men—"

"Was the woman's name Andre Cross, by any chance?" Moreau said.

"Yes, I do believe that was her name," said Wells.

"And the two men with her, Steiger and Delaney? One blond, hook-nosed, one with dark red hair, large, very muscular?"

"Yes, they are the ones!" said Wells. "They said they were scholars of some sort. Are they friends of yours?"

"Hardly friends," Moreau said. "They would not hesitate to kill me the moment they set eyes on me, in spite of which, I am enormously relieved to know that they are here."

"Why?" said Wells. "I understand none of this! What reason would they have to want you dead?"

"It is a long story," said Moreau, "but one that you must hear if I am to convince you of the danger we all face. It involves war, Mr. Wells. The greatest war of all time. A war to end all wars. And there is no telling how long it may last. It is even possible that it will never end. But first, you must meet the only other man who shares my secret. He may seem like an unlikely ally, but do not be deceived by his age or his appearance. He is a most unusual man. His name is Lin Tao . . . ."

For a change, Ian Holcombe was glad for the help. It had been a long day and after working with Conan Doyle for several hours, he no longer had any qualms about "scribblers" in the crime lab.

"I owe you an apology, Doctor," Holcombe said as they were washing up and removing their aprons. Neilson handed them fresh towels. "About my behavior towards you earlier—"

"Think nothing of it," Doyle said. "And please, call me Arthur."

"Nevertheless, I do apologize, Arthur," Holcome said. "You are a first-rate medical man. For someone not trained in pathology, you possess remarkable skill."

"Well, it's true that I am no pathologist," said Doyle, "but I served as a ship's surgeon on several occasions, which is as good a way as any that I know to learn adaptability. And I had the good fortune to study under a most remarkable man once, Dr. Joseph Bell of Edinburgh, who taught me the value of observing, rather than merely seeing. I never knew him to make a single incorrect diagnosis. His deductive faculties were brilliant. He could tell what a man's occupation was simply by observing him carefully. In fact, I modeled Sherlock Holmes on him."

"How is it that you became a writer instead of a practicing physician?" Holcombe said.

"A peculiar trick of fate, I suppose," said Doyle. "It seems that people would prefer me to stick to writing rather than practice medicine. They pay me truly exorbitant sums for my stories, but if I had to live off my medical training, Louise and I would doubtless starve." He chuckled. "I could not get any patients, and yet sometimes it seems as if the entire world is hammering down my doors, demanding more stories about Holmes. You simply would not believe the response to my killing him off. You should see my mail. I am berated with the most outrageous accusations. One woman called me a heartless brute." He sighed. "My own creation has me by the throat. And yet, I must confess, right now I almost wish I had him here beside me, in the flesh, to help us unravel this mystery and bring this maniac to justice."

"You think it is all the work of one man?" said Holcombe. "Another Jack the Ripper?"

"The evidence certainly seems to support that theory," Conan Doyle said, putting on his coat. "The *modus operandi* in all these grisly killings is the same, with the sole exception of the Crewe girl."

"The additional hair samples matched the ones you found beneath the fingernails of Constable Jones?" said Holcombe.

"Yes, we got some good ones off the late Mr. Tully. He must have grappled with the killer. That we are dealing with a madman, there can be no doubt, not only from the sheer brutality of these crimes, but from the strength the killer obviously possesses. To throw five men around as if they were no more than kittens takes much more than ordinary strength."

"A madman's strength," said Holcombe.

"Indeed," said Doyle. "But what puzzles me most is the manner in which the wounds were inflicted. I thought, perhaps, that our killer possessed some kind of weapon, a small club of some sort fixed with sharp animal claws, similar to those carried by some tribes of African natives. A minor example of the taxidermist's art. That might have accounted for the animal hairs—or at least hairs that appear to be very like an animal's. But then closer analysis suggests that they are human hairs, albeit unusually coarse. Consider the testimony of the eyewitnesses who saw the struggle from their windows. From the way things seem to have occurred during the struggle, it would have been necessary for our killer to use both hands during the fighting, which means that if his weapon were a club or something that he had to carry, he would have had to drop it and pick it up again several times during the fight."

"So the claws, or whatever they were, had to have been worn upon his hands, like gloves?" said Holcombe.

"That does seem to be the only possible conclusion that the evidence will support," said Doyle, "and yet, it seems to me that something worn upon the hands in such a manner would have to affect the killer's dexterity to some degree. And consider the manner in which Tully's hands were crushed. The bones in the fingers were all shattered, as if squeezed in a powerful vise. And at least two of the witnesses report seeing the killer catch Tully's fists as Tully tried to strike him and then force Tully to his knees. No one saw anything resembling a weapon, although with the heavy fog, the reliability of these reports is open to some question. No one was able to see the killer's face clearly, which is truly unfortunate. Still, everything we know indicates that this struggle took place hand to hand, which raises the inevitable possibility, unlikely as it may seem, that the killer actually *has* claws."

"The werewolf hypothesis again?" said Holcombe sourly. Neilson pretended to be busy cleaning up, but he was listening closely. As common with doctors working around "lesser employees," the two men spoke as if he wasn't even there.

"For obvious reasons, I am as unsatisfied with that conclusion as you are, Ian," Conan Doyle said, "but when we conclusively eliminate all probable explanations, what remains, no matter how improbable it seems, must be the truth."

"But *have* we eliminated all the probable explanations?" Holcombe said.

"We do not yet possess enough evidence to say for certain," said Conan Doyle. "Consider this. We are confronted with a killer who murders with animal savagery, and in an animal manner. A man whose hands seem to have sharp claws. A man who tears the throats out of his victims with sharp teeth. A man who seems to have inhuman strength. What if our killer is *not* human? The more we consider these facts, the less it seems that we are dealing with a man."

"But the witnesses saw a man," said Holcombe.

"The witnesses saw what *appeared to be* a man," said Conan Doyle. "In the heavy fog, how could they be certain? Remember, no one saw the killer's face. I keep thinking about the sole survivor of the struggle, Stanley Turner. A face covered with hair, he said. What does that mean, a heavy beard? He said a man appeared out of the mist and called to the killer, called to him—or it—several times while it growled, apparently eager to attack Turner and finish him off. The killer finally responded and then, in Turner's own words, '*shambled off*' after the mysterious stranger. One might describe the movements of a great ape in such terms."

"A trained ape?" said Holcombe. "Dressed in a man's clothing?"

"A great ape would have the necessary strength required," Conan Doyle said, "and the other elements would seem to fit as well, only the hair does not match that of any ape I am familiar with. Still, there are such rare creatures as the silver-backed gorilla, for example, which might have hair to match those samples that we have found. There are no such creatures in captivity in England that I know of, but great apes are very manlike and I have seen chimpanzees trained to an astonishing degree, so that they almost seem like people."

"But what motive would someone have to train such a creature to kill, apparently at random?" Holcombe said. "And how could someone keep such an animal concealed?"

"I don't know," said Conan Doyle, frustrated. "It is a maddening case. But the more I think about it, the more I consider the evidence, the more convinced I become of the fact that our killer is not human. The question is, if he is not human, then what *is* he?"

"I'd sooner accept the theory that we are looking for an ape rather than a werewolf," Holcombe said wryly.

"So would I, Ian, so would I," said Conan Doyle. "One thing seems certain, though, and that is that we are dealing with some sort of a monstrosity. I will be curious to see what happens in the next few days, if there will be any more killings after tomorrow night."

"Why after tomorrow night?" said Holcombe, puzzled.

"Because tomorrow is the last night of the full moon," said Conan Doyle.

Neilson almost dropped a tray of instruments.

"A *werewolf?*" said H. G. Wells. He removed his glasses and rubbed the bridge of his nose. "Really, Moreau, this is too much. Just how much do you think one man can absorb in just one short afternoon?"

"Not only a werewolf," said Moreau, "but I have reason to believe that Drakov may have created a vampire, as well. The template for the creature was outlined in the notes he showed me—"

"Wait, wait," said Wells, holding his hands up in protest. He glanced from Moreau to the old Chinaman, Lin Tao, then back to Moreau again. "Let me understand you. Are we *seriously* talking about werewolves and vampires, such as those described in folklore? Men who turn into wolves when the moon is full, capable of being killed only by a silver bullet? Corpses reanimated by the devil, existing by the means of drinking human blood? Beings you cannot see reflected in a mirror, who turn into bats and can be destroyed only by wooden stakes driven through their hearts?"

"No, no, of course not," said Moreau. "What *you* are talking about is fantasy, the supernatural. What *I* am talking about is science. Specifically, the science of genetic engineering and biomodification. Biological experimentation, if you will, that is my field. I had developed a new way of manipulating human DNA . . . no, that would mean nothing to you, of course. How can I put it? This werewolf we are discussing, in a way, it was I who created him. I was the one who taught Nikolai Drakov everything he knows, to my everlasting shame. I was the one who showed him how animal genetic material . . . well, how surgical procedures, for lack of a better way of explaining it to you, can create beings who are neither men nor beasts, but something in between, creatures in whom elements of both men and beasts are combined. I never dreamed that he would take it so far. It never occurred to me that he had been studying the field for years, that he was an insane genius who would be able to observe my techniques and duplicate them, even refine them, that he was using me . . ."

Moreau's voice trailed off. He balled his fists and took a deep breath, shaking his head in an agony of rage and frustration.

"I am only confusing you," he said. "I can see it in your face. How can I explain? How can I make you see?"

"Why not convince him as you convinced me, Phillipe?" Lin Tao said softly. "Why not *show* Mr. Wells how much one man can absorb in just one short afternoon?"

Moreau stared at Lin Tao. "I had considered it," he said, "but it frightens me. What if something should go wrong? I mean no offense, old friend, but you are not historically important. Wells is. He will write extensively about the future. He will leave his mark. I have already interfered too much in his destiny. I am afraid to take it any further."

Lin Tao looked thoughtful. "In the words of the poet Hakuyo, 'Over the peak are spreading clouds, at its source the river is cold. If you would see, climb the mountain top.' If time is, indeed, as you have explained it to me, like a river with no end and no beginning, then perhaps, Phillipe, you should be afraid *not* to take it any further.''

Moreau licked his lips nervously. "Creatures in whom elements of both men and beasts are combined," he murmured softly to himself. "And then the remarkable coincidence of my name . . ." He shook his head. "But that was another world, another timeline. It's true, this one is almost a perfect mirror image—"

"Moreau, in Heaven's name, man, what are you mumbling about?" said Wells. "I understand none of this!"

"Perhaps not at this moment, Mr. Wells," Moreau said, "but you will very shortly understand it perfectly. As you have already observed, the type of warp disc that I wear can generate a temporal field large enough to transport more than one individual. You have experienced one very short temporal transition, from Fleet Street to Limehouse. How would you like to experience a far greater one, from the 19th century to the 27th?"

Wells stared at him. "Do you mean that you propose for us to travel over *seven hundred years* into the future?"

"Exactly," said Moreau. "I think that would convince you of what science can accomplish beyond any shadow of a doubt."

Wells swallowed nervously, glancing from one man to the other. "I am still not entirely convinced that I am not dreaming all of this," he said. "But if it is truly possible to see the future, to actually *travel* there . . . How could any man possibly resist such a fantastic opportunity? When would we leave?"

Moreau pulled back his sleeve. "Right now."

5 ──────────────────────────

The waiting was driving Finn Delaney crazy. Andre had relieved him on the surveillance of Conan Doyle and he had relieved Steiger at the Hotel Metropole command post while Steiger took a break for some much needed sleep. Delaney had bathed and put on a silk robe. He sat drinking coffee, going over his notes on the mission, which were continually updated as new reports came in. They were making progress, but it was excruciatingly slow.

Ransome and Rizzo had been systematically eliminating names from their lists of recent leaseholds and depositors, trying to track down Drakov's alias in this time period. *If* he was using an alias and if he was even in this time period. Delaney could not believe he wasn't. It would not fit Drakov's pattern to release several hominoids in Victorian London and then clock out to another time period. He would remain close by, to watch and supervise his handiwork. Nikolai Drakov was a product of two times—the 27th century, where he had received his implant education, and the 19th, where he had received his values, twisted though they had become. Drakov was not the sort of man to remain behind the scenes for long. His ego would not allow it. He took responsibility.

Neilson was keeping them steadily posted on the progress of Grayson's investigation. Grayson was an unexpected blessing. He was doing much of their legwork for them. And Neilson's clandestine examination of Grayson's notes and files had produced an address for the missing Tony Hesketh. Rizzo had been pulled off the search for Drakov's hideout and he was now staked out in Bow Street, near Covent Garden, watching Hesketh's rooms. They were rotating their posts as best they could, shifting manpower where it was needed most, but they were still spread very thin. With the Temporal Crisis rendering the timestream unstable, the entire Temporal Corps was being spread thin. It was an insane, impossible task, trying to monitor all of history for temporal confluence points, where their timestream intersected that of the alternate timeline from which Moreau had come.

Ever since Delaney had studied Mensinger's Theories of Temporal Relativity back in Referee Corps School, he had been haunted by the feeling that irreparable damage to the timestream was inevitable. It was one of the chief factors responsible for his washing out of RCS, that and his inability to grasp the subtler concepts of temporal physics, or zen physics as the cadets in RCS had called it. Only a few could pass the stringent entrance examinations required for admission to RCS and of those only a handful ever made it through, those whose minds were capable of the intricate gymnastics necessary to arbitrate temporal conflicts as members of the Referee Corps. Delaney had not been up to the mental discipline required of temporal physicists and he had not been cold enough to maneuver battalions of temporal soldiers through historical scenarios, considering them as nothing more than factors in a point spread which determined the arbitration of international disputes. Deep down inside, Delaney had always known that he could never function as a referee, a temporal strategist; he knew he would never be able to escape the feeling that he'd be like the proverbial Dutch boy with one finger plugging up a hole in the dyke while with his other hand, planting a limpet mine to blow it open. And yet, at the same time, even while he had been frightened of the consequences of the Time Wars, he had found participation in them intoxicating. It was a life of unparalleled adventure and unprecedented risk. Once he had experienced it, he could never go back to being a civilian.

He had been among the first selected for the First Division, the elite unit of time commandos led by Moses Forrester. Until then, he had been like an anti-personnel mine, buried just beneath the surface and forgotten until some hapless individual, usually an officer, strayed too close and triggered him off, making him explode. If not for Forrester, Delaney knew he would have wound up in a stockade or, still worse, cashiered from the service. A military prison, even cybernetic re-education therapy, would have been preferable to being drummed out of the Temporal Corps. There was nothing for him in civilian life. Like an attack dog trained to kill, he could not be redomesticated without a complete change in his personality. He simply knew too much. And his personality was such that he could not take any direction from inferiors. A mundane civilian job would have been out of the question. What was left? A life of crime? His ethics would not have permitted that. What then? He would have wound up as a derelict, a drunk, no doubt, or worse, a drug addict or a cybernetic dreamer, fleeing from an unacceptable reality until his body gave up on a life of desperate fantasy and surrendered to the reality of death.

Delaney had few illusions about himself. There was no place for him in the structure of society except as a soldier and even then, it took an unusual commander who would know how best to use a man such as himself. Forrester was such a man. He didn't bother with pointless military protocol and senior officers outside his unit never fully understood his methods, although they respected Forrester's results. To the average officer in the Temporal Corps, Forrester's First Division seemed like a cadre of mavericks and screw-ups. From the strictly military point of view, that which governed the parade ground, the First Division had no discipline. They were a group of roughnecks, most of them completely lacking spit-and-polish, devoid of even the rudiments of military courtesy. They held themselves above the other units in the service, most of them had a disdain for regulations, they were often sloppy and insubordinate and given to using their fists too readily. But out in the field, on the Minus Side of time, they were a model of efficiency. The necessity of forming a unit to deal with temporal disruptions gave rise to a need for a different breed of soldier—one who could improvise and think fast on his feet, one who did not go by the book, because the book did not cover all contingencies, and one who was more than a little crazy. It called for the sort of soldier who was too smart, too aggressive, too independent and too much of a nonconformist to fit in well with any other unit in the service.

One of the first things Forrester had done when he began to form his unit was to check through the dossiers of those soldiers in the Corps who had the worst disciplinary records in their respective units. He had known what he was looking for and he had known that, in certain cases, the difference between a man confined to a military prison and an outstanding combat soldier was an officer who knew how best to utilize the unique abilities of those placed under his command.

The fact that Delaney, who held the record in the entire Temporal Army for the most promotions and consequent reductions in grade, had finally become an officer in the First Division, and a captain, no less, was one of the bizarre ironies of his career. Another irony was that he had now become not only a soldier, but a temporal agent, an operative of the TIA, which had been brought under the same umbrella with the First Division, both combined into one unit under General Forrester's command. Delaney had never liked what he referred to as "the spooks," the quasi-military operatives of the Temporal Intelligence Agency, who seemed to be recruited primarily from among psycopaths and paranoids. And now he was one of them. Part soldier, part spy, part assassin, part counterterrorist. His worst nightmares had come true—the timestream had been split and now they were at war with an alternate universe. A war which was, perhaps, impossible for either side to win.

Theoretically, Delaney knew, it was possible for there to be any number of universes existing at the same time, in different dimensions or planes of reality. Neither Time nor Space was a rigid concept. Mensinger's Theories of Temporal Relativity were, like Einstein's revolutionary concepts, only theories, after all. The fact that nothing had come along to disprove them categorically only supported the theories, it did not "prove" them in the conventional sense as "laws."

The Theory of Temporal Inertia held that the "current" (a word Mensinger used loosely, primarily as an analogue) of the timestream tended to resist the disruptive influence of temporal discontinuities. According to the "father of temporal physics," the degree of this resistance was dependent upon the coefficient of the magnitude of the disruption and the Uncertainty Principle.

The element of uncertainty in temporal relativity, expressed as a coefficient of temporal inertia, represented the unknown factor in the continuity of time. Professor Mensinger had stated that in a temporal event-location which had been disrupted, it was impossible to determine the degree of deviation from the original, undisrupted historical scenario due to the lack of total accuracy in historical documentation and due to the presence of historical anomalies as a result either of temporal discontinuities or their adjustments. In other words, if something happened to influence or alter an historical event, Mensinger maintained that it was impossible to tell exactly how the original event had taken place—because there was no way of knowing *exactly* what all the details of the original historical event were. Historical records were never absolutely accurate and there was no way of knowing the extent to which a disruption could affect an historical scenario. Consequently, if the historical event were adjusted to compensate for a disruption, there was no way of knowing if the adjustment itself had not introduced a disruptive influence, something that might not have a noticeable effect until years later.

The Fate Factor held that in the event of a disruption of a magnitude sufficient to affect temporal inertia and create a discontinuity, the element of uncertainty both already present and brought about by the disruption combined with the "force" that Mensinger identified as the Fate Factor to determine the degree of relative continuity to which the timestream could be restored. In layman's terms, this meant that history did not "want" to change and there were natural forces at work to maintain the smooth and undisrupted flow of time. However, these forces did not necessarily come into play at the exact locus of a disruptive incident. A "ripple" in the timestream could be set in motion which would result in these compensating forces manifesting themselves further down the line in some other temporal event-location—with completely unforseeable results.

The "Timestream Split" had always been the greatest danger. In the event of a disruption of a magnitude great enough not only to affect temporal inertia, but to actually overcome it, the effects of the Fate Factor would be cancelled out by the overwhelming influence of a massive historical discontinuity. The displaced energy of temporal inertia would in that event—according to Mensinger's theories—create a parallel timeline in which the Uncertainty Principle would be the chief governing factor.

Delaney remembered how one of his professors in RCS had explained it by setting up a hypothetical situation. "Suppose," the professor had said, "you were to clock back in time to the American Revolutionary War. Suppose your potentially disruptive presence there results in your having to shoot an American soldier during a battle. This, in itself, creates a temporal disruption, but if this particular American soldier was not someone who was historically significant, the combined forces of the Fate Factor and temporal inertia would work to compensate for his death. For example, if this soldier that you killed originally survived the battle and one of his great, great grandchildren eventually did something of historical significance, the metaphysical influence of temporal inertia and the Fate Factor would probably influence event-locations all the way down the timestream in such a way that someone else would wind up doing the historically significant thing that the dead soldier's great, great grandchild would otherwise have done.

"However," the professor had continued, "suppose you accidentally shot General George Washington. You would have eliminated a historically significant figure at the key event-location point in the timestream and temporal inertia would not be able to build up enough 'momentum' to compensate for that death. The Fate Factor would be cancelled out and the massive amount of displaced temporal energy that would result could split the timestream, creating a parallel timeline. The original, undisrupted scenario would then continue in a smooth temporal flow—the original timeline in which Washington had never died. The parallel timeline created by the split, however, would proceed from the point at which the event-location had been disrupted and changed—in this newly created timeline, the death of George Washington would become a fact of history and events would proceed from that point, taking Washington's death into account.

"This brings up a number of interesting problems," the professor had said, smiling grimly in a way that had sent a chill down Finn Delaney's spine. "For one thing, having initiated a disruption in the temporal event-location, you would inevitably wind up in the timeline in which that disruptive event became a fact of history. In other words, you'd probably never be able to come home. Chances are you'd be trapped forever in that parallel timeline. If you were to clock ahead at that point, you would wind up in a parallel future, not the one you came from. Now, while that might pose an immense problem for you personally, it would be nothing compared to the problem it would pose for the entire flow of time, because Mensinger believed that if such an event came to pass, the combined force of the temporal inertia in *both* timelines would eventually result in their coming together again at some point in the future, like a confluence of rivers. And nobody knows what would happen in such a case. It's pretty scary.''

It was much more than scary. It was terrifying on a scale that could not even be fully comprehended. Mensinger came closest to understanding it completely and his realizations had resulted in his suicide. The political stupidity which had brought about the Time Wars had been based on the conventional wisdom of the then-current scientific establishment, which had maintained that history was an immutable absolute. The past had already happened, they maintained, therefore, it could not be changed. By the time they knew better, it was too late to retreat. At least, from the political standpoint.

A student of history, Delaney had once written a thesis based on the folly of politically feasible halfway measures that had proved disastrous in the long run. He had used a number of examples from the past to illustrate his point.

America in the 20th century had been heavily dependent upon the use of automobiles, personal transport vehicles powered by internal combustion engines. It was the almost universally chosen mode of transportation. The trouble was that internal combustion engines emitted gases and hydrocarbon particles that polluted the atmosphere and in the more densely populated regions, air pollution resulting chiefly from the use of too many automobiles in too small a space resulted in serious health and environmental problems. A solution of some sort was needed, but the scientifically feasible solutions did not prove to be politically feasible.

One possible solution was to regulate the amount of automobile traffic allowed in any densely populated area and develop alternate means of transportation and alternate, nonpolluting fuels, but people would not sit still for being told that they couldn't drive their cars whenever they pleased and they did not want their taxes raised so that alternate—and less attractive—means of public transportation could be developed. The oil industry, with its massive political clout, was not very anxious to see a competitive fuel developed unless they could control it and they already controlled oil, so why go to the expense of developing an alternative fuel, testing it, setting up new plants and distribution networks and so forth, all of which would mean extremely long-term payouts and much smaller profits?

Another solution was to regulate the number of people who could live in any one area, controlling population density. This, too, would have been political suicide for any legislator who supported such a measure. The politicians wanted a fix that would not overly offend their constituencies. Politicians frequently wanted to have their cake and eat it, too. The fix they found was a halfway measure that made a certain amount of "common sense," given enough supportive propaganda, but it ignored economic and scientific realities. "Pollution Control" devices were incorporated into automobile engine design, additional plumbing in the engine that would help control emissions. It sounded good in theory, but the trouble was that these devices interfered with optimum performance and most were only good for about ten thousand miles before they required complete replacement—something few automobile owners ever did. The emission control testing programs instituted to enforce this were easily circumvented and little more than lip-service programs to begin with. The result was that engines so equipped not only gave performance far inferior to engines lacking these devices, but they polluted measurably more after a brief period than an engine without the extra plumbing that was routinely kept in a proper state of tune.

The populace was propagandized into believing that this "bolt-on solution" was the answer and someone else came up with the brilliant idea that if people drove more slowly, they would save fuel and thereby pollute less. Unfortunately, this had very little to do with the principles of automotive engineering. It was a "sounds good solution" that made sense only to the technologically ignorant, who knew nothing about horsepower curves, gearing and torque and therefore were incapable of understanding how a high performance sports car driven at 85 miles per hour could be made more fuel efficient than a family sedan driven at 55. They wanted simple answers, not engineering complexity. Slower speed meant less fuel used—it was wrong, but it made sense to most people, so they wrote a law limiting the speed to 55 miles per hour. Delaney had once driven an antique internal combustion engined car from Denver to Houston and he had concluded that only idiots on the densely populated east coast could have passed such a law. Had they been made to drive the same distance over the same roads at a speed of 55 miles per hour, he had no doubt the law would have been quickly repealed. But it wasn't, because it had great propaganda value and because rampant noncompliance with the law provided local authorities with easy revenue. Yet another way to fool the public and then skin them.

Nuclear energy was an even more graphic example. Before fusion was developed, nuclear power plants were potentially hazardous. If the proper safeguards were not observed, if personnel manning the plants were inadequately trained and if the plants were not constructed and maintained properly, then nuclear power plants could pose serious threats to the environment. In 1986, in the USSR, an accident occurred that was referred to in the media as a "fire"—a curious but more palatable term for a chain reaction. Dangerous levels of radiation were released into the atmosphere, an event which could have been prevented had the proper safety procedures, such as the use of concrete containment buildings, been observed. But the human factor was always the weak link. Engineering principles were only as efficient as the people who applied them. After the accident occurred, the danger was de-emphasized, the scientific ignorance of the populace facilitated political circumlocution, and the resulting "fallout" of popular opinion blamed nuclear power itself as being too dangerous, when the real answer was that nothing could be rendered absolutely safe—it was all a question of relativity and trade-offs, of acceptable versus unacceptable risks, and of scientific illiteracy prevailing over educated and informed opinion. A scenario made to order for political stupidity.

The Time Wars were the ultimate example of people making decisions who were not even qualified to hold an opinion on the matter. When the Time Wars could have been stopped, the politicians prevailed, thinking about their own livelihoods, concerned about all the support industries created by the Time Wars which were providing jobs to their constituents, thinking about the propaganda value of being able to assure the folks back home that thanks to the Time Wars, they were immune to conflicts taking place in their own time—the only ones at risk were soldiers, all of whom were volunteers, and warfare in the past meant essential disarmament in the present. Propaganda. Halfway measures. Scientific illiteracy. Lies. Now they reaped the harvest.

The accident that everyone had dreaded had finally occurred. It was impossible to pinpoint exactly what had caused it. It was even impossible to determine if one particular event had caused it or if it was a result of cumulative temporal interference. Without an event-location which could be pinpointed, there was no "fix." And yet, the politicians were screaming for a fix. The scientists of the Temporal Corps had explained it to them over and over again, they had explained it to the media, but the question still persisted, always starting with the all-too-familiar "yes, but" phrase. "Yes, but how can it be fixed?" They screamed for an investigation. Who was at fault? Who can the finger be pointed at? If enough money could be spent, surely a solution could be found. Wrong, said the scientists. There is no solution, because the problem can't be solved. We can't cure the disease, we can only treat the symptoms. As for whose fault it was, finding a scapegoat would accomplish nothing, because it was everybody's fault, the fault of all those people who thought that lunch was free, that something could be gained for nothing, that there was a way to live secure, without the threat of risk. But such an answer was politically unfeasible, and so they didn't want to listen. And they blamed the scientists.

It was similar to what happened to the space program in the latter part of the 20th century. An enviable safety record had lulled the public into complacency. Budgetary cuts voted by scientifically illiterate legislators steadily reduced the safety factors and created additional pressure to make space exploration more glamorous and relevant, to keep it in the public eye. And then, when an accident occurred, resulting in tragic loss of life, once again, the media and the legislators screamed. How could it have happened? Who was to blame?

The magnitude of the problem was too great for them to comprehend. And explaining complicated scientific principles to the public in uncomplicated terms took up too much time—it could not be reduced to a simplistic statement or two in a five-minute interview on a news program. And a five-minute attention span was the most that the media could hope for. They wanted it short, informative and simple and if they were told that it could not be short, informative and simple, they became impatient and suspected obfuscation.

Shortly after the Temporal Crisis, as the media had dubbed it, had been publicly announced, a reporter had cornered Delaney at a bar near Pendleton Base, frequented by soldiers of the First Division. She was eager for the "simple truth," as she had put it, that a "frontline soldier" could provide.

"How much time have you got?" Delaney had naively asked her.

"Take as much time as you need," she said. "We'll edit it together later for the broadcast. We just want to hear the simple truth about the Temporal Crisis as a frontline soldier sees it."

Delaney had emptied his glass in a long swallow and leaned back against the bar while they trained the camera on him.

"Well," he said, "the simple truth is not so simple. Basically, the Time Wars were a terrific risk right from the start, but people were either willing to accept the risk or else they simply didn't want to hear about it. I suspect the truth is they just didn't give a damn until something went wrong. And something was bound to go wrong, because we were screwing around with temporal physics."

"What does that mean, exactly?" she had said.

"Well, let's take a real basic example and I'll make it as simple as I can, okay?" Delaney had said. "Let's say that our country had a difference of opinion with the Nippon Conglomerate Empire. It got intense, no negotiated settlement could be reached, and so the grievance was submitted for arbitration to the Referee Corps. A ref was assigned to arbitrate the temporal action that would settle the whole thing. He asked the Nippon government to provide five hundred grunts and he asked our government to provide five hundred grunts. He selected an historical scenario for the arbitration conflict or the time war, as it's more popularly called. He decided to use World War II. The troops were cybernetically indoctrinated and clocked back into the past, to fight among the troops of World War II. One of our guys got a bit carried away and used a warp grenade instead of a regular 20th century hand grenade. He didn't exactly set off a multimegaton nuclear explosion, he only used a small portion of the energy released by the grenade, no more than would have been released by a conventional 20th century hand grenade. The only problem is, he killed General Dwight D. Eisenhower, who went on to become the President of the United States.''

"Did this actually happen?" said the reporter.

"No, of course not, it's only a hypothetical situation," said Delaney. "Well, now we've got a problem. We've got a fairly large temporal disruption and it has to be adjusted. So an adjustment team is clocked back into the past, in the hope that something can be done about it before the damage becomes irreversible and a timestream split occurs. Let's say we get lucky. We're able to replace the late General Eisenhower just in time with one of our own people, someone from a special unit formed to deal with just such a situation. It's not an easy job. This person has been surgically and cybernetically altered to *become* General Eisenhower. He has to live out the rest of Eisenhower's life, *exactly* as Eisenhower would have lived it, based on what we know of history. A chancy proposition, at best, but it's the most we can do. There are certain to be at least minor discontinuities as a result, but we can bring all of our resources to bear on this and hope that the discontinuities will be relatively minor.

"Meanwhile, things like this have been happening all throughout the timestream, every time we've had a temporal conflict. Sometimes we've adjusted the disruptions. Sometimes we've had to replace historically significant individuals with people of our own. Sometimes we haven't caught the disruption, because it was really very minor. It all started to add up. Maybe it put a strain on temporal inertia and something happened to disturb chronophysical alignment in time and space and another universe somehow came into congruence with our own. I suppose it really doesn't matter how it happened, the point is that it happened. Somehow the timestream became unstable and our timestream intersected another timestream and now the two parallel universes are crisscrossing in time and space, intertwining like a double helix strand of DNA. Every now and then, there occurs an event-location at which both timestreams exist in the same time and space. Crossover becomes possible. And the people in this other timestream are not very happy with us.

"To anticipate your next question, the reason they don't like us very much has to do with that warp grenade our temporal soldier blew up General Eisenhower with. The way a warp grenade works, you set it for the amount of energy you want to use. Let's say you only need about one-tenth of one percent of the energy of the grenade's nuclear explosion. The rest of it is warped into outer space where it goes off, theoretically, without doing any harm. Only as it turns out, the surplus energy of that grenade didn't just go off with a big bang in outer space, as we had thought. Because of the congruence, most of that energy was teleported directly into the alternate universe, where there was one hell of an explosion. And we've been setting off more than just one warp grenade. In other words, we were bombing the hell out of the alternate universe without even realizing it and, understandably, they're somewhat annoyed with us. So now we're at war with them. The Temporal Crisis, as you people in the media call it. Only neither side really wants an all-out war. Nobody could survive that. So instead they concentrate on screwing up our history, in the hope that they can split our timeline and somehow force our universe away from theirs, and we do much the same to them.''

"Where does it all end?" the reporter said.

"The hell of it is, it probably doesn't end," Delaney told her. "You see, you could wind up with timestream splits all over the damn place and nobody knows what effect that would have. We could wind up with all of them intersecting. A real mega-Time War. Their universe is almost a mirror image of ours, but it's not exactly the same. The trouble is, the forces of temporal inertia in both universes are working to bring our two timelines together, so the only thing we can do to keep that from happening is to continue creating disruptions in their timeline while they continue creating disruptions in ours. In order to keep our two timelines from becoming one timeline, we have to maintain the instability. But if we maintain the instability, we're threatening our own temporal continuity. It's a Catch-22 situation. The whole thing is liable to collapse at any minute like a house of cards."

"So what's the answer?" the reporter said, growing impatient.

"What makes you think I've got an answer?" said Delaney.

"Yes, but surely you must have some ideas about how to resolve the Temporal Crisis. There has to be an answer."

Delaney shrugged. "Not really. In a complex world, I'm afraid there are no simple answers."

"So where does that leave us?" the reporter said, still pressing for an answer.

"I guess it leaves us with a lot of questions to which there are no simple answers," said Delaney wryly. "And that's the 'simple truth' as a 'frontline soldier' sees it."

He watched the report later that night. They had, indeed, edited his answer. It ran like this:

"We just want to hear the simple truth about the Temporal Crisis as a frontline soldier sees it."

"Well, the simple truth is the Time Wars were a terrific risk right from the start. They just didn't give a damn until something went wrong. And something was bound to go wrong. It's a Catch-22 situation. The whole thing is liable to collapse at any minute like a house of cards. And that's the simple truth as a frontline soldier sees it."

Delaney had to explain to Forrester about the editing. He received an official reprimand, which Forrester promptly "filed," and specific orders were issued to all military personnel not to speak to members of the media without special authorization. Paranoia settled in to stay.

Delaney wondered what would have happened if he had told them about the Special Operations Group, the First Division's counterpart in the alternate universe, and Project Infiltrator, a genetic engineering project headed by Dr. Phillipe Moreau, aimed at creating genetically engineered soldiers to be infiltrated into their timeline? What if he had told them that Drakov had kidnapped Moreau from the Project Infiltrator labs and set him to work creating hominoids, creatures bioengineered from human clones and modified with advanced surgical and cybernetic techniques, turned into monstrosities that were no longer human, but something else entirely? And what if he had told them that aside from the Temporal Crisis, they were all faced with the threat of Nikolai Drakov, an insane criminal genius who wanted nothing less than temporal anarchy, or failing that, an apocalyptic entropy, an end to all of time?

He imagined the reporter saying, "Yes, but what's the answer?"

He imagined himself replying with a variation on an old zen koan. "If the shit hits the fan and there's no one left to smell it, is there a stink?"

He checked his watch. Ransome was late. He should have

reported in by now and gone off to relieve Rizzo at Hesketh's apartment. And it would soon be time for him to wake up Steiger, catch a couple of hours sleep himself and then relieve Andre at Conan Doyle's house, so that she could get some rest. It was monotonous. Watching and waiting. Something had to break soon. The bathroom door opened and Christine Brant came in, having been relieved at H. G. Wells' house by Linda Craven.

They were using the bathroom as a clocking in point, with each member of the team assigned a ''window'' during which they could make temporal transition. Using the bathroom as a temporal staging zone meant that they could all freely move about the rest of the apartment without having to worry about when someone might be clocking in at a certain point—it wouldn't do to be standing on the same place where someone was trying to clock in. The results would be very messy and very fatal. It also meant that in the unlikely event that someone else was present in the apartment, with the bathroom door closed, they would not see anybody suddenly materializing out of thin air. Someone clocking in could simply wait inside the bathroom until whoever it was had gone. As far as using the bathroom for its intended purpose was concerned, they resorted to the one in the adjoining suite.

''Anything?'' said Christine Brant.

Delaney shrugged. ''Ransome's late reporting in. Otherwise, no changes.''

''How's Colonel Steiger holding up?'' she said.

''I'm due to wake him in another hour. He's holding up about as well as could be expected, I suppose. He's getting anxious, as are we all. Any sign of Wells?''

She shook her head. ''Not yet. Of course, there's no guarantee he'll be coming back to his house. Can I have some of that coffee?''

''Help yourself.''

''Thanks.'' She sat down and poured herself a cup. ''What do you think Moreau's going to do with him?'' she said.

''I have no idea what to think,'' Delaney said. ''I still don't see how Wells would fit in with what Drakov seems to have planned. Unless he's planning something separate that has to do with Wells.'' He shook his head. ''There are just too many variables. The best we can hope for is that Wells will show up again, with Moreau, and we'll get a shot at taking out Moreau and snatching Wells. The problem is, what do we do with Wells once we've snatched him? He already knows too much, but can we risk having him conditioned to forget his part in all of this? Would that affect his writing?'' He shook his head again. "I don't know, Christine. It's going to be very tricky. The waiting's hard, but it's not the hardest part."

"You know, a very unpleasant thought occurred to me while I was on the watch for Wells," she said. "It's bad enough that Moreau snatched him from right under our noses, but what are we going to do if he doesn't come back?"

Delaney's hand froze with his coffee cup halfway to his mouth. "Don't even think about it," he said.

6 ─────────────────────────

They met in the rooms of the Beefsteak Society. The Sublime Society of Beef-Steaks was not in session at the moment. The tradition dated back to 1735, when John Rich, manager of the Covent Garden Theatre, founded the club for "men of noble or gentle birth," which met for a beefsteak dinner every Saturday from November to June. The badge of the society was a gridiron and its members wore blue coats and buff waistcoats, buff being a light yellow napped leather properly made from buffalo skin, though other skins were sometimes used. The motto of the club was "Beef and Liberty" and it met at the Lyceum Theatre. Grayson thought the whole thing was rather juvenile, but then there had always been a ritualistic fervor among the upper classes that he had never fully understood. If you want to meet once a week for a steak dinner, he thought, why not simply meet once a week for a steak dinner? Why make a bloody boys' club formality of the whole thing? In any case, it was a question that was never liable to concern him personally, as it was highly unlikely that he would ever be invited to join a gentleman's club. He was just a simple working class sod, happy with his station in life and if he wanted a steak dinner, he could bloody well just go down to the pub and get one.

Bram Stoker beckoned him to one of the chairs placed around the table. "Please sit down, Inspector. May I offer you something to drink?"

"No, thank you very kindly, Mr. Stoker, not while I'm on duty."

"Are you making any progress with your inquiries, Inspector?" Stoker said. "I take it that is what you wanted to speak to me about?"

"As a matter of fact, yes, it was," said Grayson. "I trust, Mr. Stoker, that we may speak in confidence?"

"Certainly, Inspector," Stoker said. "However, I should tell you that if what you have to discuss with me should happen to concern Henry Irving, I would be both honor and duty bound to take the matter up with him. He is both my employer and my closest friend."

Grayson nodded. "I quite understand. However, I don't think we will need to concern ourselves with Mr. Irving. There is certainly nothing to suggest that he is in any way involved."

"Involved in what, Inspector?" Stoker said.

"Well, frankly Mr. Stoker, at the moment I am not quite sure, but I suspect it may be murder."

Grayson watched Stoker carefully. The man suddenly became silent, but he did not avoid Grayson's steady gaze. He pressed his lips together and gave a couple of curt nods.

"I see," said Stoker. "Then if I understand you correctly, Inspector Grayson, you believe that Angeline Crewe was murdered, but you have no proof."

"No proof that I would feel comfortable presenting at the Old Bailey," Grayson said. "At least, not yet. However, there is no question but that Miss Crewe was subjected to at least one violent assault shortly prior to her death and it appears possible that she may even have cooperated in it."

Stoker frowned. "Exactly what are you implying, Inspector?"

"Those wounds on her throat were made by teeth, Mr. Stoker," Grayson said, watching the man for a reaction. "Human teeth."

"You're certain of this?" Stoker said.

"Beyond a shadow of a doubt," said Grayson.

"You are telling me that she was bitten in the neck by someone and, as a result, she died?" said Stoker.

"She died from loss of blood," said Grayson.

Stoker took a deep breath. "Is each of us wondering who will say it first?" he said. "Very well, then, *I* will say it. Her killer bit her in the neck and drank her blood. In other words, a vampire?''

Grayson pursed his lips. ''I see that the thought had already crossed your mind,'' he said. ''Tell me, are you a superstitious man, Mr. Stoker?''

''People in the theatre are always superstitious,'' Stoker said. ''But let's speak plainly, shall we? If you're asking me if I believe in the existence of such creatures, I can only answer by saying that I would be disinclined to, but to my certain knowledge, I don't know. There are many things in this world which we cannot explain to our satisfaction. Frankly, when I saw those marks upon Angeline's throat, it was the first thing that crossed my mind, but then I had only recently read a novel by Sheridan Le Fanu about a woman who was a vampire. Are you familiar with the work?''

''You mean *Carmilla?*'' Grayson said.

''Yes, that's the one. You've read it then?''

Grayson nodded.

''So what do *you* think?'' Stoker said.

''I found it entertaining, but to borrow your own words,'' said Grayson, ''I am disinclined to believe in the existence of such creatures.''

''You would prefer to seek a more rational explanation,'' Stoker said, nodding. ''Has it occurred to you that there are legends about vampires dating all the way back to ancient times, to Greece and Rome? And that there have been many apparently reliable reports concerning vampirism scattered throughout history since then? Even up to and including recent times?''

''Yes, I am aware of that,'' said Grayson. ''In fact, I recently had an interesting conversation concerning that very topic with Dr. Conan Doyle and he was able to explain to me convincingly how such stories might have been sustained as a result of ignorance and improper observation.''

Stoker smiled. ''Yes, that sounds like Arthur. There's a man with both feet planted firmly on the ground, just like his detective, Sherlock Holmes. He claims the character was based upon an old professor of his, but the truth is that there's a lot of Arthur in old Sherlock. No, I don't imagine he would sit still for a moment to listen to any farfetched notions about vampires. And yet there is the tragic, albeit fascinating case of Angeline Crewe. Did Arthur offer any theories about that?''

"As a matter of fact, he did," said Grayson. "And I am inclined to accept them. One of the things that he suggested was that . . . well, how can I put this delicately?"

"Please don't bother," Stoker said. "We have agreed to speak plainly, if you'll recall."

"Yes, well, meaning no offense," said Grayson, "but people associated with the theatre have a certain reputation for rather irregular behavior. And one of the things that Dr. Conan Doyle suggested is that we may be dealing with a case of sadistic perversion here. This theory seems to be supported by the fact that Miss Crewe apparently never made any mention of having been bitten in the throat and one would think that if she had been assaulted forcibly in such a manner, she would certainly have said something about it to someone. And if she had actually permitted such an act to be committed upon her person, and actually allowed the drinking of her blood, then what other conclusion could there be except that she was a willing participant in an act of such depravity?"

"I see," said Stoker. "It is an interesting speculation, to be sure. And, purely in terms of degree, certainly more rational than the vampire theory. However, has it occurred to you that the reason Angeline Crewe never said anything about having been so cruelly used might have been that she was frightened and humiliated?"

"I should think that if she had been frightened," Grayson said, "she would have been all the more anxious to speak out and have the blackguard who did it brought to justice, so that he would never be able to menace her or any other young woman again."

"One might well think so," Stoker said, "if one is a man. However, try to consider the situation from a woman's point of view, Inspector. A woman who is an actress and, unfortunately, as you have already pointed out, suffers from an entirely undeserved reputation for irregular behavior, as you put it. Just because a woman is an actress, Inspector, that doesn't mean she is immoral. And in this particular case, we have a young woman who comes from a good family, a family which has already suffered a certain amount of distress due to her chosen vocation. If the matter were to come to court, it would be purely her word against that of her assailant and you can be sure that the man's counsel would do everything in his power to discredit her testimony by attacking her reputation. I personally know of no woman who would not flinch from such an ordeal.''

"Your point is well taken," Grayson said, nodding. "I had not thought of that. It is the sort of thing that might give some comfort to her family when all of this eventually comes to light—as it shall, rest assured on that account—but for the moment, let us leave the question of Miss Crewe's reputation aside and concentrate upon the fact of her demise. Whether she was a willing participant in depravity or whether she was forcibly imposed upon, it seems obvious that whoever was responsible cannot possibly be sane. Which brings us back to Dr. Doyle's observations upon this matter. And again, I remind you that we speak in confidence.''

"Of course," said Stoker.

"I have been attempting to reconstruct something of Miss Crewe's recent past," said Grayson. "I know, for example, that she was seen frequently in the company of a young man named Tony Hesketh. You yourself confirmed this in our last discussion. Hesketh is missing, disappeared without a trace. I find this highly suspect. I have also managed to learn that Mr. Hesketh's character is not altogether what one might consider proper. I have established to my satisfaction that he was intimately associated with at least one young man of questionable moral character, if you get my meaning.''

"You're saying that Tony Hesketh was a homosexual," said Stoker. He shrugged. "Frankly, that does not surprise me. I always thought that young Hesketh was a bit overly flamboyant and rather effeminate. I did try to dissuade Angeline from fraternizing with him. He seemed like a bad sort to me. You're suggesting that one mode of abnormality might breed another?''

"It is certainly possible," said Grayson. "I have the impression that young Hesketh straddled the fence, as it were. A jaded appetite that is already immoral and decadent to begin with could easily turn to more depraved pleasures. Hesketh may not be sane. Dr. Doyle cited a number of historical examples of so-called vampirism, but vampirism practiced by insane living persons rather than satanic dead ones. A form of perversion, if you will. And if this sounds farfetched, you should hear the details of some of these cases. Dr. Doyle mentioned one that comes vividly to mind, the case of a 15th century warlord named Dracula who murdered thousands of people in the most grisly manner—''

Stoker started. *"What* did you say that name was?'' he said.

Grayson was surprised at the reaction. "Dracula,'' he said. "A prince of some sort, Vlad Dracula, known for his cruelties as the Impaler. Why do you ask?''

"Because I have met a man named Dracula,'' said Stoker. "And quite recently, too. A wealthy Balkan aristocrat. I remember the name because I liked the sound of it. It rolled rather ominously off the tongue. Count Dracula. He came to the theatre on a number of occasions. And he was a friend of Tony Hesketh's.''

Wells stood at the hotel window, clutching Moreau's arm as if terrified of letting go. Below them, people surged past in a ceaseless wave of humanity, moving quickly and purposefully across pedestrian spanways high above the ground. The skyscrapers towered above them on all sides and far below, Wells could see other spanways, both vehicular and pedestrian, crisscrossing in a webwork of suspended roads and walkways. Just below them was a vehicular spanway that snaked among the buildings and tiny vehicles which were completely enclosed and shaped like sleek teardrops in a wide and dazzling array of colors traveled at amazing speeds just above the surface of the suspended roadway. Above them, machines flew through the air, small craft with stubby, swept back delta wings, occasionally diving down like kingfishers into the steel, glass and concrete jungle, often passing so close to one another that Wells could not see how it was possible for them to avoid collision.

"I cannot believe my eyes,'' he said. "Where *are* we?''

"London,'' said Moreau.

"London!''

"The London of the 27th century, to be exact,'' Moreau said. "The year 2626.'' He pointed out the window. "If you will look between those two large buildings over there, you will see the Thames. You will not see Tower Bridge, which no longer stands, but I think you will recognize the Tower of London beneath that dome, where it remains perfectly preserved.''

"Incredible!'' said Wells. "Absolutely incredible! Can we go outside?''

"It would be safer to remain here," said Moreau.

"What is this place?" said Wells. "Is this your home?"

"Not exactly," said Moreau. "It is a hotel room. I pay for it by bringing certain coins and stamps from the 19th century and selling them privately to collectors in this time period. In this way, I have managed to establish accounts here, as well as a false identity. If my true identity were known, it is almost a certainty that I would be arrested. I am telling you this because I want you to understand that I am being completely honest with you."

"It is all so overwhelming, I do not know where to turn! Such astonishing growth! I would never have thought it possible that buildings of such amazing height could be constructed! And all those flying machines buzzing about like bees around a hive, how do they keep from colliding?"

"They are equipped with guidance systems," said Moreau. "Far too complicated to explain, just think of them as devices which are capable of sensing everything around them and communicating with each other as they navigate."

"Amazing!" said Wells. "Moreau, can't we go outside for just a moment? Please?"

"Well, all right," Moreau said, "but only for a moment or two. However, you had best change into some different clothing first."

Moreau went to a closet and opened it.

"What manner of clothing is this?" said Wells, touching the sleek, shiny material and feeling it stretch. "It is made from materials such as I have never seen!"

"Synthetics," said Moreau.

"Synthetic materials?" said Wells, touching the futuristic garments hanging in the closet.

"A blend of synthetics, created in a laboratory," said Moreau. "Form fitting, easily cared for. They will stretch to accommodate your size."

"But . . . it is all of one piece. Is this all there is to the costume?" Wells said.

"It will serve," Moreau said.

They changed and moments later, Wells stood before a mirror, examining himself in the black clingsuit. "I cannot say it flatters me," he said. "It seems terribly revealing. And what makes it shine so? It looks as though it is soaking wet.''

''It is the nature of the material,'' Moreau said somewhat impatiently. ''And rest assured, in this time period, it is considered a conservative fashion. I should warn you that we are liable to see people, women in particular, wearing costumes that are far more revealing. Customs are very different here. Try not to be shocked.''

They went outside into the hallway and took a drop tube to the lobby. Wells could barely contain himself. He wanted to know how the lighting in the hallway operated, how the drop tube functioned, what made the indicator lights work and where the cool air was coming from. Moreau made no attempt to reply to his torrent of questions, saying merely that it was impossible to explain hundreds of years of scientific development to someone who could not even comprehend most of the terms and Wells had to satisfy himself with brief explanations of what the function of various things was, rather than how they functioned.

They came out into the lobby and Wells gasped at the immensity of it, at the height of the ceiling, which was several dozen stories over their heads, at the huge colored fountain playing in the lobby's atrium and the strange music, coming from nowhere and created by instruments he could not even identify. As they walked across it and approached the large, ornate glass doors leading outside, Wells was stunned to see them open by themselves and Moreau was unable to restrain him from repeatedly stepping on and off the sensor panels, making the doors open and close repeatedly, as a small child might do.

''Please, Herbert,'' Moreau said, finally dragging him away. ''We must try not to attract attention to ourselves.''

They went outside into the street and walked for a short distance, Wells craning his neck backward, looking up above them at the impossibly tall buildings and the traffic overhead. He stopped in the center of the sidewalk, gazing up with rapture, and in moments, there were a number of people around them, likewise looking up, wondering what he was looking at.

''Herbert, for God's sake, *please!*'' Moreau said, dragging him on.

They hadn't walked a block before an adolescent girl with varicolored hair cut in a geometric style and wearing high black boots, scarlet clingpanties and a see-through halter sidled up to them and propositioned Wells. Moreau grimaced and waved her off.

Wells grinned. "Well, in some respects at least, things have not changed very much at all."

"If you had accepted her proposition," Moreau said sourly, "I think you'd have found that things have changed more than you might think. Come, let us go back to the hotel. I do not wish to expose you to so much that your mind will be shocked by overstimulation. We have much to talk about."

"Please, can't we stay a little while longer?" Wells said. "Can't we walk about? There is so much to see! I have a thousand questions bursting from my brain!"

"Later, perhaps," Moreau said. "Regrettably, we cannot remain here for long. Bringing you here was a great risk and I am still not certain that it was the right decision. However, perhaps it was for the best. Perhaps now you will possess enough perspective to fully appreciate what I have to tell you. It would take hours to even begin to answer some of those questions you have, but I needed to eliminate your doubts."

"And that you have," said Wells, glancing all around him. "To think that I have traveled *hundreds of years* into the future! What a world awaits us! What astonishing accomplishments! Please, Moreau, can't we stay awhile longer?"

Moreau smiled. "Very well. But keep close to me. If we were to become separated, you would become truly lost, forever."

"I do not know that I would mind that very much," said Wells.

"Don't even joke about it," said Moreau.

"What would happen if we did not go back?" said Wells. "Purely for the sake of argument, of course."

"There is no way of knowing exactly what would happen," said Moreau, "but you can be certain that history would be changed. The results could be disastrous on an unimaginable scale. By the act of bringing you here, I have already altered history, but the risk is slight if we follow proper precautions. It is nothing compared to the risk we all face back in your own time. And now that you have seen all this, perhaps you might begin to understand. Come, I will tell you about myself, about who and what I am and where I came from, and about the crowning achievement of my career, which has now turned into a nightmare that threatens all humanity. And it all began when a device known as a chronoplate was invented and man achieved the capability of traveling through time . . ."

"Count Dracula?"

The tall dark man in the black opera cape paused as he was about to get into his coach outside the Lyceum Theatre. "I am Dracula," he said, turning around.

"Inspector William Grayson, Scotland Yard. Might I ask you to give me a moment of your time?"

"Certainly, Inspector. How may I help you?"

"I should like to ask you a few questions. I understand that you were one of the last people to see Miss Angeline Crewe alive."

"Yes," said Dracula, "I suppose I must have been. I had heard about her collapse during rehearsal. Poor girl. A tragedy to die so young. But why should the police be interested? It was an illness, no?"

"We have reason to suspect that it may not have been," said Grayson. "Why, did she seem ill to you?"

"I thought she seemed a trifle pale," said Dracula.

"You had dinner with her and another young woman from the company, a Miss Violet Anderson?"

"Yes, that is correct."

"And there was another gentleman present, a Mr. Anthony Hesketh?"

"Yes, it was Mr. Hesketh who introduced me to Miss Crewe."

"I see. When was the last time you saw Mr. Hesketh?"

"I believe it was that evening, when we all had dinner together."

"And you have not seen him since?"

"No, I think he said something about going abroad on business."

"How well do you know him?"

"We occasionally take in a play together. We met here, at the Lyceum. He was kind enough to share his box with me and assist me with the language. English is not my native tongue, you know."

"You seem to speak it very well," said Grayson.

"Thank you, but my fluency is not all that I would like it to be. The theatre is an excellent place to hear it spoken properly. I never tire of listening to Mr. Irving.''

''So you and Mr. Hesketh are not very close, then? You see each other only at the theatre?''

''And sometimes for dinner, afterward,'' said Dracula. ''I am a very private person, Inspector. I generally keep to myself and only go out at night. Mr. Hesketh seemed like a very pleasant and well-educated young man, but he is only an acquaintance, nothing more. I could not even say what business he is in. I do not recall ever discussing it with him. Such matters bore me. We spoke mainly about music, literature and the theatre. I fear that I am not being of much help to you.''

''On the contrary,'' Grayson said, ''every little bit of information helps. Might I ask what brings you to London?''

Dracula smiled. ''I am a very wealthy man, Inspector Grayson, thanks to the fortunes of my family. I devote most of my time to travel. There is not a great deal to occupy one's time in my native country. The night life of London is so much more fascinating.''

''I see. May I ask where you are staying?''

''For the present, I am taking rooms at the Grosvenor. But I enjoy sampling your hotels as much as I enjoy sampling your theatre. In fact, I am enjoying England so much that I am considering purchasing a home here. Perhaps nothing quite so grand as my family castle in Transylvania, but on the other hand, nothing quite so old and drafty, either.''

''Speaking of your family,'' said Grayson, ''I once heard a fascinating story about a prince from your country whose name was the same as yours. He was also known as Vlad the Impaler, I believe.''

''Yes, I am descended from him,'' said Dracula. ''Not many people outside my country know of him and those that do, such as yourself, invariably ask me if it is true that my ancestor was as bloodthirsty as the legend has it. He was, indeed. However, he is a national hero in my country for having driven out the Turks, who were quite savage in their own right. It is fortunate for all of us that we live in times that are so much more civilized. I fear that my ancestor would not have approved of me. He was a merciless warlord, a *voivode,* and I am merely an extravagantly wealthy vagabond. No one shall ever tell stories about me. But now I have forgotten what we were discussing. Ah, yes, Miss

Crewe and Mr. Hesketh, was it not? They seemed quite taken with each other. Such a pity. They made such a delightful couple. Have I answered your question, Inspector . . . Grayson, was it?''

"Yes, thank you, Count," said Grayson, "I will not be taking up any more of your time. Sorry to trouble you."

"No trouble at all. Good night to you, Inspector."

"And good night to you, Count."

Grayson held the door for him as he climbed in, then he shut it and waved up at the coachman. For a moment, he froze, startled at the sight of the coachman's face staring down at him. The lower half of the man's face was covered by a muffler. He had long grey hair and he wore a high-collared tweed coat and a bowler hat, but it was the eyes that startled Grayson. They were looking down at him with an absolutely feral gaze. For a brief moment, they almost seemed to glow in the dark and then the coachman cracked the whip and the horses took off at a trot. Grayson stared after the coach until it disappeared into the fog.

Private Paul Ransome woke up strapped to a bed in a large, luxuriously appointed bedroom. He had been drugged and he did not know how long he had been unconscious. The restraints would not allow him any motion beyond some slight movements of his head and neck. He felt ill, disoriented, and there was a maddening itch at a spot on his throat which he could not scratch. He felt nauseous and he had a fever. The sheets were damp with his sweat.

The bedroom door opened and a man dressed in a dark butler's suit entered, the same man who had answered the door of the sprawling Richmond Hill estate that Ransome had come to investigate. He had long, steel grey hair that hung down to his shoulders and he was powerfully built. He was swarthy looking, with sunken eyes, a high forehead and a prominent jaw. The mouth was wide, thin-lipped and cruel. He saw that Ransome was awake, turned and left the room before Ransome could say anything.

Ransome desperately tried to remember what had happened, but his mind was a complete blank. He could not seem to concentrate. He knew he was in trouble. Bad trouble. And that knowledge was confirmed when the door opened once again several moments later and a tall, dark, well-built, striking looking man with emerald green eyes and a long scar down the side of his face came in and stood over his bed, looking down at him.

"Drakov!" Ransome said.

"Good morning, Private Ransome," Nikolai Drakov said in a deep voice. He smiled. "How do you feel?"

"Sick as a dog," said Ransome. "What did you do to me?"

"A number of things," said Drakov pleasantly, as if they were merely discussing the weather. "Nothing fatal, however."

"But I assume that's coming, right?"

"Oh, on the contrary, I want you alive. I have some very special plans for you."

"What happened?" Ransome said. "How did I blow my cover? I don't remember anything."

"You remember what happened before you came here, don't you?" Drakov said.

"Yes, but after that it's all a blank."

"Good."

"What did you do, damn you?"

"Well, you might say I've influenced you somewhat, in more ways than one," said Drakov. "You see, I was prepared for you people this time. I no longer take any chances. You were scanned when you approached this house and your cybernetic implants were detected. I'm really very well protected here. Just the same, it now appears that I shall have to leave this comfortable house. A pity, but if you found me, the other members of your team cannot be far behind."

"It won't work, Drakov," Ransome said. "I'm not going to tell you anything."

Drakov chuckled. "Spare me the *esprit de corps* heroics, Ransome. You may not know it, but you have already told me everything I wished to know. I am quite looking forward to another confrontation with my father's first string team. You were just an appetizer. It's Delaney, Cross and Steiger that I want. And you are going to help me."

"The hell I will," said Ransome. "I'll die first."

Drakov grinned. "In a manner of speaking, yes, you will," he said. "But never fear, you shall be reborn. Your rebirth is in progress even as we speak."

Ransome felt a knot forming in his stomach. "What have you done to me?"

"How does your throat feel, Ransome?"

"My—" Involuntarily, Ransome tried to raise his hand to his throat, but the restraints wouldn't let him move. "Jesus," he said. "Oh, Jesus."

His eyes went to the butler standing by the door, watching him silently.

Drakov followed his gaze. "No, it wasn't Janos," he said. Drakov beckoned the butler forward. "However, Janos *is* someone you've been looking for. I thought you might like to be properly introduced. Pvt. Paul Ransome, Janos Volkov. Janos is, in a manner of speaking, one of my children. I'm really very proud of him. Janos is the very first of his kind, a triumph of genetic engineering and biomodification. He is the werewolf you've been seeking. I'm sorry to say that you will not be able to see Janos in all his hirsute splendor, as he has reached the end of his monthly cycle, but take my word for it, it is an impressive sight."

He nodded to the butler, who turned and left without a word.

"My plans for you, however," Drakov said, "do not call for infection by lycanthropic genes. No, for you, Ransome, I have something infinitely more interesting in mind."

Ransome was breaking out in a fresh sweat and he started to shiver. He fought to keep his teeth from chattering. "Whatever you've infected me with, Drakov, it'll never work, I promise you. I'll kill myself."

"Yes, I'm sure you would," said Drakov, "which is why I have conditioned you with a number of programmed imperatives. A relatively simple matter of neutralizing your cybernetic implants and installing some of my own in a minor surgical procedure. When I have completed your programming, you will no more be able to commit suicide than you will be able to discuss what's happened to you with the other members of your team. I had hoped that it would be Finn Delaney who fell into my hands; he would make a splendid werewolf, don't you think? Or Andre Cross, what a wonderfully seductive vampire she would make. But you'll do for the moment."

The door to the bedroom opened once again and a tall, slim, middle-aged man with a drooping moustache and jet black hair combed into a widow's peak entered. He was sharp featured, with an aquiline nose, a high forehead, sunken cheeks and thin red lips. He was dressed in dark evening clothes and a long black opera cape with a high collar. His dark eyes were those of a psychotic.

Drakov smiled. "I could never resist a touch of melodrama," he said. "Allow me to present Count Dracula."

7 _____

Sgt. Anthony Rizzo waited for his relief, warming his hands over the glowing coals in his pushcart. The sweet and musty aroma of roasting chestnuts rose from the cart, which had become a familiar feature to the residents of Bow Street over the past week. Each morning, he arrived at the corner with his pushcart, near the old Bow Street Police Court, and many of the local residents had made a habit of buying a small bag of roasted chestnuts from him on their way to work. Dressed as an Italian immigrant, Rizzo addressed his customers in a sort of broken Cockney, a mangled dialect spiced with Italian phrases and delivered in a robust, gesticulatory manner. It was a ''purloined letter'' method of surveillance, based on the principle of being so completely obvious that one would be overlooked.

The streets of London were full of vendors and musicians. Around Covent Garden, it was not unusual to see entire string quartets playing in the street, collecting money in the battered cases for their instruments, which they placed open before them on the sidewalks. The costermongers were a prominent fixture on the city streets. There were ice cream sellers; fruit vendors; men selling various wind-up toys for children; balladeers who performed songs of their own composition, often based on headlines in the newspapers, then sold the sheet music; muffin men ringing their bells and the ubiquitous flower girls, who were usually not girls at all, but mostly elderly women wrapped in shawls, selling bunches of flowers or fresh buttonholes for gentlemen to wear in their lapels. Sometimes these street vendors were regarded as a nuisance, but no one ever objected to Rizzo's presence on Bow Street, because Rizzo did not disturb the residents with any vendor's street cries. He depended instead on the aroma of the roasting chestnuts to draw his customers. It worked well enough and he usually did a nice bit of business in the morning, less throughout the afternoon, and towards evening, as people started to return home from work, business picked up once more for several hours. Meanwhile, he kept his eye on Tony Hesketh's apartment just across the street.

Surveillance work was often very boring and Rizzo's stake-out was especially ennervating. Anything that could have made the long watch more bearable, such as reading a book or newspaper, was out of the question since it would distract him from his duties, so there was nothing for Rizzo to do except stand on his feet all day and sell his chestnuts, all the while keeping alert for any sign of Hesketh. By the end of the day, he was worn out. Someone would show up in the evening to relieve him, someone who could take advantage of the darkness and the fog for concealment and did not require a pushcart. Then Rizzo would go back to the Hotel Metropole command post to soak his feet and get some sleep. But now it was getting late and his relief had not yet arrived. His feet were tired and his back was sore. Rizzo was not especially worried. He knew the team was being spread thin and relief would arrive as soon as they could spare someone, but just the same, he hoped they would send someone soon. He was tired and it would start to look unusual if he remained too late on the corner with his pushcart.

He sold a bag of chestnuts to a grey-haired gentleman in a long tweed Inverness and a bowler hat, apparently on his way out for the evening.

"Working a bit late tonight?" the man said with a smile.

Rizzo shrugged elaborately. "Aah, eez the wife, she 'ave 'er seezter comma to veezit. All night long, ya-ta-ta-ta-ta, like cheekens." He made rapid gestures with his hands, fingers together and outstretched, thumb and index fingers coming together and apart quickly in a representative gesture of cease-less chatter. "Aah," he said, waving his hand in derision, "I stay late anda sell my cheznoots."

"Don't blame you one bit, old man," said the man,

grinning. "Know just how you feel. My sister-in-law's a bloody horror herself."

"*Grazi*," said Rizzo, accepting the man's money and putting it in the little cash box on his cart. "*Ciao, signori.*"

"*Ciao* to you, too, Sergeant Rizzo."

Rizzo glanced up quickly, too late, his eyes focusing on the small plastic pistol held in the man's right hand. There was a faint chuffing sound, halfway between a cough and a hiss, and the tiny dart struck him in the chest. He barely had time to realize he had been shot before he lost consciousness.

Pvt. Linda Craven crooned a Cockney song to herself while she sat on an overturned basket by the curb, making fresh button-holes from some of her flowers. She wore a long dress made out of coarse black linsey-woolsey, lace-up ankle high boots with rundown heels, a black plush jacket, a long black shawl and a feathered hat. Every now and then, when someone would pass by, she would stretch out a handful of flowers and make a halfhearted, plaintive-sounding pitch, punctuated by a sniffle, and then she would return to her song, a song about how "loverly" it would be to have a room somewhere far away from the cold night air, with lots of chocolate to eat and an enormous chair to sit in. Sung in an ear-gratingly Cockney whine, it sounded perfectly in keeping with the time, even though it wouldn't be written for years to come.

There was still no sign of H. G. Wells. She felt utterly miserable about the whole thing. She blamed herself for having slipped up badly. It did not occur to her that perhaps the reason Steiger hadn't given her hell was that there really wasn't anything she could have done about the situation. The odds of her having been able to prevent what happened would have been infinitesimal. Even if she had recognized Moreau, a man she had never seen before, it would have been necessary for her to notice him activating his warp disc, an action easily concealed, and move quickly enough to kill him before he could clock out with Wells.

It would have seemed rather incongruous, to say the least, if a Victorian woman had suddenly opened up on a man in a London teashop with a laser or a disruptor pistol, which was one of the reasons why she wasn't armed with one. If anyone in the teashop had wondered where the two men at the table by the window had suddenly gone, they would have been struck dumb by the sight of a man being killed by molecular disruption, briefly wreathed in the glowing blue mist of Cherenkov radiation and then disintegrating right before their eyes. Paranoia ran high at TAC-HQ. The warp discs they all wore were failsafed and, in case of an emergency, there was an arms locker back at the command post, likewise failsafed to self-destruct unless it was opened properly. To remain on the safe side, the team had been issued weapons more in keeping with the time. In her purse, Linda carried a Colt Single Action Army revolver, otherwise known as a .45 Peacemaker. It weighed almost 3 pounds and it packed a wallop. It was an 1873 design and, although it would have been regarded as highly unusual for a young woman in London to be carrying such a gun, as a visitor from America, it was not beyond the realm of possibility that she might have one.

She knew what she would have to do if Moreau showed up again with Wells. She would have to make certain she could get a clear shot at him without endangering Wells or anybody else, which meant she might have to place herself in a position of vulnerability. She'd have to move fast and get in close, kill Moreau as quickly as possible and then either prevail upon Wells to return with her to the command post or take him by force. Wells would have to be debriefed. She had no doubt that she could handle Wells and she felt reasonably certain that she could take care of Moreau. After all, the man was a scientist, not a soldier. Still, it would be very risky. There was a good chance that Moreau could return with Wells during someone else's shift on surveillance duty, but Linda hoped it would happen during her shift, so that she could redeem herself for having lost him in the first place. She didn't even want to think about what could happen if Wells never returned from wherever it was Moreau had taken him.

She was only twenty-two years old, still a rookie, green and on her first mission. She was painfully aware of her lack of experience compared to the other members of the mission support team. She was thrilled to be working with the First Division's number one temporal adjustment team, but she also felt intimidated. Andre Cross was a legend in the service, as was Finn Delaney, already a veteran when she was still learning how to crawl. Steiger was Gen. Moses Forrester's second-in-command and prior to that, he had been the TIA's senior field agent. She knew they couldn't have been happy to have a rookie assigned to their support team. None of them had said as much, but she was certain that on a mission of such importance, they would have preferred more experienced personnel.

Scott Neilson seemed to understand. Like her, he was a rookie, though he wasn't quite as green as she was and he seemed to think much faster on his feet.

"Look," he had told her one night while they were having dinner in a pub, "nobody's going to hold it against you that you're a rookie. They were all green themselves once. It's really very simple. You either learn fast or you don't make it."

"That's just what I'm afraid of," she had said. "It's not so much that I might not make it myself that worries me, but the idea that I might screw up due to my inexperience and it could result in temporal interference, a disruption or maybe even a timestream split. The idea of all that responsibility is simply staggering. The pressure's unbelievable. It gives me migraines—"

"And it makes you nauseous and upsets your stomach and you can't sleep and when you do sleep, you have recurring nightmares," Neilson said. "I know, I've been there. They've *all* been there, except maybe Steiger. Nothing seems to bother him much, but then you've got to be pretty cold to be a TIA agent to begin with."

"So how do you handle it?" she said.

"You don't," he said. "Believe it or not, after a while, it sort of handles itself. There's only so much pressure you can take before you either break or you just get used to it. You even become casual about it. You have to, otherwise you simply can't function. If you were the type who was liable to break, chances are it would have come out in your psych profile and you never would have made it this far. But almost everybody goes through what you're experiencing the first few times out to the Minus Side. Nobody expects a rookie to take it like a veteran. They're not going to cut you any slack, but they won't hold your inexperience against you, either. Anybody can mess up, even someone like Delaney, who's got more years in the service than both our ages combined."

"How long did it take before you learned to handle the pressure?" she said.

Neilson had laughed. "Are you kidding? I still have nightmares. Almost every night, except when I'm so exhausted that I don't even dream. And I'll tell you a secret—I don't really believe that anyone ever learns to handle it. They just learn to live with it. It's no accident that the First Division has a reputation for being such a bunch of hellraisers in Plus Time. You get drunk; you fight; you fuck; you get into high risk sports; whatever it takes to give you an outlet for the pressure.''

''What do you do?'' she said.

''Well, I don't drink and I'm afraid I'm not much of a fighter,'' Neilson had said. ''I barely made it through combat training.''

She had smiled. ''So what does that leave?''

Neilson grinned self-consciously. ''Well, actually, not what you might think. I get into a lot of hand-eye coordination things.''

''Like what?''

''Quick-draw target practice with antique revolvers and semiautomatic pistols. Knife throwing. Darts. Sleight-of-hand . . .''

''What's that?''

''It used to be called close-up magic. Tricks with cards and coins and such.'' He had demonstrated by ''walking'' a coin across his fingers. ''It requires lots of practice and concentration,'' he had said. ''It takes your mind off other things and it sharpens your reflexes. Helps you think fast. Maybe you should give it a try.''

''Well, antique firearms are noisy, I don't have any knives or darts, I'm not really in the mood for any magic tricks and I don't much feel like getting drunk and waking up with a hangover.'' She smiled. ''What does that leave? You want to run down that list again?''

They had spent the night together and their lovemaking had been frenzied and intense. Afterwards, they went to sleep holding each other and, for a change, there had been no nightmares. But then Moreau had abducted H. G. Wells and now the pressure was back on, savage and relentless. It felt as if her every nerve synapse were charged with adrenaline-induced, hair-trigger sensitivity. She was scared, yet at the same time, there was an intoxicating rush associated with it, almost an orgasmic high, the intense, heightened perceptions of a sword dancer. She didn't realize just how intense it was until someone came up behind her and addressed her in a deep voice.

"Excuse me, Miss, how much for a buttonhole?"

It wasn't until almost a full minute later that she fully realized what had happened. None of it had taken place with any conscious thought. She had turned and, in a galvanizing, white hot blast of instinctual response, the sight of the gun had registered and she reacted, throwing herself to one side as the dart missed her by scant millimeters. She clawed for her revolver, fired—but he was already gone and the bullet passed through empty air where he had been standing just a second earlier and struck a lamppost, ricocheting off it and whining away into the distance.

"*Damn!*" she shouted. "God *damn* it! *Jesus* . . ." And then she noticed several people on the street staring at her with astonishment and she felt the delayed stress reaction kicking in. She quickly hit her warp disc and clocked out, materializing in the Hotel Metropole command post just as the dry heaves began. At some point, she became aware of Delaney standing over her and holding her while she retched, gasping for breath.

"We're blown," she said. "Dammit, we're blown! Drakov almost got me!"

Delaney didn't even pause to wait for an explanation. He bolted into the other room to wake up Steiger and then Christine Brant was steadying her, helping her to the couch as the shakes began.

It did not occur to her until much later that she had survived an encounter with the Temporal Corps' worst nemesis. Nikolai Drakov had the drop on her and she had lived to tell the tale. She wasn't a rookie anymore.

Pvt. Dick Larson stood over the body, numbly staring down at what was left of Cpl. Tom Davis. The corpse was lying in a crumpled heap next to a pile of refuse in the alley. Blood was everywhere, covering the chest and spattered on the alley wall. The head was barely attached by a few ragged threads of flesh. Someone . . . or some*thing* . . . had twisted his head around completely, severing the spinal column, and then the body had been *thrown* across the alley. A large splatter of blood marked the spot where Davis had been killed and then another one marked the wall at about shoulder level where the thrown body had struck it and then dropped down to the ground.

"Thought you should see this," Inspector Grayson said. "That's your friend Davis, from the *Telegraph*, isn't it?"

Larson nodded mutely.

"I'm sorry," said Grayson. "He seemed a decent sort. It looks as if he may have found our killer. Or the killer found him. I know the two of you were working together on this story. I thought perhaps you might be able to tell me what he was on to."

Larson shook his head and turned away from the grisly sight. "I honestly don't know, Inspector."

"What was he doing down here?" Grayson said.

"Same thing I've been doing, I imagine," Larson said. "Canvassing the pubs, questioning the locals. He must have stumbled onto something."

"Yes, apparently," said Grayson with a sour grimace. "Look, don't misunderstand me, I appreciate the restraint you've shown in writing about these killings and you've lived up to our bargain in keeping certain details confidential, but if you've discovered anything that you're not telling me, I want to know about it now."

"I wish I did have something to tell you, Inspector," Larson said, "but if Davis had uncovered something, he never had the chance to tell me."

"You're quite certain?" Grayson said, watching him carefully.

"Tom Davis was no fool," said Larson, "nor was he a hero. If he had learned the killer's identity, he would never have kept it to himself and he certainly would not have risked confronting him alone."

"Not even for the sake of an exclusive story?" Grayson said.

"Tom was much more than a colleague, Inspector," Larson said. "He was a close friend. I knew him. He wouldn't do anything like that."

"Well, I hope you're right," said Grayson. "I'd hate to think that a man died for something so foolhardy. I suppose the newspapers are truly going to scream about this. Losing one of their own and so forth. I don't wish to seem callous, Larson, but I do hope you will employ some discretion when you write your story. The manner of death is, after all, not quite like the others. There is no real evidence that the killer was the same."

"But you don't really believe that," Larson said.

Grayson looked down at the ground and pursed his lips thoughtfully. "No, I don't," he said after a moment. "Whoever killed poor Davis had to possess astonishing strength. Much like what happened in the courtyard, when those men were thrown about like so much chaff. Perhaps we'll be able to learn something from an examination of the body, but I'm almost beginning to believe that we may be faced with something beyond our ability to understand. There is some sort of horror loose in London, something that—" He caught himself and glanced up at Larson quickly. "I hope you will not quote me," he said.

Larson shook his head. "I have already forgotten what you said, Inspector."

Grayson looked relieved. "Thank you. My superiors are making things difficult enough for me as it is. For what it's worth, I promise you that I won't rest until I find this fiend and bring him to justice. And I *shall* find him. I swear it."

Larson nodded and looked back at the body. "I'll have to inform his . . . his family."

"Would you rather I do that?" said Grayson.

"No, I think it would be best if they were to hear it from me," said Larson. "I'd better go and see to it, before the news reaches them some other way."

"I understand," said Grayson. "Forgive me if I seemed a bit—"

"No need," said Larson. "You have your job to do."

"Yes, and I'd best be on about it," Grayson said. "Please pass on my condolences to the poor chap's family."

"Thank you, Inspector. I'll do that."

Grayson looked at him strangely for a moment. "Larson . . . do be careful."

"God damn it, no!" Delaney said. "It's much too dangerous."

"We have no choice," said Steiger. "If we're blown, we've got to move the command post now and that means someone has to stay behind and get word to all our people."

"We know where most of our people are," Delaney said. "We could set up a rendezvous and clock out separately, pass the word on to everyone directly—"

"And what happens if some of them clock in while we're out looking for them?" Steiger said. "They'd have no idea that we're blown and they'd be sitting ducks if Drakov made a strike on the command post. Besides, I don't want to risk having everyone spread out all over the place. That makes us vulnerable. We have no idea where Davis and Larson are—"

"Davis is dead," said Larson, entering the room.

"What!" said Steiger. "How? What happened?"

"I've just left Grayson. They found Davis in an alley behind a pub in Whitechapel," Larson said. "His head was twisted around 360 degrees, practically torn right off his neck."

"Ransome must have talked," Delaney said.

"What about Ransome?" Larson said.

"He's missing," said Christine Brant. "He was late checking in and there's been no sign of him."

"Drakov must have got a hold of him somehow," said Delaney. "We're blown. Ransome must have told him about the entire operation."

"I don't believe it," Larson said. "Paul would never break."

"The hell he wouldn't," Delaney said. "Be realistic. Anyone can be deprogrammed. How else could we have been blown?"

"It might have been Rizzo," Andre said.

"*Rizzo's missing, too?*" said Larson.

Andre nodded. "I showed up to relieve him and there was no sign of him. I found his pushcart abandoned in the street. No one even had a chance to steal it yet."

"And Drakov made a try for Linda," Christine Brant said. "She got off a shot at him, but he was too quick."

"Jesus," Larson said. "He's picking us off one at a time!"

"Which is exactly why I don't want everyone spread out now," Steiger said. "We've got to pull in and regroup. And the sooner we're out of here, the better."

The door opened and Paul Ransome walked in.

"What's going on?" he said.

"Ransome!" Steiger said. "Where the hell have you been?"

"Checking out the estates on our list, as I was supposed to be doing," he said.

"You missed your check-in by four hours!" said Delaney.

"Yes, sir, I know," said Ransome. "I'm sorry, but I discovered something and I wanted to make sure before I pushed the button."

"What are you talking about?" said Steiger.

"I found Drakov's base of operations," Ransome said. "He's at an estate in Richmond Hill."

The sprawling Victorian mansion stood atop the hill overlooking the Thames Valley in Richmond, Surrey. The furnishings were all still in place and the pantry was fully stocked, as was the wine cellar. Otherwise, the house was empty. If there had been any servants employed in the mansion, they were gone now. There was nothing to indicate that anyone from another time had been present in the house and, for that matter, the mansion didn't even look abandoned. It simply looked as if no one was home, but the clothes closets were all empty and toilet articles were missing from the bathrooms. On closer examination, they found where the security systems had been concealed and then hastily removed.

"That's it," said Steiger. He glanced at Ransome and nodded. "Drakov was here, all right, but he apparently cleared out in a hurry."

"Sir," said Larson, "take a look at this." He showed Steiger a sheaf of newspaper clippings about the killings in Whitechapel. "They were lying on a table in the library. Along with this." He handed Steiger a handsome first edition of *Dracula*, by Bram Stoker. A book that Stoker hadn't even written yet.

"Cute," said Steiger. "Obviously left behind for us to find. He's awful goddamn sure of himself."

"It may not be safe for us to stay here," Andre said.

"You think Drakov would booby-trap this place?" Delaney said. "That's not his style. Much too impersonal."

"Maybe, but I wouldn't want to bet on that," said Steiger. "Be careful what you touch."

"So it was Rizzo, then," Andre said.

Steiger nodded. "It had to be. He's the only one left unaccounted for. We can probably assume he's dead by now. We'd better get someone down to the crime lab at Scotland Yard to warn Neilson. He'll be getting off duty there soon and I don't want him going back to the Metropole."

"What do we do about a new base-ops?" Andre said. "If Rizzo's talked, we can't use any of our fallback safehouses."

"I've been thinking about that," Steiger said, "and I have an idea. Probably the last place Drakov would expect us to use. And maybe it would let us kill two birds with one stone."

Ransome coughed and sagged against a doorframe.

"Ransome," said Delaney, "are you all right?"

He nodded. "Yes, sir. I'm just tired, I guess. I'll be okay."

"You look a little pale."

"Nothing to worry about, sir, I'm fine, really."

"We're all tired," Andre said. "And we're not getting anyplace. At this rate, we'll all be asleep on our feet soon. We need another safehouse. What did you have in mind, Creed?"

"Number 7 Mornington Place," said Steiger.

"But that's H. G. Wells' house!" said Christine Brant.

Steiger nodded. "Wells is the only really solid lead we've got. He's become the primary focus of temporal interference in this scenario. Forrester was right. We're going right back to square one. Moreau must have had a reason for abducting Wells. He's got to be in this with Drakov and they must have a plan for using Wells somehow."

"But if Rizzo's been wrung dry, then Drakov knows we've been keeping Wells under surveillance," Brant said.

"And he also knows we've lost him," Steiger said. "He'll expect us to continue watching Wells' house and we won't disappoint him. Drakov won't expect us to be using a house we're keeping under surveillance."

"What about Amy Robbins?" Brant said.

"We'll have to keep her prisoner inside the house," said Steiger.

"But what are we going to tell her?" said Christine.

"We don't tell her anything."

"I don't think that's wise, Creed," Delaney said. "I see what Christine's getting at. The poor woman will be terrified enough, it'll be even worse if she has no idea what's going on. It would be easier if we could get her cooperation. If we get Wells back, he's going to have to be debriefed anyway and we can have her debriefed at the same time. And if we don't get him back, Amy Robbins will be the least of our problems."

"All right," said Steiger reluctantly, "but she doesn't leave the house for even a second. And she's to be watched every moment."

"Sounds like you're taking yourself off command post duty," Andre said.

"You got that right," Steiger said. "We've lost two people and I'm not losing anymore. Brant, as of right now, you're in charge of logistics at the new command post."

"Sir," she said, "with all due respect, regulations specify that the senior officer—"

"Screw regulations. I'm tired of sitting on my hands. Besides, since you're so concerned about Amy Robbins, you can babysit her. You're in charge and that's a direct order."

"Yes, sir."

"All right, Larson and Craven, you get to Scotland Yard and brief Neilson. I'm pulling him out of there. If we're blown, then so is he. Wait till it's dark and then get over to Wells' house. Make sure nobody sees you going in. We'll meet you there."

"What about Conan Doyle?" said Andre.

"I'm tempted to pull all surveillance off him," Steiger said. "We're spread too thin as it is. But if Drakov knows we've been watching him, he might decide to take advantage of our cancelling surveillance on him. No, it's too risky. And I want someone on Bram Stoker from now on, as well."

"I can handle that, sir," said Linda Craven.

"All right. You'll work shifts with Neilson," Steiger said. "Larson, cover as much ground as you can on your own and keep in close touch with Grayson. Andre, you cover Conan Doyle. Ransome will relieve you. Ransome, I want you to get some rest first. You look dead. Between the rest of us, we'll cover Wells' house, the docks and Whitechapel."

"That's a lot of territory to cover," said Delaney.

"We've got no choice," said Steiger. "We were counting on the advantage of surprise, but Drakov's turned it around on us. Damn it, I wish to hell we could get some reinforcements." He took a deep breath. "Hell, it's worth a try. I'm going to clock back to base and see Forrester. We've got to have more manpower. In the meantime, if anyone catches sight of Hesketh, take him. Alive, if possible. The same goes for Moreau, but if you can't take him, burn him. As for Drakov and any of his creatures, they're to be killed on sight, regardless of the risk. Any questions?"

There were none.

"All right. Let's move out. We'll rendezvous at Wells' house."

• • •

Something was happening. Jasmine had no idea what it was, but something was clearly happening. She was far from ignorant of her grandfather's activities, the ones that had nothing to do with running the apothecary shop. Lin Tao was the head of the Green Dragon tong, a secret society of overseas Chinese which he had founded shortly after they first arrived in London. The organization had grown quickly and it had become the most powerful fighting tong in London. Its aims were primarily to help smuggle Chinese into England and to protect those already there. Even before he had left China, Lin Tao had learned how Europeans often looked down on Orientals and he knew that Chinese immigrants were frequently taken advantage of. And despite his advanced age, Lin Tao was not one to suffer insults meekly. He had once been a powerful man in his own country and now, in Limehouse, he had become a powerful man again.

From time to time, it became necessary for the Green Dragon tong to exert some influence. The police were familiar with the Green Dragon tong. That is, they knew of it and they had seen the results of some of its actions, but they knew almost nothing about its membership, much less who its leaders were. More often than not, the actions of the tong were never reported to the police. One such case was that of a factory owner who hired Chinese laborers, refused to pay them the same wages he paid his occidental workers and frequently had his foreman beat the "heathens," as he called them, "for good measure." He also had some of the younger Chinese workers brought to his home, where his wife directed them in their household duties with the aid of a braided leather riding crop. The factory owner was requested to desist from these practices. He not only refused, but he redoubled his efforts.

One night, a group of masked men broke into his home. The factory owner awoke in his own bed to find himself bound and gagged, his terrified wife beside him, likewise restrained. Neither the servants nor the children were disturbed. They were never even aware of the late night visit. The uninvited guests stayed for just under an hour, long enough to leave a souvenir of their visit tattooed on the lower abdomen of the man's beautiful young wife, just above an extremely private part of her anatomy. It was a very intricate tattoo of a coiled green dragon, about three inches long and beautifully executed. Thereafter, each time the factory owner attempted to have sexual relations with his wife, the sight of the tattoo brought home the memory of the late night visit and he was rendered impotent. Eventually, his beautiful young wife became quite proud of the tattoo. She delighted in showing it to all her lovers.

Of course, Jasmine knew nothing of such things. She knew the tong existed; she had long ago surmised that her grandfather was its leader, but she knew little of the actual workings of the secret group. She had never discussed the subject with her grandfather and his manner indicated that it was not a subject that was open to discussion. Jasmine had been raised in the traditional ways of her people. She did not question her elders. She did not speak unless she was first spoken to. But some things had changed from the way they might have been back in the old country. Jasmine no longer kept her eyes downcast when she was speaking to a man, unless that man was her grandfather, though in most other respects, she still followed the old ways—western influence was coming to her very slowly.

Every day now, men were coming into the apothecary shop—young Chinese men, men who were not customers—and they were asking for her grandfather in the most respectful tones. Her grandfather would peek out from behind the curtains and beckon them into the back room, where they would converse for a short while in soft, low voices, almost whispers, and then the young men would leave, bowing to her grandfather, some to come back the next day, some a day or two later, some only several hours later, and then the process would repeat itself.

Something was happening. The men of the Green Dragon tong had been mobilized. They were searching for something—or someone—and Jasmine was certain that it had something to do with Dr. Morro and the new gentleman, the Englishman named Wells. And somehow, Jasmine knew, the man named Drakov had to be involved, the evil man with whom Dr. Morro was obsessed.

She wanted to help in some way, but it was not her place to offer, much less admit that she even knew anything about it. Her sense of helplessness and frustration was causing her to lose sleep and it was because of this that she had overheard a conversation between her grandfather, Dr. Morro, and Mr. Wells.

She had been coming down the stairs, on her way down to the shop to get some herb tea that was good for sleeping. She had been barefoot and she was walking softly, quietly, so as not to disturb anyone else, when she heard the low voices of her grandfather and the two men coming from the back room. The man named Wells had raised his voice briefly, but was quickly silenced by Dr. Morro.

"Absolutely not!" said Wells, his voice lower, though no less intense.

"Herbert, please try to understand," Moreau said. "There really is no other way."

"I cannot and *will* not be a party to murder," Wells said vehemently. "No matter what the man has done, we still have laws—"

"Which cannot possibly avail us," said Moreau. "What would you have us do, call in Scotland Yard and tell them that an insane renegade from another time has created a vampire and a werewolf, perhaps several of them, and released them in the East End? That the reason he has done this is that he wishes to create a disruption in the flow of time and alter history? That right here, in Victorian London, there are agents from the future, on the trail of this man and undoubtedly on my trail, as well, a fugitive from another time in a parallel universe? How do you think they would react to that?"

"Granted, if we told them that, they would be sure to think us mad," said Wells, "but we do not have to tell them everything. We need only tell them that it is Nikolai Drakov who is behind these murders and—"

"And where would be our proof?" Moreau said. "Even if we could supply it to them, don't you see, they would be as children to a man such as Drakov. They simply do not possess the skill, the intelligence, the experience or the technology to deal with such a man. There is not a jail in this time period that could hold him and even if there were, he is far too dangerous to be allowed to live."

"And who are *we* to make such a decision?" Wells said. "If we take the law into our own hands, then we become no better than Drakov. In that event, we must abandon reason altogether."

"Listen to me, Herbert," said Moreau, "I understand what is troubling you, but think a moment. This curious phrase, 'taking the law into our own hands,' what does it mean? What is the law, after all, but an agreement reached by men such as ourselves who, in the act of formulating the law, have taken matters into their own hands? It is not my intention to become embroiled in a philosophical debate with you. I have neither the time, the energy, nor the inclination. Drakov must be stopped and his creatures destroyed along with him. We are bound by an imperative far greater than any British law. But if you must have some form of justification for what I am proposing, then consider this: if a citizen of another country were to come to England, someone who is a wanted criminal in the nation of his origin, and if officials of that nation were to request his extradition so that this criminal might be tried under the laws of his own land, then there is a process whereby such a thing might be accomplished, is there not? Well, the three people who came to see you at your home are representatives of the law in their own time and they have come here to bring Drakov to justice for his crimes. For obvious reasons, they cannot approach the officials of your government and ask them for assistance. However, *we* are in a position to give it to them. It is our moral duty to do so, mine because I have given Drakov the means to do what he has done and yours because you respect and believe in the laws of your country, but have no recourse to them. If you will not take the law into your own hands, then avail yourself of the law enforcement agents from the future. In either case, it would make no difference, I can promise you. Either Drakov dies, by their hand or by ours, or we all die by his. The question is not one of principle, but of survival.''

"The first question is that of finding the one we seek," Lin Tao said. "It may serve to consider the example of the Siamese fighting fish. When two males are present, they must inevitably do battle to the death. But if a third male should be present, he will wait until one of the first two combatants has died and then he will engage the weakened winner, thereby greatly increasing his chances of a victory. We would do well to emulate his example. Let us pit Drakov and these agents from the future against each other while we wait and watch. If these agents from the future should succeed, so much the better. If they fail, then we shall be fresh, strong and prepared to act. Let us not attract too much attention to ourselves while these other fish do battle. Our turn will come. In the meantime, we must locate our adversary's sanctuary and identify his minions. In that regard, we have already made some progress.

"I have had my people making discreet inquiries," Lin Tao continued, "and every Chinese man, woman and child in London has been enlisted to help us in our cause. Now it has come to my attention that a certain unused warehouse near the docks has been the site of some unusual activity. Although it is locked and apparently still empty, it has been visited by several people, always very late at night, most notable among them being a certain wealthy gentleman. Sometimes he brings servants with him and they carry large sacks from their coach into the warehouse. One of these sacks was heard to moan. On two separate occasions, I have had men attempt to search this warehouse. They have not been seen again. I have had this gentleman followed and it has been reported to me that he has rooms at the Grosvenor Hotel. He does not answer to Drakov's description, yet his name is curiously similar. It is Count Dracula."

"*Dracula!*" said Moreau. "Are you absolutely certain?"

"Yes," said Lin Tao. "The name means something to you?"

"It does, indeed!" Moreau said. "Your people must be very careful, Lin Tao. They have found our vampire!"

Jasmine had listened, awestruck by their conversation, and then she quietly tiptoed back upstairs, all thoughts of sleep-giving tea forgotten. Sleep would now be an impossibility. She remained awake all night and by the time the morning came, she knew what she would have to do.

8

"Excellent," said Drakov, watching Rizzo through the iron bars of the cell. "He's young and strong, in peak physical condition. I was afraid he might not stand up to accelerated treatments, but he's doing splendidly."

Rizzo repeatedly threw himself against the bars of the cell, howling like a beast. His hairy, clawed hands reached between the bars, vainly trying to get hold of Drakov. His face was sprouting hair from the eyeball sockets down and his forehead was covered with new growth as well. His teeth were elongated and saliva dribbled down onto his torn shirt as he snarled, frothing at the mouth, biting his own lips with frenzy.

"He appears to be resisting the imperative programming," said the tall, dark, moustached man standing beside Drakov. He was wearing an elegant black suit and a long opera cape. There was a ruby amulet at his throat. He spoke with an Eastern European accent. "I thought you said that was not possible."

"It is always possible to *try* to resist," said Drakov, "but in the long run, such efforts prove futile. Most people would be unable to resist after the first full session, however, this one seems to be one of the rare exceptions. He is using pain and rage to fight the conditioning."

"It seems to be working."

"Yes, Volodya," Drakov said, using a familiar, Russian

diminutive form of the name Vladimir, "but for how long?" He smiled. "He cannot keep it up forever. And if we become impatient with him, all it would take would be another session and he would become completely pliable, just like his friend, Ransome. Rizzo seems to be made of sterner stuff. One has to respect such determination. Let him resist. He is only prolonging the inevitable."

Rizzo growled and launched himself against the iron bars again, as if he could batter them down by such repeated assaults, but the bars were set deeply into the old stone of the castle dungeon and all he succeeded in doing was bruising and bloodying himself as he ran at the bars again and again.

"Keep at it, my friend," said Drakov, grinning at him. "The release of adrenaline and endorphins brought about by all this strenuous activity is only speeding up the change."

Rizzo screamed in anguish, but it came out as a prolonged, bone-chilling howl, like that of a wolf baying at the moon. The cry echoed in the cold, damp dungeons and became multiplied, as if joined by the howls of the tormented souls of all those long dead prisoners who had been tortured in the subterranean cells of the ancient castle.

They were not in London anymore. Above them were the ruined battlements of a medieval keep situated high in the Transylvanian Alps, a castle once occupied by the real Dracula, a warlord and a high-ranking member of the Order Draconis, founded by the Holy Roman Emperor Sigismund. Dracula meant "son of the dragon" and although the Dracula who stood at Drakov's side was not in any way descended from the warlord who had once fought the Turks and impaled thousands of them upon wooden stakes, he was in every other respect a true son of the dragon.

He was a genetically engineered creation, born of human DNA which had been radically modified and raised through the expedient of time travel. Nurtured within an artificial womb, he had been born in a laboratory and then sent back into the past and given to a childless family who had been carefully selected and paid well to raise their very special charge. At prescribed intervals, Vlad had been brought back from the past to Drakov's laboratory once again, so that Drakov could embark upon the next stage in the development of his creation. Programming through cybernetic implants, surgical biomodification, serum treatments . . . for the child who was the first true vampire, years passed between the times he saw his creator, but for Drakov, it had been only a matter of days, hours or even minutes. Once he had planted his seed back in the past, he needed only to program his warp disc to take him back five or ten or fifteen years later, any interval of time he chose, to see his creation literally growing up before his eyes and guide its physical and intellectual development. And now that he had what he referred to as his "breeding stock" in the ironically named Vlad Dracula and Janos Volkov (the name meaning "son of the wolf"), he could use them to create others through the medium of infection in a fraction of the time. It could be done via an infectious bite, as had been the case with Hesketh, or with an injection of the genome taken from one of the creatures. And they were creatures, human in a sense, yet at the same time both more and less than human. A new and different species.

With Tony Hesketh, Drakov had decided to go the "traditional route," as he referred to it with amusement, following the elements of folklore associated with the vampire myth—the seduction, the mutual drinking of the blood, sleeping in coffins during the day and establishing a psychosexual rapport with the victim. He found it useful to follow the traditions of the legend, to take advantage of Hesketh's susceptible and superstitious mindset.

In time, Hesketh would discover that whether he slept during the day or night was purely a matter of setting his biological clock and that a bed with clean sheets would be far more comfortable and would work equally as well as a coffin lined with "native earth." He had already learned that there was no reason for him to avoid mirrors, since his image was obviously reflected in them, and he had learned that crossing running water posed no problem, either. He would be able to enjoy as much garlic in his dinner as he wished and, if he chose to, he could wear a silver crucifix without the least bit of discomfort. Try as he might, he would never be able to assume the shape of a wolf or turn into a bat and fly, nor would he be able to transform himself into a mist and seep beneath a doorway. And, if he was careless, he would learn that a wooden stake hammered through his heart would certainly kill him, as would a knife stuck between his ribs or a bullet fired into his brain. But for the time being, Tony Hesketh functioned as the vampire of folklore, believing only that there were inaccuracies in the myth, that since he had no need to fear the cross, a mirror or a string of garlic bulbs, a vampire was even stronger in his "powers" than the legend would have people believe. And in his new "eternal life," Dracula was his spiritual guide. Hesketh would make the legend real and it did not matter much if he was killed, so long as he was able to infect at least a few more victims. They, in turn, would infect others, and it would spread. Biological warfare combined with murder and superstitious terror would achieve the desired result. The craving and the need for blood was real and it was that which would perpetuate the plague.

With Rizzo, as with Ransome, it was a different matter. No trappings of vampiric folklore for them. There was no point to it. They were the first pawns taken in a far more intricate, and for Drakov, much more personal game. Ransome was already infected with the vampire DNA and brainwashed through the medium of cybernetic programming to function as Drakov's agent. Rizzo would be next. Through them, Drakov planned to attack the temporal agents and, if he was successful, they would each become infected with a frightening disease.

"I would love to see the expression on my father's face when he realizes that I've struck back at him through his finest agents," said Drakov. "I will have disrupted the timestream irreparably and, at the same time, I will have shown them all the ultimate folly of their conceit, their insufferable arrogance in flouting the laws of nature."

"And when you have done this," said the vampire hesitantly, "what will become of us, of Janos and myself?"

"What do you mean?" said Drakov, frowning.

"It is a question I never dared to ask before," said Vlad, "but I feel that I must ask it now. Janos and I have talked of this and it is a matter of great concern to us. All our lives, we have been prepared for this one moment and now it is at hand. What shall become of us when it is finished? What are we to do? You now have Hesketh, Ransome and this man, Rizzo. Soon you will have others. You will have no further need of us."

Drakov put his hand on the vampire's shoulder. "You and Janos are like my children," he said. "You are my firstborn, Volodya. Did you think I would abandon you?"

"I did not know what to think," the vampire said. "I have always known that you gave me life for a purpose and I have always wondered what would become of my life once that purpose was fulfilled."

"It will become your own," said Drakov. "You will be able to go anywhere you please, choose any time you wish, pick any identity you like. I will see to it that both you and Janos are well provided for."

"And we shall be able to live as normal people do?" said Dracula.

"As normal people? What do you mean?" said Drakov.

"The craving for blood," said Dracula. "The change Janos experiences every month. You will remove these?"

"*Remove* them?" said Drakov. "Don't be absurd! How can I remove them?"

"But . . . you have made us as we are," the vampire said.

"And you think I have the power to turn you back into ordinary men?" said Drakov. He chuckled, then shook his head. "Volodya, you disappoint me. Have you learned nothing in all these years? You can never be ordinary. I have made you extraordinary! You are a predator! A superior being! The first of a new race! You are stronger than they are, more intelligent, quicker and with a far greater life-span. You are a wolf among sheep. How can you even entertain the thought of being like other men? Whatever gave you this ridiculous idea?"

"Wherever we may go and whatever we may do, we shall always be hunted," said the vampire. "We shall be hated and misunderstood . . . indeed, how can we even hope for their understanding when our very nature compels us to prey upon them? You taught us to kill them, so that we could avoid creating others like ourselves before the time was ripe, but now that the time has come, where will it end? Now that you want us to create others like ourselves, will there come a time when there are no more humans, only hominoids like us? Where shall we turn for sustenance then? We shall have to kill each other, feed on our own kind. What will happen then? What will become of us?"

"You have intelligence," said Drakov impatiently. "Use it. It will be up to you to control your population. I have shown you how. Besides, even if you were to fail in that, it would take many generations before you would have totally exhausted your food supply. Humans breed quickly and they will always be a dangerous prey. I have not made you invulnerable. Unlike the

Dracula of legend, *you* are not immortal. Although your life-span is far greater than that of any ordinary human, you can be killed far more easily than the vampire of folklore. In order to survive, you and your kind will have to become canny hunters, keen competitors. Your greatest weapon will be that humans shall find it impossible to believe in your existence.''

Drakov snorted with derision. ''The fools have always lacked imagination. A few short centuries from now, they will have killed off all their predators and eliminated all the diseases which controlled their population, allowing themselves to spread unchecked until their cities are all choked with life and their wilderness despoiled, their water not fit to drink and their air no longer fit to breathe. They will crowd together in increasingly dense concrete warrens, too many people in too small a space, and the stress of such proximity will affect their emotional stability and they will all start going mad. They will become base, unstable creatures who will understand only the artificiality of their own urban existence. They will have lost touch with nature, having brought her to her knees, and they will forget how to survive. And then they will begin to die.''

He glanced at the vampire. ''In creating you and Janos, I have introduced a predator into their midst that is at least their equal in intelligence, if not their superior. One that will not be easily destroyed. I have done them all a favor.''

He looked back through the iron bars at Rizzo. The transformation was complete. The werewolf crouched on the floor of the cell, exhausted from its efforts, its chest rising and falling heavily, saliva dribbling onto the floor as it panted like a dog, staring at him balefully.

''What a look!'' said Drakov.

''He hates you,'' said the vampire. ''He would kill you if he could.''

''I do believe he would,'' said Drakov, ''and do you know why, Volodya? Not because I have transformed him, but because I have revealed him to himself as he really is. A loathsome animal. A predatory beast.''

As I am a loathsome animal and a predatory beast, the vampire thought, but he said nothing. He merely stared at the pathetic creature huddled in the cell and felt unutterable sadness.

• • •

"Arthur, it's good to see you," said Bram Stoker, rising to his feet. It was early evening and the pub was crowded. Conan Doyle had worked his way through the crowd unrecognized. He approached the table Stoker was holding for them and took Stoker's hand.

"How are you, Stoker?"

"Reasonably well. Don't know that I can say the same for you, however. You look a bit the worse for wear. Sit down. Are you all right?"

Conan Doyle sat down heavily and leaned back wearily in his chair. Stoker waved for another pint of bitters. "I have not been sleeping well," said Doyle. "These killings have all of my attention at the moment. I can think of nothing else. The matter is driving me to complete distraction. I sit up half the night, smoking pipeful after pipeful, filling the room with a latakia fog, racking my brain, attempting to arrive at some sort of rational explanation for the whole affair, but every line of reasoning I try to follow leads me nowhere. Nowhere, that is to say, near an explanation that is rational. I have just come from Scotland Yard. There has been yet another murder."

"Another one!" said Stoker. "When?"

"Apparently sometime last night," said Doyle, pausing a moment while the drink was set before him and then lifting the glass and drinking deeply. "A young man, perhaps nineteen or twenty years old, found in the most appallingly disgusting condition. Decency forbids me to describe it. Yet the cause of death itself was almost identical to that of Angeline Crewe. Insult to the system brought about by a profound loss of blood."

"Human teethmarks on the throat?" said Stoker.

Doyle sighed. "Yes, I am afraid so. It seems certain that we are faced with two separate fiendish killers, and yet I cannot help feeling that these killings are connected somehow, despite the fact that we are looking at two different methods of murder. I have no sound basis for drawing this conclusion, but I feel it as an exceedingly strong intuition. You said in your message that you had some information connected with this case."

"Well, I knew, of course, that you were involved in the investigation," said Stoker. "Inspector Grayson took me into his confidence. Has he discussed our last meeting with you?"

Doyle shook his head. "Not beyond telling me that the two of you spoke about that young man, Tony Hesketh, whom Grayson has been anxious to question in this case.''

Stoker pursed his lips thoughtfully. "He didn't mention the name Dracula to you?''

''Dracula?'' Doyle frowned. "What, you mean Vlad the Impaler? Oh, I think I understand. No, actually, it was I who mentioned the name to Grayson, while telling him about—''

"No, no, I did not mean in that connection," Stoker said. "Grayson mentioned the name while telling me about the conversation that you had with him, about the vampire legend and how it may have come about. No, what I was referring to was the fact that it was a name I recognized as belonging to someone I had recently met. An Eastern European nobleman whose name is also Dracula.''

"Coincidence," said Doyle, shrugging. "Doubtless that was why Grayson never mentioned it. You mean that was all you had to tell me?'' He was unable to hide his disappointment.

"Not quite," said Stoker. "This Count Dracula was in the company of young Hesketh when I met him. Also a coincidence? Perhaps. They came backstage to speak with Angeline Crewe. The Count seemed quite attentive towards Miss Crewe. She seemed to know him. Hesketh invited one of the other young women in the company, Miss Violet Anderson, to join them for dinner. The Count seemed quite attentive towards Violet, as well, and she did not seem to mind. All four of them left together. Now Angeline is dead, Hesketh is missing, and no one has seen Violet for at least a week.''

"I see. How very curious. Has anyone inquired after Miss Anderson?''

"She had sent word that she was ill," said Stoker, "and we replaced her with an understudy, but when there was no further word from her, I became concerned and sent round to her flat to see how she was feeling. She was not at home and her landlady has neither seen nor heard from her.''

"And you mentioned this to Grayson?'' said Doyle.

"Well, yes and no," said Stoker. "That is to say, I mentioned having met a man named Dracula, because it seemed a singular coincidence when he brought up the name in that context, but it wasn't until after I had spoken with him that it occurred to me to look into Violet's situation, so I did not discover that she was missing until only this morning. Under the circumstances, I became alarmed and, knowing you were involved, I at once sent word to you.''

"Why to me and not to Grayson?" said Doyle.

"Well, frankly, because I know that you have already predisposed him not to consider certain possibilities inherent in this case. I thought we should discuss the matter further.''

"Precisely what are you suggesting?"

"I am suggesting that perhaps the reason you have not been able to find a rational explanation for these events is that there *is* no *rational* explanation.''

Doyle set down his glass and sighed, shaking his head. "Really, Stoker! Are you seriously suggesting that there is some sort of supernatural manifestation behind all of this? That we are dealing with a werewolf or a vampire?''

"Perhaps both," said Stoker. "According to legend, vampires often have servants, familiars of a sort, to protect them during their periods of vulnerability.''

"Oh, come now, Stoker!" Doyle said. "What utter nonsense! Do you honestly expect me to believe that a 15th century Wallachian *voivode* has been resurrected from the dead and is now among us as a vampire? With some sort of lycanathropic manservant, no less? I fear you have become carried away by your own imagination.''

"What was it your detective was so fond of saying," Stoker said, "that if you eliminate all the probable explanations, what remains, no matter how improbable, must be the answer? Something like that, wasn't it?''

"Something like that, yes," said Doyle irritably. "However, we are still a long way from eliminating all the probable explanations. For example, has it occurred to you that what we are dealing with may be a madman who, in his perverse dementia, believes himself to be a vampire?''

"No, quite honestly, that had not occurred to me," said Stoker. He grimaced, wryly. "I must admit, it makes more sense than my own theory.''

"Well, don't feel too badly about it, old fellow," Doyle said. "That was not something that just came to me. In the course of racking my brain over these murders, I considered a number of seemingly outrageous theories. One was that the murders were accomplished with the aid of a trained gorilla. Another was the possibility that we could be faced with a madman who believed himself to be a werewolf. Interestingly enough, those werewolf killings, as Holcombe and I have started to refer to them, took place during the time of the full moon and they have apparently stopped now. But in their stead, we now have these vampire-style murders. As if . . .''

''What is it?'' Stoker said.

''I am not certain,'' Doyle said. ''Perhaps I've been infected by your active imagination, Stoker, but what if, indeed, the killer were a madman who believed himself to be a werewolf? According to legend, werewolves are active only during the time of the full moon, so if his delusion were associated with the lunar phases, then it would follow that the killings would correspond accordingly. And the werewolf murders have stopped now. However, what if our madman's compulsion to murder were so strong that he could not bring himself to stop until the next full moon? He would have to find some sort of justification that would allow him to continue killing and since he already believes himself to be a werewolf, could he not also convince himself that he was a vampire, as well?''

''And you say *my* imagination is overactive?'' Stoker said. ''Still, I must admit that it is a fascinating hypothesis. One that certainly sounds more rational than my own.''

''Well, in any event,'' said Doyle, ''I would say that, all things considered, our first order of business must be to speak with this Count Dracula of yours.''

''*Our* first order of business?'' Stoker said. ''You mean I am to join you in this investigation?''

''You have already met this Count Dracula, whereas I have not,'' said Doyle. ''And surely you wish to get to the bottom of this matter.''

''Indeed, I do!'' said Stoker.

''Then we must seek out Count Dracula and confront him to see what we can learn. Do you have any idea where he may be found?''

''He has a box at the Lyceum,'' Stoker said. ''He attends our performances with regularity. I expect that we may find him there tonight. The curtain should be going up on this evening's performance within the half hour.''

''Then there's no time to lose,'' said Doyle. ''Come, Stoker! The game's afoot! We must make haste to the Lyceum Theatre!''

• • •

Scott Neilson had left the crime lab early, much to the disgust of Ian Holcombe, who was rapidly coming to the end of his rope as a result of all these killings. Neilson had begged off on a pretext, anxious to get back to the command post at the Hotel Metropole and report the latest developments, so he was no longer there when Linda Craven arrived with Dick Larson to warn him that their cover had been blown and that they were moving the command post.

Neilson had wanted to waste no time. There had been another murder, but this time Neilson had no doubt as to who the killer must have been. The corpse had been that of a young male, about nineteen years old, found nude in the bedroom of his boarding house. From the state of the body on the bed when it was found and the subsequent examination in the crime lab, it was obvious that the dead man was killed during a sexual encounter and the autopsy left no doubt as to what sort of sexual encounter it had been. It seemed certain now that Tony Hesketh had become a vampire and he had claimed his first victim.

A gay vampire, thought Neilson. What a diabolical creature to release upon Victorian London! Hesketh would be able to prey upon the male homosexual population of London with relative impunity. In Victorian England, with homosexuality still largely locked up in the closet, it would be almost impossible for the police to gather evidence about such murders. And those Hesketh victimized but did not kill would not be very likely to report the assaults. Given the sexually repressed Victorian morality, a young man trying to make his way up in society would hardly admit to having been bitten in the neck and had his blood sucked by another young male. So he would doubtless hide the wound, and soon he would sicken as the infection spread within his body and a new craving began to manifest itself—an insatiable appetite for human blood.

Neilson also wanted to report that Conan Doyle had received an urgent message from Bram Stoker and had rushed off to meet with him. Doyle had crumpled up the note he had received from Stoker and thrown it into a wastebasket. Neilson had retrieved it at the first opportunity. From the message, it seemed that Stoker had stumbled upon something. He was very anxious to discuss the case with Conan Doyle. The significance of these two meeting and discussing the murders could not be overlooked. Neilson felt that Steiger had to know at once. Only Steiger was not at the command post. No one was.

Neilson stood inside the empty suite in the Metropole Hotel, puzzled, uncertain what to do. The team had not checked out of the hotel, but the suite was abandoned. He could make no sense of it. Something must have happened, but what? The arms locker had been opened and it was empty. There were no signs of violence, nothing had been disturbed, there simply wasn't anybody there. Neilson started to feel apprehensive. Something told him he should get out of there, fast. Just as he turned to leave, there came a knock at the door.

Neilson quickly reached inside his jacket and removed the Colt Model 1873 from its specially made leather shoulder rig. It was similar to the gun carried by the other members of the mission support team, a single action .45 with a 7 ½ inch barrel, a primitive weapon by the standards of the 27th century, but Neilson was deadly with it. Trick shooting with antique firearms was his hobby, something he had learned from his father during his childhood in Arizona, and he felt far more comfortable with the heavy Colt than he would have with a laser. His "fast draw" had been clocked at over a hundred miles per hour and, in one smooth motion, he could cock and fire a single-action revolver like the Colt faster than most people could fire a more modern double-action handgun. For safety's sake, the revolver's cylinder held only five rounds, so that the hammer could rest over an empty chamber. Otherwise, a dropped gun could easily go off. Having only five shots did not worry Neilson. If he could not get the job done with five rounds, he had no business carrying a gun.

He stood just to one side of the closed door, just in case anyone fired at him through it. The knock was repeated.

"Who is it?" Neilson said cautiously.

"H. G. Wells."

Wells! It could be a trap.

"Just a moment," Neilson said, and at the same time, he yanked open the door, grabbed Wells with his free hand and pulled him hard into the room, ready to fire at anyone who stood behind him. But there was no one there and Neilson immediately shifted his aim to Wells, who had fallen sprawling on the carpet.

"*Don't shoot!*" said Wells. Remaining motionless upon the

floor, he raised his hands up in the air, his posture comical and awkward.

Neilson checked the hallway quickly, then closed and locked the door. He glanced at Wells and put away his gun.

"Really, you Americans!" said Wells, getting to his feet and brushing himself off. "I see you've brought some of your Wild West with you to London. Loaded for bear, I see. Or perhaps for werewolf? I have come seeking your three compatriots or whichever of you is in charge."

"Mr. Wells, my name is Scott Neilson. You obviously know a great deal already, but I have a feeling that we may be in danger here. Everyone else seems to be missing and it's not like Colonel Steiger to leave the command post unmanned. It is imperative that we go somewhere where we can speak safely."

"Have you a place in mind?" said Wells.

"For the moment," Neilson said, "the best solution seems to be to keep in motion, at least until I can figure out what's happening."

They left the hotel and hailed a coach. Neilson held the door for Wells as he got in, looked around quickly, then got in after Wells and told the coachman to drive them to Trafalgar Square.

The coach headed down Northumberland Avenue towards the intersection of Strand and Charing Cross Road, the central point of London, at the southeast corner of Trafalgar Square, where the monument to Lord Nelson stood. The coachman drove slowly, sitting atop his seat and smoking a bent Dublin pipe. Inside the coach, Neilson leaned back against the seat and drew a deep breath.

"I hardly expected to see you, of all people," he said to Wells. "How did you escape from Moreau?"

"Escape?" said Wells. "There was no need of escaping. I was never a prisoner of Phillipe Moreau. He is my friend."

"I wonder how much you know about your new friend," said Neilson wryly.

"I know that he is from another time," said Wells. "More specifically, from another time *line*, as I believe you people put it, a universe which exists alongside this one. I know that he had developed the techniques to create the creatures that you seek as part of a wartime laboratory effort known as Project Infiltrator and I know that he abandoned that project to work with Nikolai

Drakov, whom you people from the future are pursuing. I have met three of you before, you are the fourth, but I do not know for certain how many of you there are. In any event, I have come to offer you my help and that of Phillipe Moreau.''

"Jesus," Neilson said, "he told you everything!"

"And I am satisfied that he was telling me the truth," said Wells. He had decided not to mention his trip into the future. "Your reaction merely confirms it."

"Only you don't realize that Moreau is the one behind all this."

"Apparently, Mr. Neilson," said Wells, "it is you and your compatriots who do not realize that Phillipe Moreau had nothing to do with these killings. He blames himself for having taught Nikolai Drakov the art of creating these creatures, but they were solely Drakov's work and not Moreau's. Moreau had tried to stop him when he realized what Drakov had done, how he had used him, and they fought. Drakov left him for dead, but Moreau survived and has been on his trail ever since. We met utterly by accident, when he came to the offices of the *Pall Mall Gazette,* in search of more detailed information about one of the murders. He had tracked Drakov to London and he was convinced that a hominoid had been responsible for the murder. He had no idea that he would find me there and, in fact, he did not know who I was at first. When I became suspicious, he tried to leave, but I would not let him. Then he found out who I was and decided to take me into his confidence. When I mentioned to him that I had heard the name of Nikolai Drakov before, and the circumstances in which I had heard it, he immediately realized who my three visitors had been and he told me that they were law enforcement agents from the future and that there might be more of you than just the three I met. He also told me that he was enormously relieved to hear that you were on the scene, because it meant that the chances of stopping Nikolai Drakov and his creatures were increased."

"And you *believed* all this?"

"Implicitly," said Wells. "Moreau warned me that you would be incredulous and I see it as my responsibility to convince you that what he told me was the truth."

Neilson exhaled heavily. "If all that's true, then why didn't Moreau come to us himself?"

"Would you have listened to him?" Wells said.

Neilson recalled Steiger's order to shoot Moreau on sight and shook his head. "No, probably not. We would have killed him. And chances are it would probably have been the right thing to do."

"Chances?" Wells said. "You would take a man's life merely on the *chance* that it was the right thing to do? I see Moreau was right in not coming to you himself. What sort of people *are* you?"

"Not very noble ones, apparently," said Neilson. "And not very trusting, either. I don't think you fully understand just what it is you've become involved in, Mr. Wells. Liberal principles are something we just plain can't afford. There's far too much at stake. Even if what Moreau told you was the truth, and he has obviously convinced you, we simply could not afford to trust him. As reprehensible as it may seem, we could take the chance that killing him would be the right thing to do, but we could not afford to take the chance that trusting him would be. In the case of the former, if we were wrong, only one life would be affected and it would be a life that does not belong in this timestream. In the latter case, it could affect billions of lives and I am not exaggerating. We are at war and Moreau is the enemy. Given such a choice, what would *you* do?"

"War," said Wells reflectively. "Do you know what Oscar Wilde said about war as it may take place in the future? He said, 'A chemist on each side will approach the frontier with a bottle.' And from what I understand, he was far closer to the truth than he ever realized. I don't think I will tell him. He would be aghast at the thought of one of his cynically ironic observations reduced to a mundane reality." Wells shook his head. "And now it is I who am becoming cynical. I, who have sought to kindle a love of science in students, look about me now and see that we in this time are in the midst of a sort of 'dis-ease' about technology and industry, that we are not certain what to make of it exactly, that it frightens us more than a little, and then I look at you and think perhaps that it should frighten us a great deal more. The forceps of our minds are clumsy forceps and they crush the truth a little in taking hold of it. That is why every scientific generalization is tentative and every process of scientific reasoning demands checking and adjustment by experiment. But you seem frightened by the process, afraid that the truth may not justify the risk. You would rather pulverize the truth in your clumsy mental forceps rather than take the chance that it may not bear out your hypothesis. What would *I* do if I were in your place, Mr. Neilson? I tell you frankly that I would take the risk, because to destroy a life so casually, merely on the *chance* that it might endanger others, whether it be millions, billions or even trillions, is to place all those other lives in jeopardy of the direst sort merely by the fact of setting a precedent for such a draconian philosophy.''

Neilson sat silent for a moment. ''You argue most persuasively, Mr. Wells,'' he said at last. ''However, the decision is not mine to make. I am a soldier and I am under orders to shoot Moreau on sight.''

''In that case,'' said Wells, ''I shall have to make certain that Moreau stays out of your sight, at least until I am able to convince your superiors of the truth.''

''But how do you *know* it is the truth?'' said Neilson. ''Have you any *proof*? Isn't it possible that Moreau is actually in league with Drakov, as we suspect, and that they are using you as a pawn in their plan? Either way, we have to find Moreau. I have explicit orders concerning you, as well. You have been exposed to things that you have no business knowing. I have to take you back with me to my superiors.''

''Only it seems that you do not know where they are,'' said Wells. ''That would appear to pose something of a problem.''

''And I can think of only one solution,'' Neilson said. ''We have been keeping your house under surveillance. Unless something has occurred to change that, we're sure to encounter at least one of our people there. Whatever happens, I can't let you out of my sight. You know too much and you could be in danger.''

''Am I to take it, then, that I am your prisoner?'' said Wells.

''I would prefer if you thought of me as your bodyguard,'' said Neilson. ''At least for the time being, until we can sort things out.''

Wells nodded. ''It really makes no difference. We both want the same thing. You want to deliver me to your superiors and I want very much to speak with them. I will put myself into your hands. Shall I direct the coachman to take us to my home?''

9 _____

The curtain had already gone up on the play by the time the coach pulled up in front of the Lyceum Theatre. Bram Stoker led Conan Doyle backstage, to a place where they could stand in the wings and peek out from behind a curtain at the audience in the theatre. Stoker pointed up towards a section of box seats to stage left.

"We're in luck," he said. "There, you see? Third one over, in the well-tailored evening clothes and opera cape, the chap with the downward pointing black moustache and widow's peak."

"I see him," Doyle said.

They spoke in low voices while Henry Irving declaimed his lines as Becket, performing as usual in his highly idiosyncratic, mannered style, his voice rising to the rafters, his gestures elaborate and flamboyant.

"Your count does not look very dead to me," said Doyle wryly. "However, there is, I must admit, a certain malevolence about him. The intensity with which he stares down at the actors . . ."

"He has seen the play half a dozen times, at least," said Stoker, "and yet he keeps returning, seeing it again and again."

"Merely an avid theatregoer?" Conan Doyle said. "Or is there something about this play in particular which so impresses him?"

"I cannot say," said Stoker. "Henry noticed him about the third time he came back and asked me to find out who he was. When I discovered that he was a nobleman, I suggested to Henry that it might be a nice idea to invite him to the Beefsteaks. Henry thought it a capital idea, but the chap refused. He gave no explanation, he simply declined. He did so politely, but, well, after a response like that, one simply does not press the issue. I mean, after all—"

"Yes, I quite understand," said Doyle absently, staring up at the man intently. Stoker suddenly had the impression that Doyle wasn't even listening to him, that he was completely absorbed by the man in the box. "I want to speak with him."

"Perhaps we should wait until the intermission," Stoker said.

"It might be a bit awkward in the crush," said Doyle.

"Not at all," said Stoker. "The Count has yet to leave his box during an intermission. He either remains there and converses with some guests or, more often, sits there by himself, staring fixedly at the curtain until it goes up once again. I'll take you up and introduce you."

They waited, watching from the wings. The audience was highly receptive to the play, and Irving's performance in particular. Irving's formula for success at the Lyceum was historical themes and the story of Thomas Becket was a familiar one to the English theatregoing public. He had adapted the play with Stoker's help from Lord Tennyson's work and Stoker had consulted with the great man himself in the process of bringing the drama to the stage. Irving spared no expense when it came to set design and costumes. His productions were lavish and the effort paid off in packed houses. Shortly before the curtain came down for the intermission, Stoker led Conan Doyle around to the lobby and up into the tiers of box seats. They waited outside until they heard the audience applaud as the curtain came down, then went into the box. The sole occupant heard them enter and rose to face them as they came in.

"Good evening, Count," said Stoker. "I trust you are enjoying the performance? It has not palled on you by now?"

"Good evening, Mr. Stoker," said the vampire, inclining his upper body forward slightly in an abbreviated bow. "No, the play is as fascinating to me now as when I first saw it. There is something noble and compelling in its theme, the redemption of the soul. Mr. Irving's performance is inspired, as usual. I seem to find something new in it each time I attend."

"I am sure he will be pleased to hear that," Stoker said. "Allow me to introduce a friend of mine, Dr. Arthur Conan Doyle. Dr. Doyle, Count Dracula."

"How do you do, sir," Doyle said, extending his hand.

Dracula took it and repeated his short bow. "A pleasure to make your acquaintance, Dr. Doyle. Are you, by any chance, the same Arthur Conan Doyle who wrote those fascinating stories about the consulting detective, Mr. Sherlock Holmes?"

"I am," said Doyle. "I am surprised that you would be familiar with them. To my knowledge, they are not available in the Balkan countries and I perceive by your name and accent that you are from Transylvania."

"An excellent deduction, Dr. Doyle," the vampire said, smiling very slightly. He did not bare his teeth when he smiled. "No, regrettably, your work is not available in my homeland, but I have read your stories here, in the editions published by George Newnes, Ltd. I was sorry to read about the unfortunate demise of Mr. Holmes. Perhaps he may yet return from the dead, no?"

Doyle smiled. "An interesting turn of phrase," he said. "Return from the dead. No, I do not think so. After all, once people die, they stay dead, don't they?"

"Except, perhaps, in fiction or in legend," Dracula said. "And the abilities of your Mr. Holmes are certainly legendary, Dr. Doyle. It would not surprise me if you were to inform us all that he had somehow cheated death and come back from the grave."

Doyle pursed his lips, maintaining eye contact with the Count. "Indeed. Speaking of legends, I am familiar with one from your own homeland, that of a certain Wallachian prince whose name you share. Vlad Dracula, also known as Vlad Tepes, the Impaler."

"An ancestor of mine," said Dracula. "Much maligned by history, I am afraid."

"You are saying that he did not kill all those thousands of people he is reported to have done away with so savagely?" Conan Doyle said.

"My ancestor lived in savage times," said Dracula, "and savage times demand savage measures. There are times when it is necessary to kill in order to survive. My ancestor was at war against the Turks. How many people has your British Empire killed in its wars for survival and colonial expansion?"

"A great number, I am sure," said Doyle. "Still, there is a difference between killing in wartime, on the field of battle, and torturing people in dungeons and impaling them on wooden stakes. I would find it difficult to justify such barbarous acts."

"Would you find it easier to justify the acts of your English privateers, pirates with a license from the Crown to pillage, rape and torture on the high seas and in the West Indies?" said Dracula. "And what of the acts of your English kings, such as Henry VIII and Richard III? Or the acts of your crusaders, for that matter? What of all the implements of torture that I have seen in your Tower of London? The thumbscrew; the rack; the iron maiden. Is your English history so free of bloodshed that you can throw stones at that of my own country?"

Doyle cleared his throat. "Your point is well taken. Forgive me. I did not mean to be rude. It is only that the senselessness of violence has been much on my mind of late, becoming something of an obsession. Apparently, I cannot even enjoy an evening at the theatre without dwelling on them. I am referring to these crimes in Whitechapel, the hideous murders the police have been investigating. I have been consulted by them, in a purely medical capacity, as they have been quite baffled by the manner in which the unfortunate victims met their deaths. As it happens, one of them was a girl who was a member of this very company. You knew her, Stoker, what was her name again?"

"You mean Miss Angeline Crewe?" said Stoker, picking up his cue.

"Yes, that was her name," said Doyle. "I understand you knew the young woman, Count Dracula."

"Yes, I knew her slightly," said the Count. "I had the pleasure of her company at dinner with some friends. A charming creature. A tragic loss. So young. So beautiful. So innocent. Have the police made any progress in their investigation?"

"Well, I am not privy to all the details," said Doyle, "since they consulted me only in my capacity as a physician, but I understand that they are seeking several of her friends to question them about the case. A Mr. Tony Hesketh and a Miss Violet Anderson, I believe. I do not suppose that you would be familiar with them?"

"Miss Violet Anderson was the other young woman in the aforementioned dinner party," said the Count, "and Mr. Hesketh was the other gentleman. I have attended the theatre with Mr. Hesketh on a number of occasions, as I think you knew already, Dr. Doyle. However, I have not seen him in some time. I think that he has gone abroad on business of some sort."

"And Miss Anderson?" said Doyle. "Have you seen her recently?"

"No, I have not," said the Count. "And I have already said as much to the police. Or are you pursuing your own investigation, Dr. Doyle?"

"I was merely making conversation," Doyle said. "It was you who asked me if the police were making any progress."

Stoker pulled out his watch and held it up in front of him. "The second act will be starting in a moment," he said, holding the watch out almost level with his eyes. A small silver crucifix dangled from the watch chain.

"How interesting," said Dracula. "You are a Catholic, are you not, Mr. Stoker?"

"I beg your pardon?"

"I was merely noticing the little crucifix upon your watch chain," said the Count, smiling slightly. "It is of Eastern Orthodox design. A lovely little cross, may I see it?"

He reached out and touched it as Stoker held on to the watch, staring at him. He turned it slightly.

"Beautiful engraving. Was that purchased here in London?"

"I . . . I found it in an antique shop," Stoker said, his face flushed. "I took a fancy to it and . . . and had my jeweler attach it to my watch chain."

"Yes, well, I see the play is about to start," said Dracula. "Perhaps we shall speak again later."

The lobby emptied as the signal for the conclusion of the intermission was given and Stoker and Conan Doyle stood outside alone, Doyle smiling slightly.

"Couldn't resist, could you?" he said.

Stoker grunted. "I feel like a bloody fool."

"Perhaps you should have eaten some garlic before we came and worn some wolfsbane in your buttonhole," said Doyle, grinning.

"All right, no need to rub it in," grumbled Stoker. "I was obviously wrong, carried away by my own imagination. I made myself out to be an utter idiot. I hope you're satisfied.''

"No need to be so hard on yourself, Stoker," Conan Doyle said. "I believe your instincts were correct. I strongly suspect that Count Dracula may be our murderer. However, what we lack is proof and that is what we must obtain and soon. We are dealing with a savage, brutal killer, a maniac, one so certain of himself that he plays at word games with us, teasing us like a coquette. I think we should follow our Transylvanian friend when he leaves the theatre tonight. Whatever we do, we must not let him out of our sight.''

"Who are you people?" Amy Robbins said. "How dare you force your way into this house! Get out this instant or I shall summon the police!''

Steiger took the woman by her arms and gently, but firmly, forced her down into an armchair. "I'm sorry, Miss Robbins, but I'm afraid we can't do that. We don't mean you any harm, but if you attempt to resist or cry out, I will be forced to restrain you.''

"I remember you!" she said. "You're one of the Americans who came to see Bertie!''

"That's right," said Delaney, "and I was here, too, remember? Please don't be frightened, Miss Robbins, no one is going to hurt you. We've come here to protect you. Mr. Wells is in great danger and we need your help.''

She looked from one face to another, panic-stricken, not knowing what to do. "Bertie's in danger? How? Why? From whom? I don't believe you! Where is he?''

Christine Brant knelt down beside her. "It's a long story," she said gently, "and one that you're going to find very hard to believe, but we can prove it to you. My name is Christine Brant. Sgt. Christine Brant. We are all special agents of our government, on the trail of a wanted criminal, a very dangerous man named Nikolai Drakov. He has an accomplice named Moreau and I'm afraid that H. G. Wells has fallen into his hands.''

She shook her head, her eyes wide. "No, I don't believe it! Why would anyone wish to harm Bertie? He's done no one any harm. You're lying!''

"I'm not lying," said Christine. "It's true. One of our agents saw him being abducted. It has to do with the murders you've been reading about in the newspapers. We're here to try and stop them. Several of our people have already been killed. Now listen carefully. What I have to tell you is going to sound incredible, but it's very important that you believe me and try to understand. You must, if you want to help Bertie. Will you try?''

Mutely, Amy Robbins shook her head.

Christine took a deep breath and while the others checked out the house and set about making it ready as their new command post, she started to explain to the frightened and bewildered woman.

"Now what?" said Dick Larson.

"We go back to the Hotel Metropole," said Linda Craven.

They were standing outside Scotland Yard, having just been informed by an impatient Ian Holcombe that Scott Neilson had left for the day and that he might not have bothered coming in at all, for all the use he was being. Holcombe had no time for them, but they had learned all they needed to know. Scott Neilson had left early; he hadn't received word that they were blown and that the command post at the Hotel Metropole was being abandoned as a security risk.

"Not smart," said Larson. "We shouldn't risk it. What we should do is report back to Steiger."

"And meanwhile Scott goes back to the hotel, finds no one there and has no idea what's going on," said Linda. "I don't know about you, but I'm not about to leave him sitting there, vulnerable, waiting for someone to show up."

"What if he's not back at the hotel?" said Larson. "Then what?"

"Then we report in," she said. "The point is, Scott's wide open and it's our fault. Actually, it's Steiger's fault. He should have left someone on duty at the command post, just in case."

"He wanted to, but Delaney was against it and he was right," said Larson. "It would have been too risky. There was no way of knowing Neilson would leave the crime lab early. In any case, it doesn't matter now. We don't know where he is and we'll be taking a hell of a chance if we go back there now."

"And what about the chance Scott will be taking?" she said. "Without even knowing it?"

"Neilson's a big boy," Larson said, "and he's not stupid.

When he sees there's no one on duty at the hotel suite, he'll put two and two together and figure something went wrong. He'll get out of there.''

"Maybe," Linda said, "but I don't want to take that chance."

Larson gave her a questioning look. "You letting personal feelings get in the way?" he said.

"What if it was you?" she said.

"I wouldn't want anybody taking any needless risks on my account," he said. "And I don't think Scott would, either. We've already got one member of the team at risk. If we go back to the hotel, that'll make it three."

"Fine," she said. "You don't have to go. Report in to Colonel Steiger. I'll go back to the hotel alone and if Scott's there, fine. If not, I'll leave a message that we're blown and get right out of there and meet you back at Wells' house."

"And if anything happens to you, then Steiger will have my ass," said Larson. He sighed. "All right, we'll take a chance. I'll go back with you. But if he's not there, we report in, understood? We don't go running all over London looking for him."

"Fair enough," she said.

They went into an alley, out of sight, and programmed the transition coordinates for the suite in the Hotel Metropole into their warp discs. They clocked out together and appeared inside the suite, weapons held ready. The suite looked empty.

"Scott?" said Linda.

There was no response.

"There's no one here," said Larson.

"Maybe we should check the adjoining suite," she said.

"Linda, there's no one here," said Larson.

The door to the adjoining suite suddenly flew open and Volkov fired. The dart struck Linda Craven in the chest. She collapsed to the floor before she knew what hit her. As Volkov quickly brought his gun to bear on Larson, Larson fired his revolver. The .45 slug took Volkov in the shoulder and threw him backwards through the doorway, into the adjoining suite. Larson felt the dart whiz by his neck, missing him by millimeters. He cocked the hammer on his revolver and started towards the doorway that led into the adjoining suite, but just as he approached it, Volkov came out in a flying leap, snarling, hands outsteadily towards Larson's throat. Larson fired again just as Volkov hit him and they both went down. Larson dropped his gun. They grappled, but even with two .45 slugs in him, Volkov's strength was superior to Larson's. He lifted him up off the floor and hurled him across the room. Larson struck the wall hard and fell down to the floor, stunned. Volkov grabbed him and lifted him high over his head. Then, with a roar of rage, he threw him through the windows. The glass shattered and Larson screamed as he fell to his death on the street below.

The blood was pouring from Volkov's shoulder and from the wound in his chest. He brought his hand to it and it came away wet with blood. He staggered and braced himself against the wall, his breath rasping in his throat. Even though he was in human form, Volkov started to whimper like a dog. Linda Craven lay unconscious on the floor. Volkov moved towards her, unsteadily, gasping for breath, blood frothing on his mouth. He collapsed just as he reached her, falling down on top of her.

Moreau wasn't taking any chances. He did not think Wells would betray him to the temporal agents, but there were ways of making men talk who didn't wish to and if they put Wells through a debriefing session, Wells would have no choice but to reveal Moreau's hideout above the apothecary shop. It was time to move. Lin Tao would accompany him, leaving the apothecary shop in Jasmine's hands. If the temporal agents questioned Jasmine, she would not be able to tell them anything, since she had been kept ignorant of the whole affair. Or at least so Lin Tao and Moreau believed, not realizing that since the first time she accidentally overheard them talking, she had made a habit of going upstairs to bed and then sneaking back down quietly to eavesdrop on their discussions. They told her they would be away for some time and that, if she needed any help, she could count on Chan, a young member of the Green Dragon tong who would stay with her while they were gone. Chan would protect her and just to be on the safe side, they made sure he did not know where they were going, so even if Wells proved unable to convince the temporal agents and they traced Moreau to the apothecary shop, the trail would end there. However, neither of them had counted on Jasmine's growing sense of independence, nor had Lin Tao anticipated the full effect of western culture on his late-blooming granddaughter.

To both men, Jasmine was no more than a child, sheltered and naive, and in some respects, she was just that. But at nineteen, she possessed the body, if not the emotional development, of a full-grown woman. And though, in some respects, Jasmine had led a sheltered life, she had lived in two widely divergent cultures and knew more about the world than many other young women her age. What she didn't know, she filled in with her imagination, fueled by her private fantasies and by the novels she purchased without telling her grandfather—for fear that he might disapprove—and read at night in the privacy of her room above the shop.

And Lin Tao would indeed have strongly disapproved of the works his granddaughter had chosen to complete her western education, novels such as Gustave Flaubert's *Madame Bovary* and Thomas Hardy's *Return of the Native* and *Tess of the D'Urbervilles,* works that were highly controversial in the atmosphere of Victorian morality, works which dealt openly and frankly with themes such as lust, adultery, illegitimate birth and murder. Flaubert had been brought to trial on the basis of his novel's alleged immorality and narrowly acquitted and Hardy's work had scandalized proper Victorians. Jasmine had even read *Dorian Gray,* by Oscar Wilde, but it was Hardy who had captured her imagination, with his tragically romantic heroines. Their grand, frustrated passions became Jasmine's own. In her mind, she and Moreau were lovers linked by destiny, despite the fact that Moreau was completely ignorant of her feelings towards him. That made it even more romantic and now there was the added impetus of her "lover" being in danger. Like her literary role models, Jasmine was prepared to throw everything else aside and give way before the torrent of her feelings. But unlike the women of Hardy and Flaubert, she was Chinese, with oriental values, and her outward delicacy was not an indication of fragility. She was not going to remain idle at home while the two people she cared about the most went out to risk their lives.

The decision made, escaping from the watchful gaze of Chan was simple. She made an infusion of spearmint and chamomile, sweetened with honey. Into Chan's cup, she stirred ten drops of her grandfather's favorite sleeping draught—a tincture of opium and belladonna. The honey masked its bitter flavor and the opium-laced tea quickly did its work. The moment Chan dozed off, she ran upstairs and changed her clothing, then slipped out of the shop. She had heard them talking and she knew where they had gone. What she did not know, exactly, was what she would do when she arrived there. She had never before been to a house of prostitution.

The last thing Neilson expected when Amy Robbins opened the door of the house on Mornington Place was to find Sgt. Christine Brant standing just inside the doorway, armed with a disruptor pistol.

Amy Robbins rushed up to Wells and threw her arms around his neck. "Oh, thank God!" she said. "Thank God you're safe! They told me that you had been abducted!"

"I'm perfectly all right," said Wells. "What's happening here? Who *is* this woman?"

"She's one of us," said Neilson quickly. "What's going on? There was no one at the command post—"

"We're blown," she said. "We've moved the command post here."

"What? How?"

"Didn't Larson and Craven tell you? Where are they?"

"I haven't seen them," Neilson said, frowning.

"What do you mean, you haven't seen them? Didn't they contact you at the crime lab?"

Neilson shook his head, mystified. "No, something came up and I left early. There's been another murder, a nineteen-year-old male. It looks like Hesketh was responsible. The deceased was gay."

"The deceased was *gay?*" said Wells.

"It's just an expression, Mr. Wells," said Neilson. "It means the dead man was a homosexual."

"Is *that* what you Americans call it?" Wells said. "I shall have to remember that if I ever go to America. If someone asks me how I'm feeling, I would not wish to give the wrong impression."

"Please, Mr. Wells," said Christine Brant impatiently. "Go on, Scott."

"Well, Doyle was at the lab. He received a message from Bram Stoker and rushed out. The note said Stoker had some information about the murders. I thought I should get back right away and let Colonel Steiger know, but there was no one at the hotel. I saw that the arms locker had been opened and I was afraid something had gone wrong. I was just about to leave when Wells arrived, looking for us.''

"Looking for *us?*" Christine said. "Did you search him?"

"Search him?" Neilson said, glancing at Wells and then back at her. "What for?"

"They've been picking our people off one at a time," she said. "Davis is dead, Rizzo's gone, and now Larson and Craven are missing! Moreau could have planted a homing transmitter on him! You could have led them right to us!"

She spun the astonished Wells around and shoved him up against a wall, then started frisking him quickly and professionally.

"Really, madame!" Wells said, blushing. "I must protest! This is highly improper! I assure you that I am concealing nothing!"

"I'm sorry, Mr. Wells," she said, "I just can't take that chance."

"You're probably going to have to," Neilson said. "If Moreau was going to do that, you can be sure he'd plant a bug you'd never find without a full body scan. Besides, if what Wells told me is true, Moreau is on our side."

"*What?*"

Quickly, Neilson recounted everything that Wells had told him, glancing at Wells from time to time for confirmation. "So with nowhere else to go," he finished, "we came here. Unless something had gone seriously wrong, I figured the house would still be under surveillance and I could contact whoever was on duty here to find out what the hell had happened. When I didn't spot anyone outside, I started to get a little worried, but—"

"I *knew* I was forgetting something!" Brant said, rushing to the window. She parted the curtains and gazed outside for several moments, then turned around to face them once again, a grim expression on her face. "Ransome was supposed to be on surveillance duty outside. I was wondering why he didn't warn me you were coming. Now there's no sign of him. He wouldn't leave his post. Something must have happened to him."

Neilson glanced quickly at Wells.

Wells shook his head. "If anything has happened to your friend," he said, "I swear to you that I did not have anything to do with it. Neither did Moreau."

Neilson's .45 was in his hand. "I wish I had your confidence," he said.

"Oh, Herbert!" Amy said. "What's happening?"

"You two had better go into the study," Brant said to them, checking the windows once again.

Wells quickly sized up the situation. "If my home is about to be invaded, I am not about to hide quaking in my study while—"

"Mr. Wells, *please,* I don't have time to argue!" she said. "Scott, get them in there and make sure they stay in there until I tell them to come out!"

"Please, Mr. Wells, do as she says," said Neilson. "Above all else, we have to keep you safe."

Reluctantly, Wells complied.

"Anything?" said Neilson, glancing at her quickly while he crossed the room to check the other windows.

She shook her head. "Nothing. I hope like hell it stays that way, but I've got a nasty feeling that it won't."

"Where the hell is everybody?" Neilson said.

"Delaney left awhile ago to cover the docks," she said. "You and Craven were supposed to cover Stoker. Along with some newspaper clippings of the Whitechapel murders, we found a copy of Stoker's book in Drakov's abandoned headquarters. It had obviously been left there for us to find. Andre left to cover Conan Doyle. You didn't see her?"

Neilson shook his head.

"Terrific," Christine said wryly. "Well, it looks like it's just you and me, kid. Steiger clocked ahead to Plus Time just before you came to see if Forrester could send us any reinforcements. You'd better hope like hell that he gets back with some and soon."

"I can't do it, Creed," said Moses Forrester, sitting behind the large mahogany desk in his well-appointed office. He was a massive man, completely bald and wrinkled with age, but he was in superb physical condition. His arms were as big around as most men's thighs and his thick chest filled out the blouse of his black base fatigues, unadorned except for his insignia of rank and his division pin. "I'm sorry. I just haven't got the available manpower."

"You've got a battalion of commandos in reserve on standby

duty,'' Steiger said. ''All I'm asking for is some additional personnel, let me have ten commandos, just ten—''

''I can't do that,'' Forrester said, cutting him off. ''You know that just as well as I do. I'm required to keep the counterinsurgency battalion at full strength in case of a temporal alert, a crossover by troops from the alternate universe. Besides, they're all combat commandos. None of them are trained temporal adjustment personnel. Even if my hands weren't tied by regulations—''

''Screw regulations!'' Steiger said, losing his patience. ''Who the hell is going to miss ten soldiers? I'm telling you—''

''And I'm telling *you*, Colonel,'' Forrester said, rising from his chair and towering over Steiger, ''that I am in no position to spare you any additional personnel!''

Forrester was the most informal of commanders and it was always a danger signal when he started addressing his junior officers by their rank.

''Now I made you my executive officer and I sent you out to do a job,'' he said. ''I expect to see you get it *done*. I sent you out on this assignment with more support personnel than I ever gave your predecessor, Major Priest. You're not the senior covert field agent for the TIA anymore. The days of the agency being able to function without justifying itself or its expenditures are over. It's been made part of the regular army and placed under my command and I have to account to the Referee Corps for every single soldier I send out to Minus Time. I was originally allocated only one adjustment team for this mission, but I fought to get you a support unit. Now you're telling me that's not enough. If you can't take the heat, get the hell out of the kitchen and I'll appoint somebody who isn't so sensitive to pressure.''

Steiger stiffened. ''That's not how it is and you know it,'' he said. ''You sent us out on an investigative mission, but it's become a great deal more than that. We're faced with a terrorist infiltration by genetically engineered creatures capable of spreading a contagion that's a far greater threat to temporal stability than any invasion by enemy troops. We're looking at a biowar aimed at making our species self-destruct, for God's sake. And you know who's behind it.''

Forrester's eyes went hard. ''I don't need to be reminded of that, Colonel.''

"Maybe you do," said Steiger, losing his temper. "After all, 's your mess we're trying to clean up!"

The color drained out of Forrester's face and Steiger instantly regretted his outburst.

"Damn it," he said. "I'm sorry, sir. That was way out of line."

Forrester seemed to deflate. He sat down slowly. Steiger gritted his teeth and clenched his fists, wishing he could take back what he had said.

"Sir, I—"

Forrester held up his hand and Steiger clamped his mouth shut, his jaw muscles working.

"There's no need to apologize," said Forrester. "You're absolutely right." He took a deep breath and expelled it slowly. "My son is my responsibility. I should have killed him when I had the chance. I couldn't bring myself to do it. There's no excuse."

"Sir, I had no right to say that. I know what you must have been going through—"

"Do you, Creed?" Forrester said softly. "Do you really? How could you possibly know? People have died because of my mistake and all I've done is pass the buck. I can't remember the last time I had a good night's sleep. It just keeps eating away at my guts, chewing me up . . ."

Steiger stood there silently, hating himself. There was nothing he could say. The Old Man was right, the pressure had been getting to him and he had lashed out, thoughtlessly, hitting Forrester below the belt. It was hard enough knowing you had a son who was insane and hated you without having to send people out to hunt him down and kill him.

"I've seen my son face-to-face just once in my entire life," said Forrester, "and that was over the blade of a knife. And even then, I don't believe he was a criminal. He was angry, hurt, confused, but he wasn't evil. He wasn't insane, at least not then. Whatever's happened to him, whatever he's become, it's my responsibility and I'm going to have to live with that."

He opened the top drawer of his desk, took out a warp disc and strapped it on.

"Sir," said Steiger, "what are you doing?"

"What I should have done a long time ago," Forrester said. "Take responsibility. Clean up my own mess."

"Sir, with all due respect, you can't do that," Steiger said. "That would be abandoning your post in wartime. Under the regulations, the penalty for that is—"

"To use your own words, Steiger," Forrester said, "screw regulations."

He summoned his administrative adjutant, Lieutenant Cary.

"I'm clocking out to the Minus Side," he told the startled young woman. "I'm not sure how long I'm going to be back there, but I'm programming my disc for clockback coordinates five minutes from now. Cover for me. If anything comes up, I'm relying on your best judgment to issue orders in my name. Wait six minutes. If I'm not back by then or if a crossover alert comes down while I'm away, get on the horn to Director General Vargas and report me A.W.O.L. on the Minus Side."

Her eyes grew wide. "But, sir—"

"That's an order, Cary."

"Yes, sir," she said, swallowing hard, "I understand that, but if I report you A.W.O.L. to Director Vargas, do you realize what that means?"

"It means I'll probably be dead," said Forrester, "so I guess it won't matter much to me one way or another." He strapped on his sidearm and glanced at Steiger. "Let's go."

10 ———————————

"I shall ask you one more time, madame," Grayson said, pacing back and forth across his office at Scotland Yard, "what is your real name and what is your purpose here in London?"

"I've already told you," Linda Craven said. She was sitting in a straight-backed wooden chair placed against the wall. A uniformed policeman stood beside her. "My name is Craven, Linda Craven, and I am an American citizen. I am part of a research group preparing a series of texts—"

"You're lying," Grayson said, stopping directly in front of her. He did not raise his voice.

"Inspector, I resent your accusation," she said stiffly. "Why am I being treated like this? I have been assaulted and the gentleman I was with was murdered in a horrible manner, yet you are questioning me as if *I* were the criminal! What possible reason would I have for lying to you?"

"That is precisely what I am attempting to discover, madame," Grayson said. "I have been in touch with the American consulate and they have no knowledge whatsoever of any research project such as you describe. I would think that if there really were such a project, the American embassy would be aware of it. Additionally, there is the matter of your passport. It is an extremely clever forgery. And let us not forget that singularly unacademic revolver of yours. Quite a large revolver, too, especially for a woman. Mr. Larson also had such a revolver. A Colt .45 Peacemaker, as I believe it's called. Hardly the sort of item one might expect to find among the personal effects of an American research scholar or a British newspaperman. A British newspaperman who seems to have no past, I might add. It seems that prior to his being hired on at the *Police Gazette,* Mr. Larson appears not to have existed. I find that very curious. But it becomes still more so.

"Members of the hotel staff report having seen the late Mr. Larson at the Metropole on numerous occasions, visiting that very suite where you were found unconscious, pinned beneath the body of your assailant. Now why would a British newspaper reporter investigating a series of brutal murders in Whitechapel be paying frequent visits to a group of young American scholars engaged in writing a textbook concerning the social history of England?"

"As it happens, we were seeing each other socially," said Linda.

"Entirely possible," said Grayson, "but, I think not very likely. I have here a list, kindly supplied by the hotel, of the names of individuals who were part of this supposed 'research group' of yours. The name Richard Larson does not appear on this list, but interestingly enough, the name Richard Locker does and several members of the hotel staff have positively identified the remains of the unfortunate Mr. Larson as those of Mr. Locker. Remembering that Mr. Larson had been working very closely with the late Mr. Thomas Davis of *The Daily Telegraph,* it occurred to me to show a photograph of the remains of Mr. Davis to the hotel staff and, lo and behold, we discover that Mr. Thomas Davis was apparently also Mr. Thomas Daniels, whose name appears right here on our list of members of this 'research group.' Further inquiries lead us to the realization that prior to being taken on by *The Daily Telegraph,* Mr. Davis also appears not to have existed. We begin to uncover a tissue of lies and misrepresentation, forged credentials, faked references, all pointing to some sort of ambitious and illegal undertaking.

"Now," continued Grayson, "I find it very fascinating that two British newspapermen are also apparently members of an American research group, headed by two so-called 'professors' named Steiger and Delaney, whom the American consulate has never heard of and who are nowwhere to be found. I also find it fascinating that both you and Mr. Larson visited the crime lab here at Scotland Yard earlier today, asking after Mr. Scott Neilson, and when you learned that Mr. Neilson had left early, you apparently went directly to the Metropole Hotel. Now, having an inordinately suspicious nature, I decided to question some of the hotel staff about our Mr. Neilson. It seems they had never heard of anyone by that name. But when I described him, lo and behold once more, comes the reply, 'Why, that sounds like Mr. Nelson, one of those nice young American scholars!' The plot, it seems, grows thicker. Mysteries abound and the trail keeps leading us back to the Hotel Metropole, all roads leading to Rome, as it were. That it was a headquarters of some sort I have no doubt, but a headquarters for what, specifically? An academic project? No, madame, I think not.''

He went around to his desk and opened one of the drawers. He took out the plastic dart pistol Volkov had used and a pair of black bracelets—Craven and Larson's warp discs.

He picked up the plastic pistol. ''I have never seen anything even remotely like this weapon before,'' he said. ''I cannot even identify the material it's made from. Lightweight, yet incredibly strong. It does not appear to be metal, at least none such as I have ever seen. What is it?'' She shrugged. He put it down and then picked up the warp discs. ''And would you mind telling me what these peculiar items are?''

''They are only bracelets,'' she said. ''Jewelry, nothing more.''

''Indeed?'' said Grayson. ''And what, then, is the purpose of all these little numbered knobs? Mere decoration?''

''Here,'' she said, reaching for the warp disc, ''I'll show you.'' Grayson handed her the bracelet. ''It's merely part of the catch, that's all. There's a little trick to opening it. . . .'' As she spoke, she tried to activate the disc, but she quickly realized that Grayson must have already played with it, because the failsafe designed into the disc had fused it, melting the particle level chronocircuitry and rendering it useless. Her spirits sank.

''Yes?'' said Grayson.

She shook her head. ''It seems to be broken now,'' she said.

He reached out his hand for it and she returned the useless warp disc to him. ''I was examining it earlier and it suddenly became quite warm,'' he said, watching her carefully. ''How do you account for that?''

She shook her head, staring at him as if he were speaking Greek. "I have no idea what you're talking about, Inspector."

"Don't you? Apparently, there is no way to disassemble it or to break it open. You still maintain that it is merely a piece of jewelry and nothing more?"

She nodded.

"And this peculiar little pistol, which fires some sort of strange, envenomed darts?"

"It isn't mine," she said. "I have no idea what it is."

"You are lying again, Miss Craven, or whatever your name really is," said Grayson. "Who was that man who attacked you and murdered Mr. Larson?"

"I don't know."

"Why did he attack you?"

"I don't know."

"What is your connection with Mr. Scott Neilson?"

"Mr. Larson wanted to question him on some point concerning a story he was writing for his newspaper."

"Mr. Larson? I thought his name was Locker."

"It was Larson," she said. "I never knew him by any other name."

"And he was a member of your research group?"

"He was a reporter for the *Police Gazette*."

"Then why is it that several members of the hotel staff have identified him as Richard Locker, a member of your research group?"

"I have no idea. I never really noticed any particular resemblance."

"I see. So if Mr. Larson isn't Mr. Locker, then where *is* Mr. Locker?"

"I don't know."

"Is it merely a coincidence that they had such similar names?" said Grayson.

"I suppose it must be," she said. "I had never really thought about it."

"And is it also a coincidence that they happened to resemble one another?"

"I suppose it must have been. I never thought of them as resembling one another."

"What about Mr. Thomas Davis and Mr. Thomas Daniels? Does the same coincidence apply to them?"

"What do you mean?"

"The names are similar."

"Yes, I suppose they are."

"And the photograph of Mr. Davis was identified by members of the hotel staff as that of Mr. Daniels."

"Well, I suppose they were similar types, but I personally don't think they looked very much alike."

"Yours appears to be the minority opinion. You've met Mr. Davis, then?"

"I met him once in the company of Mr. Larson. I didn't really know him very well, which is to say, not at all, actually. He was Mr. Larson's friend."

"Then where is Mr. Thomas Daniels?"

"I don't know."

"Were they not, in fact, the same person?"

"Of course not. Inspector, I really do not see what you are driving at," she said. "You are browbeating me as if I were a common criminal. I am guilty of no offense! I have done nothing! I was in the company of a gentleman friend and we were brutally attacked. My poor friend was killed. I might have been killed myself, and yet you are interrogating me as if *I* were the one who had committed the assault. I don't understand you! Why are you doing this to me?"

"Because, madame, I intend to get at the truth," said Grayson. "And we shall remain here until I start to hear some of it."

There was a knock at the door of his office.

"Yes?"

A policeman came in and handed him a wire. Grayson read it, nodded to himself, then held it up so that she could read it.

"This is a wire I have just received from the Boston Police Department in answer to my inquiry," he said. "There is no record of the existence of a Foundation for Educational Research in Boston, Massachusetts. You still maintain that you were employed by this fictional organization?"

"I don't understand," she said. "There must be some mistake."

"You maintain that there *is* such an organization?"

"Yes, of course! I am employed by them. What *else* would I be doing here?"

"Where are their offices?"

"I don't know," she said. "I was taken on by Dr. Steiger. I was hired through the mail, in response to a newspaper advertisement."

"Indeed? And where is Dr. Steiger?"

"I don't know."

"Where is Professor Delaney?"

"I don't know that, either."

"Where is Mr. Nelson?"

"I don't know."

"But you expected to find him at the crime lab?"

"No, that was Mr. *Neilson* we were looking for," she said, not falling for the trap. "I don't know where Mr. Nelson is."

"Another coincidence, I suppose, the similarity of names? And the fact that they both answer to the same description?"

"I have no idea what you are implying, Inspector. You seem to think that everyone resembles someone else. Am *I* being accused of something?"

"Where is Mr. Neilson?"

"I have no idea, Inspector. I don't even know the man! He was Mr. Larson's acquaintance. Why am I being kept here? Why are you hounding me like this? What am I being accused of?"

"Of being an accomplished liar, madame," Grayson said. "And a very clever actress. Of those facts, I have no doubt whatsoever. We are here to determine precisely what *else* you are."

Grayson kept hammering away at her, but she stubbornly stuck to her story. She was an American citizen, employed by a research foundation based in Boston, in London to participate in a research project aimed at producing a series of textbooks. She had been attacked by an unknown assailant, whom Larson had shot before being killed himself. She had no idea where the other members of the research group had disappeared to. They were supposed to be at the Hotel Metropole. The fact that they weren't there coupled with the fact of the assault on her obviously suggested that there was some sort of foul play involved in their disappearance. Why wasn't Grayson investigating *that* instead of hounding her? She maintained that she had no idea why her passport had turned out to be a forgery. It was a complete surprise to her. She didn't understand it at all. It had been obtained for her by the foundation and she had assumed that it was all in order. Nor did she have any idea why the Boston Police Department had reported that there was no such organization. There *had* to be, she insisted. How else could she have been able to afford coming to London?

No matter what Grayson said to her, she played the innocent, sticking to the same story, refusing to change it in spite of the fact that it was obviously lame. She knew that the moment she changed so much as one small detail of her story, all hope of deceiving Grayson would vanish utterly. It was precisely what Grayson was trying to get her to do. He wanted to trap her in an inconsistency and then batter away at her with it until her entire story fell apart. She could not afford to make the least little slip. Grayson was far too good a cop. He had almost completely unraveled it all. It was a war of nerves, a battle of psychology. If she slipped, Grayson would come at her like a hungry shark and it would be all over. But if she was careful, if she maintained her innocence and stuck to the same story, if she answered as many questions as possible with ''I don't know'' instead of inventing things off the top of her head, she might avoid being trapped and Grayson might start to believe that she actually *was* an innocent victim, duped by this mysterious foundation and used in some sort of criminal plot of which she knew absolutely nothing. It was a question of who would wear whom down first.

She pretended to be growing more and more tired, more and more confused, all the while staying on the alert, wary of being trapped in a contradiction. She cried; she complained of ill treatment; she called Grayson a heartless brute. Grayson fought to keep his temper under control, keeping his voice level, never raising it, not abusing her verbally so much as addressing her in the tone of a strict, paternal disciplinarian. He was certain she was keeping something back from him, but he could not trick her into deviating from her story. He couldn't understand it. No woman could hold up to such determined questioning for so long. Was it possible that she really *was* telling the truth?

There was a knock at the door.

''Not now,'' Grayson said.

''Thought you'd want to hear this right away,'' said Holcombe, coming in without being invited.

''For God's sake, what is it, Ian?''

''You must have a guardian angel whispering in your ear,'' said Holcombe. ''You were right. I compared those hair samples of Dr. Doyle's with some samples of hair from the man killed in the Hotel Metropole. Identical. No question about it. Whoever that chap was, we've got our Whitechapel killer right here in the morgue. Thought you could use some good news for a change.''

"You're absolutely certain?'' Grayson said. "There can be no mistake?''

"Feel free to confirm my findings with Dr. Doyle if you like,'' said Holcombe. "I can understand your wanting to be certain, but he'll tell you the same thing, I guarantee it. This one's our man, all right. No doubt about it.''

"Thank you, Ian,'' Grayson said.

"Pleasure to be of service,'' Holcombe said. "If you feel like celebrating, I'll buy you a drink.''

"Sorry, Ian, I'd like to, but I still have a great deal more to do and I simply cannot spare the time. Thank you just the same.''

"Right. Another time, then.''

"Another time.''

Holcombe left with a casual "Evening, miss'' to Linda. Grayson stared at her, frustrated, his stride broken. He was getting nowhere and he had no real grounds on which to hold her except for the forged passport, but if he detained her on that basis, that might be the end of it and he was certain that she knew more than she was telling him. Somehow, all these things were interconnected and he felt that if he could only locate the main thread, he could unravel the tangled web.

"Very well, madame,'' he said wearily. "I see no point in detaining you any longer. Perhaps you really are innocent of any wrongdoing, but I would be far easier to convince if you were to contact me the moment you saw any of your fellow 'research associates' again. I would very much like to speak with them. I am afraid that I shall have to hold on to your forged passport. I suggest that you contact the American consulate in regards to obtaining a genuine one. Might I inquire as to where you will be staying?''

"I—I don't know yet,'' she said, looking relieved and confused at the same time. "I shall have to make other arrangements. I really don't understand any of this. Right now, all I wish to do is rest, then see about my passport and return home as quickly as possible. I think I have had about enough of England!''

"Try not to think too harshly of us, madame," Grayson said. "And do please let me know where you will be staying the moment you make your new arrangements."

"Yes, I will. I don't want any more trouble. Am I free to go now?"

Grayson indicated the door. "One of my men will escort you out."

The moment she left, Grayson went to the door. "Thorpe!"

Constable Thorpe came rushing over. "Sir!"

"That young woman who just left. Follow her. Don't let her see you. Let me know where she goes and everything she does. And if you lose her, I'll have your guts for garters, understand?"

"Yes, sir. You can count on me."

"Right. Go to it."

He watched Thorpe hurry off, wondering what the young American woman's connection was to the horrible events in Whitechapel. It wasn't over yet. There were still linkages to follow. Little by little, he was collecting the pieces of the puzzle. There were many more than he had thought. The difficulty was in making them all fit together. The dead man had no name as yet, but Grayson had an excellent memory for faces and he felt certain that he had seen that face before.

There were already vampires and werewolves abroad in Whitechapel, so Finn Delaney was not greatly surprised to see a ghost. He was searching the warehouse district when Dr. Darkness materialized in the fog-shrouded street before him, his body not quite substantial. The lamppost across the street was visible right through him. Dressed in a long grey wool Inverness, carrying a blackthorn walking stick and wearing a shapeless felt hat with a wide brim, he seemed to be a creature of the mist.

With a loud clatter of horses hooves upon the street, a coach suddenly came careening through the fog. The man who was faster than light stood motionless upon the cobblestones. The driver of the coach suddenly saw a man standing before him in the street and shouted, trying to rein in. Too late. The horses, blindered and unable to see well directly ahead of them even under conditions of good visibility, barreled right through him.

Darkness tached, translating into tachyons and disappearing, reappearing beside Delaney even before his image several yards away had vanished from Delaney's sight. The horses reared and the coachman fought to get them back under control, but the animals bolted, panic-stricken, running away with the coach, the clatter of their hoofbeats receding quickly in the fog.

"Where did that idiot learn to drive?" said Darkness irritably.

"Well, if it isn't my favorite *deus ex machina*," Delaney said. "Evening, Doc. Come to lend a hand? We sure could use the help."

"You're beyond help, if you ask me," said Darkness. "Why on earth would anyone wish to wander around in the middle of the night in this godforsaken slum?"

"Well, if it were up to me, I'd rather be in the Caribbean," Delaney said, huddling in his coat against the chill, "but as it happens, I've got a job to do. I'm looking for a needle in a haystack, only in this case the needle happens to be a werewolf. A werewolf and a vampire, to be exact. At least two vampires, at last count."

"I knew it," Darkness said. "It was bound to happen. You've lost your mind at last."

"No, I haven't, but the man who's responsible for this mess has," Delaney said. "Our old friend Drakov has teamed up with the former head of S.O.G.'s Project Infiltrator and he's whipped up some monsters to release on Victorian London. A werewolf created by genetic engineering. If you survive an attack, you come down with a case of lycanthropy you just wouldn't believe. And he's created a genetically engineered vampire, as well, don't ask me how, whose bite is equally contagious. They've been killing people in this area and half the city believes they've got another Jack the Ripper on their hands. There'll be mass hysteria if they discover the truth. We're supposed to get the whole thing back under control somehow and Drakov knows we're here. We've already lost several members of our team. We're getting nowhere. Steiger's clocked ahead to ask the Old Man for some reinforcements. We've had some bad ones, Doc, but this mission is particularly nasty."

"I see," said Darkness. "Well, that explains why Forrester has clocked out to the Minus Side."

"He's done *what?*" Delaney said.

"He's here, somewhere," Darkness said. "I tached in to

headquarters to see him and he was nowhere to be found. Lieutenant Cary informed me that he had clocked out to Minus Time with Steiger, leaving her with instructions that if he had not returned within five minutes, Plus Relative Time, she was to report him Absent Without Leave to Director General Vargas. She was beside herself with worry and begged me to go after him. Unfortunately, the reason for my visit was that I had discovered a problem with the symbiotracers I gave you. Apparently, they are not quite perfected. Their cellular chronocircuitry is subject to organic degeneration. Steiger received his before any of you did and I can no longer home in on him. I was able to track you down, but I have no way of telling how long your symbiotracer will remain active. I shall have to issue new ones to you periodically until I can solve the problem of the degeneration. In the meantime, I have no way of finding Forrester and Steiger.''

''They'll be clocking back to the command post we've established at H. G. Wells' house,'' said Delaney. ''Don't ask, it's too complicated to explain now. We'd better get back there right away. If the Old Man's clocked back, disregarding wartime regulations, it can only mean one thing. He had a chance to kill Drakov during the Zenda mission and he couldn't do it. He's been blaming himself for it ever since. It looks like he's determined to make up for it. Only if Vargas discovers that he's left his post, he'll have no choice but to break him and I'm not about to let that happen.''

''You think Forrester will go back just because you insist upon it?'' Darkness said. He shook his head. ''Not the Moses Forrester I know. There is only one solution. Drakov and his creations must be terminated.''

''Sure,'' Delaney said. ''But first we've got to find them.''

''Can you see anything?'' said Neilson, glancing briefly towards Christine Brant before turning back to the window. She was keeping watch at the window on the other side of the room, her weapon held ready.

''Nothing,'' she said. ''I wish to hell Steiger would—''

Paul Ransome suddenly materialized in the middle of the living room. ''Christine . . .,'' he said, sagging down to his knees and clutching at his stomach, ''help me . . .''

She rushed over to him as Neilson turned around. The window behind him suddenly shattered in a rain of glass and a dark shape came flying through. Neilson was hit from behind and was brought down to the floor. His revolver was ripped from his hand and thrown across the room and he found himself flat on his back, staring up into the slathering face of a werewolf. Christine Brant cried out as Ransome grabbed her and threw her to the floor. She screamed as he fastened his teeth in the soft flesh of her throat.

Neilson fought against the creature with a strength born of desperation as they wrestled on the floor, knocking over furniture, but the werewolf's strength was greater and within seconds, Neilson was pinned. And then a shot cracked out.

The .45 slug took Ransome in the back. Wells cocked the hammer of Neilson's revolver and aimed it at the werewolf. The creature leapt off Neilson and launched itself at Wells. Wells fired. With a doglike squeal, the werewolf fell to the floor. Wells cocked the hammer and fired again.

At that moment, Steiger clocked in with Forrester and Wells quickly recocked the weapon and aimed it at them, but Steiger shoved Forrester aside and yelled, *"It's me, don't shoot!"*

Wells almost shot him, but the revolver was suddenly plucked out of his hand as if by an unseen force and Wells gaped at the ghostly figure that suddenly materialized before him.

"Jesus Christ!" Delaney said as he clocked in. *"What happened?"*

Amy Robbins, who had been watching thunderstruck from the doorway to the study, fell to the floor in a faint. Wells rushed to her side.

Christine sat up slowly, her hand pressed to the wound in her throat. "Oh, damn," she said, wincing with pain. "I've had it now. He got me."

"Ransome?" said Delaney.

"Rizzo," Steiger said.

"What?" said Delaney.

"Look," said Steiger. Neilson and Delaney joined him where he stood over the body of the werewolf. Before their eyes, it was slowly changing, reverting in death to human form. "It's Rizzo."

"Will someone please tell me what the hell is going *on* here?" Forrester said.

"We've been hit," said Steiger. "He's turned our own people against us."

"*Christine, no!*" shouted Neilson.

She had picked up her disruptor pistol and before any of them could move, she stuck the barrel in her mouth and squeezed the trigger. For a brief moment, she was enveloped in the blue aura of Cherenkov radiation and then she was gone.

11 _____

The House of Blue Lights was located in an unassuming, soot-blackened building off the Limehouse Causeway, near the River Thames and not far from the East India Docks. It was not among the more elegant of London's bordellos, but it was still a far cry from the tawdry whorehouses of Whitechapel. Madame Tchu's young ladies were of considerably higher quality than the Cockney streetwalkers who plied their trade in Whitechapel's cribs and alleyways. There were gentlemen among the clientele, as well as sailors, dock workers and merchants, but despite the rough character of many of her patrons, Madame Tchu maintained the house in a refined and genteel style. Few people knew that the House of Blue Lights was, in fact, operated by the Green Dragon tong and was one of the secret organization's major sources of revenue.

Jasmine did not know Madame Tchu. Their paths had never crossed before and there was no one in the House of Blue Lights who would know her, unless she were to identify herself as Lin Tao's granddaughter. Part of her wanted to walk boldly up to the front door, announce herself, demand to be taken to her grandfather, confront him with what she knew and insist on being allowed to help, while part of her was afraid of what her grandfather would do when he discovered that she had followed them and had been eavesdropping on their private conversations. She hesitated, thinking perhaps it would be best if she were to remain outside and watch, but watch for what and for how long? There was no telling when they might come out again. And meanwhile, even though the idea of going inside the house of prostitution frightened her, she was fascinated by the prospect. She wondered what it would be like inside, what sort of women they were, how they dressed and spoke and acted.

She was still debating what to do when she saw her grandfather come out with three young Chinese males. The small group stood in front of the entrance for several moments and she could see her grandfather talking to the three young men and making gestures, but she could not hear what he was saying. Finally, Lin Tao finished talking and two of the young men bowed to him and left. The third one remained with him and they walked off quickly in the opposite direction, Lin Tao moving with a sprightly energy that belied his age. That meant Dr. Morro was still in there, alone. Or was he, in fact, alone? What if the man she was secretly in love with had decided to sample the pleasures of the house? That decided her. Taking a deep breath, Jasmine started across the street.

Once she reached the door, however, her resolve faltered once again. She was walking back and forth in front of the entrance to the building when she noticed an open window on the third floor, on the side facing the alleyway. And some fifteen or twenty feet away from it, running down the side of the building, was an iron drain pipe.

She looked up and down the alleyway and then, bracing herself against the brick wall with her soft-soled shoes, she started to climb hand over hand up the drain pipe. The pipe was fastened solidly and she did not weigh much, but years of martial arts discipline had given her wiry body suppleness and strength. She made the climb quickly, like a monkey, and within moments she had reached the cornice at the top of the building.

She reached out with her right hand and grabbed the ledge of the cornice just above her, then let go of the pipe with her other hand and quickly clamped her fingers over the ledge, allowing her legs to swing out and away from the wall. Both hands clamped over the cornice ledge, she slowly started to inch across towards the open window, her forearm muscles feeling the strain as her fingers pressed down hard against the stone. Dangling high above the ground, she moved slowly, so as not to start her

body swinging. When she reached the open window, there was a
distance of about two and half feet separating her from the
building wall and the window ledge. She licked her lips and
pulled herself up slowly, allowing herself to swing outward a
little. Then she swung her legs up and dropped at the same time,
shooting her arms straight out in front of her, like a gymnast on
the uneven parallel bars making the transfer from the top bar to
the lower one. She grabbed on to the window ledge and winced
as her body struck the side of the building, then she grunted and
pulled herself up. She looked inside the room quickly and was
relieved to see that it was empty. A second later, she was inside.

She straightened up, massaging her forearms and flexing her
fingers, and looked around with wonder at the room she had
entered through the window. The floor was covered with soft,
thick Oriental rugs and the walls were hung with tapestries,
there to hide cracks and peeling paint as much as to provide
decoration. Everything was red and purple and gold, from the
upholstery on the chairs to the canopy above the bed, which
dominated the small room. She walked around the bed,
marveling at the size of it, and saw with surprise that there was a
mirror fastened just below the canopy. She heard footsteps
approaching outside and quickly looked around for a place to
hide. Briefly, she considered diving down underneath the bed,
but then she realized that the bed would be the first place they
would come to and instead she chose to duck behind the curtains
on the other side of the painted wooden screen standing in a
corner.

The door opened and a couple entered. The man was
middle-aged, dressed in a dark frock coat, an elegant waistcoat
with a gold watch chain and a bowler hat. The girl was young,
Chinese, no older than Jasmine, wearing a form-fitting, bright
red dress slashed deeply up the side with green and gold dragons
embroidered on it. The man had a red face and a huge handlebar
moustache and sidewhiskers and the girl had long black hair
hanging straight down to her waist. Jasmine watched wide-eyed
from her hiding place as the man closed the door behind them
and then swept the girl up in his arms, crushing his lips to hers.
The girl lifted her bare leg and rubbed it against the outside of
the man's leg, hooking it around him.

It was nothing like what Jasmine had imagined from the

novels she had read. Instead of whispered words of endearment and loving, affectionate caresses, it was an impatient, clumsy pawing and clutching, a hurried, awkward shrugging out of clothes and a playful, adolescent wrestling. Instead of emotion-laden sighs and languorous moans, there was panting and giggling and squealing. Instead of a transcendent, blissful floating in one another's arms, it was a grunting, bouncing, spring-creaking thrusting and groaning and when it was over, the man lay spent for several moments, then immediately got up and started to dress while the girl came behind the screen and, while Jasmine held her breath behind the drapes, she quickly cleaned herself using the washstand that the screen concealed, slipped into her dress, straightened it, brushed the stray strands of hair away from her face with a completely indifferent air and then went out to escort the gentleman back downstairs. Jasmine was at the same time both fascinated and incredibly disillusioned. Was that all there was to it?

Somehow, she had imagined something much more spiritual and romantic. The sight of the man's unclothed body had repelled her. He had looked so much better in his clothes! Without them, his stomach had hung down like a buddha's and his chest had sagged. He had been covered with unattractive, thick, coarse, curling hair and his legs looked spindly, grotesquely out of proportion with the rest of him. Naked, he had looked ugly, comical, ungainly, and as for his manhood, it was all Jasmine could do to refrain from giggling at the sight of it. She could not believe that Dr. Morro would look so silly and pathetic with his clothes off, but at the same time, a telling blow had been delivered to her romantic fantasies. She was not embarrassed by what she had witnessed. She was merely surprised and disappointed.

She slipped out from behind the drapes and moved quickly to the door. She opened it a crack and peeked out into the hallway. She could hear sounds coming from behind several of the closed doors, but for the moment, the hallway was clear. However, she had no idea which way to go. She stepped out into the hall uncertainly and, at that moment, a door opened right in front of her and an old woman carrying a pile of bedclothing stepped out. Startled, Jasmine gasped.

The old woman smiled toothlessly. ''I haven't seen you

before,'' she said, speaking in Chinese. ''You must be new.''

''Yes, I . . . I am not sure which way to go,'' said Jasmine, forcing a smile.

The old woman looked at her questioningly. ''Is there a gentleman waiting for you?''

''Yes, he has only just arrived,'' said Jasmine, and she described Moreau.

''Ah, the important visitor who came with Master Tao,'' the old woman said, nodding. ''Yes, he is to stay with us for a time. He is in the room at the far end of the corridor, but I was told he is not to be disturbed.''

''I was sent to see if there is anything he wants,'' Jasmine said. ''I am to bring him whatever he asks for.''

''Ah, well that is different,'' the old woman said. ''It is good that there will be someone else to look after his needs. I have more than enough to do. There is no end to work around here. You are one of the new servant girls, then?''

Jasmine nodded.

The old woman shook her head. ''You will find it harder work than pleasing gentlemen,'' she said. ''You will see. You may soon prefer working on your back to scrubbing on your knees. There is time enough for that. You should not waste your youth. I was young and pretty once, like you. Now I wash floors and empty chamberpots.'' The old woman cackled and waddled off down the corridor, carrying her pile of bedclothes.

Quickly, before she ran into anybody else, Jasmine made her way down to the door at the far end of the hall. She hesitated when she reached it. Now that the moment had arrived, she was suddenly afraid of declaring herself. What would he say? Would he be angry? What if he rejected her? There was no turning back now. She bit her lower lip and knocked on the door.

''Yes? Who is it?'' she heard him say.

She shut her eyes, took a deep breath, opened the door and stepped inside.

''*Jasmine!*'' Moreau said, astonished. ''Dear God! What on earth are *you* doing here? *How* did you get here?''

''Do not be angry, Dr. Morro,'' she said. ''I had to come!''

It all came spilling out of her in a torrent of impassioned words, words that tumbled over one another in her rush to get them out, afraid that if she paused for breath, her fear would paralyze her or, worse yet, that he would stop her.

Moreau stood there in astonishment, unable to get a word in edgewise. She finally ran out of steam and stood before him, looking down at the floor, stripped bare in all but the literal sense, her face flushed, her lower lip trembling, her eyes ready to flood with tears.

Moreau started to say a dozen different things and realized that each one of them would have been wrong. What was he to tell her? That he was old enough to be her father? It was a cliche and he was not her father and, in any case, the only time age made any real difference to a woman was if a man was too immature for her, a factor that was more often than not measured emotionally and not chronologically. And Jasmine was a woman, naive, perhaps, certainly inexperienced, but a woman none the less. And just as one did not treat a girl as if she were a woman, one did not treat a woman as if she were a girl. Was he to tell her that he did not love her? What purpose would that serve? Besides, she had not asked him if he loved her. She had opened up her heart to him, imposing no conditions, asking nothing, offering everything. A gift like that was not rejected out of hand. It was accepted in the same spirit in which it was offered. Whether or not it was reciprocated was another, much more complicated matter.

"Are you going to send me away?" she said, drawing herself up proudly, prepared to accept rejection with dignity.

"No," he said. "Please, sit down. It seems that we have much to talk about."

Andre was having a hard time keeping track of all the bodies. It was difficult enough, shadowing the indefatigable Conan Doyle, now she also had Bram Stoker to worry about and the man that *they* were following and the people who were following *them*.

She had picked up Conan Doyle as he left the crime lab at Scotland Yard, almost missing him as he came hurrying out of the building, heading for a nearby pub. She had followed him to the pub, where he met Bram Stoker. As the two men left the pub together, Andre became aware that they were being followed by someone other than herself. She kept her distance, so as not to give herself away, and watched as the other shadower hopped on a bicycle and followed the coach taken by Conan Doyle and

Stoker. She quickly hailed a hansom and set off in pursuit as well, wondering who else besides herself would be following the two writers.

There should have been someone from their team assigned to cover Stoker, but this was someone she had never seen before. A young Chinese man, dressed all in black, keeping to the shadows as much as possible, effortlessly pedaling the bicycle, even over cobblestoned streets.

They drove to the Lyceum Theatre and went inside. Andre lost track of the Chinese bicyclist inside the theatre. She had caught quick glimpses of him darting through the streets, following the coach, but he seemed incredibly adept at disappearing into the fog and shadows. Now she had no idea where he was. Conan Doyle and Stoker were nowhere in sight. She moved stealthily through the darkened theatre as the play progressed, but she was not able to catch sight of them until she sneaked backstage and saw them standing in the wings. She found a place to hide among the backstage clutter and kept an eye on them. They, meanwhile, were apparently keeping an eye on someone else, out in the audience. They kept glancing up at the box seats, but from where she was hidden, Andre couldn't see whom they were looking at. And if the Chinese man was still around, she couldn't see him, either.

However, she spotted him in the crowd during the intermission, when Conan Doyle and Stoker went out through the lobby and upstairs, to the box seats. She was unable to follow them into the box, where they spoke with someone for a short time and she was unable to get close enough to hear what was being said, because the Chinese man had already beaten her to it. She spotted him skulking just outside the box, eavesdropping on their conversation. She pulled back quickly, before he could spot her.

In the crush that followed the conclusion of the play, she lost the Chinese man once again, but she was able to spot Conan Doyle and Stoker leaving in their coach. Without waiting to try and hail a hansom amidst the bustle of the audience dispersing and risk losing them, Andre took off after their coach on foot, jogging through the streets, cursing the Victorian clothing which made running difficult and interfered with her breathing.

Fortunately, thanks to her being in superb physical condition and the coach having to drive slowly in the reduced visibility due to the fog, she was able to keep up without too much difficulty. But after several blocks, it became obvious that Conan Doyle and Stoker were following another coach, albeit at a distance, and there was another hansom following them, as well as the Chinese man on his bicycle.

"What the hell is going *on* here?" she said to herself, as she paused on a streetcorner to catch her breath. "This is turning into a goddamned parade!"

The "parade" proceeded along the Strand, to Fleet Street, past the offices of *The Daily Telegraph* and St. Paul's Cathedral, winding along roughly parallel to the course of the Thames. They passed London Bridge and proceeded on a rough diagonal away from the river, towards Whitechapel Road and the London Hospital before plunging into the maze of Whitechapel itself. Finally, the lead coach stopped and a tall man in a high silk hat and opera cape got out and started walking rapidly down a narrow street, disappearing into the mist. Conan Doyle and Stoker followed after paying off their driver and the last hansom disgorged a single man, dressed in a brown tweed coat and bowler hat, who hurried after Conan Doyle and Stoker. Once again, the young Chinese was nowhere to be seen, but Andre had no doubt that he was there as well, hidden somewhere in the mist.

She wished she was not alone, that Delaney was with her or Steiger. There were too many people to keep track of and she had no idea what was happening. She was exhausted from the long run. She unbuttoned her dress and loosened her corset, cursing the ridiculous garment, wishing there was time to take it off entirely. Breathing hard from her very long run, her feet hurting from the high-button shoes, she quickly closed the distance between her and the shadowers, using the fog for concealment.

Who was the man everyone was following? Could he possibly be unaware that he was being followed by so many people and was it possible that they were all unaware of each other? In the thick London fog, it was more than possible. But the same fog that offered such good concealment also made it difficult to keep everyone in sight. Andre slipped around the corner of a building, into a narrow alleyway, and fell sprawling as her foot struck something soft and large.

She quickly got up to see what she had tripped over. It was the man in the brown tweed coat, lying facedown on the cobblestones, his forehead bleeding. He was alive, but unconscious. Andre quickly searched his pockets and came up with a badge. The man was a policeman, an inspector from Scotland Yard. He had been knocked out by someone. By the Chinese man? Andre quickly looked around, suddenly feeling vulnerable in the fog-enshrouded streets. She had long since lost her hat, now she grabbed her dress and ripped it up the side, so she could have greater freedom of movement. She squinted hard, trying to penetrate the mist. She could see nothing.

Standing motionless, she strained to hear the sound of footsteps. In the distance, she heard the clatter of horses' hooves upon the cobblestones. Closer, she heard a baby cry; a man and woman's voices raised at one another in the dark; a chorus of far-off, drunken singing . . .

And then another sound, close, too close, right behind her—

Linda Craven knew she was being followed. She tried not to show it as she walked down the street, waiting for an opportunity to lose the policeman. He wasn't very good. She had spotted him within two blocks of leaving Scotland Yard. It made sense that Grayson would have had her followed. He hadn't believed her for a second. But unlike some of the men under his command, such as the one now tailing her, Grayson was very good indeed. He had put it all together very neatly, only he had no idea what it meant. When he realized she wasn't going to tell him anything, he had put a tail on her, obviously hoping that she would lead him to Steiger and the others. Well, thought Linda, he was in for a major disappointment.

She had to lose this cop and do it quickly, so she could get back to Steiger and the others and let them know what happened. She was sick over the death of Dick Larson. It had been entirely her fault. He had argued that it was too dangerous to go back to the suite at the Metropole, but she had insisted, shaming him into going along with her, and now he was dead. And Scott Neilson was probably dead, too. Larson had been right. She had allowed personal feelings to get in the way of duty, to get the better of her professional instincts, and it had cost Larson his life. "Professional instincts," she thought ruefully. What a joke. She wasn't a professional at all. She had no business being on this mission, which had turned into a complete disaster, a large part of which was her responsibility. She had cried back in Grayson's office and it hadn't been entirely an act. It was all falling apart and she felt utterly helpless to do anything about it.

At least there was one thing she could do right. She could lose the policeman Grayson had set upon her trail and get back to the command post, face Colonel Steiger and tell him what had happened. Own up to her responsibility. At least they got one of them. Perhaps it wasn't much, but it was something. If only the cost hadn't been so high.

She headed towards Charing Cross, at the junction of the Strand, Whitehall and Cockspur Street. It was the place where proclamations were once read, criminals were once pilloried in stocks and executions had been carried out. Now, in the late nineteenth century, it was one of the busiest intersections in London. A large cross stood atop an ornate pedestal with eight statues of Queen Eleanor of Castile, wife to Edward I, who had ordered the first crosses erected there in her memory at the close of the Thirteenth century. Linda quickened her pace, heading towards the Charing Cross Hotel.

She went into the hotel lobby, then quickly mingled with a group of people coming out, using their bodies to shield her from the policeman who was pursuing her. He ran into the hotel just as she was coming out. They passed within several feet of one another and he never saw her. Quickly, she hailed a hansom and jumped inside, directing the driver to take her to Mornington Place, near Regent's Park.

Having shaken the policeman, she leaned back against the cushion of the seat and shut her eyes, feeling miserable. Her first assignment in Minus Time and she had made a complete mess of it. She had allowed Moreau to escape with Wells; she had been the only one of the entire team who had a shot at Drakov and she had flubbed it and now she had caused Dick Larson's death. She would not be surprised if she was court-martialed, assuming they ever made it back to their own time. It was a nightmare. Scott had told her about the pressure, about how he did not believe that anyone ever really learned to handle it, but she didn't see anyone collasping under the weight of it, either, as she felt herself about to do. She simply didn't have anything left. She wondered whatever made her think she had what it took to be a temporal agent in the first place. She looked down at her hands and saw they were shaking.

She tortured herself with self-recriminations all the way to Regent's Park. She felt numb by the time the hansom reined up in front of H. G. Wells' house. She paid the driver and started towards the house, then saw the shattered window and the front door standing ajar.

"Oh, God," she whispered, "no, please . . ."

Without thinking of the danger, she ran straight up to the entrance and inside the house, where she was confronted by two uniformed policemen standing in the living room, talking to Amy Robbins and H. G. Wells.

"Wells!" she said, astonished.

"And who might you be, miss?" said one of the policemen.

"I . . . I . . ."

"Linda!" Neilson said, coming in from the next room with Delaney, whose hand was bandaged.

"Do you know this young lady, sir?" said the policeman.

"Of course," said Neilson quickly. "She's my sister. It's all right, Linda. No need to be alarmed. We've just had a minor accident."

"It is all entirely my fault," said Wells. He turned to the policemen once again. "I can see that I have only managed to upset everyone, including my poor neighbors. I shall have a devil of a time explaining it to them. I must ask you to forgive me, Linda," he continued, looking at her apologetically. "I invite you all for dinner and instead, it turns into a veritable disaster."

"Now let me see if I have it all correctly, Mr. Wells," one of the policemen said. "You were showing this Colt pistol to Mr. Neilson here, believing that the weapon was unloaded; Mr. Neilson cocked the hammer, squeezed the trigger—thinking the revolver was empty—and it went off, startling you and causing you to knock into that lamp there, which fell and broke the window, is that correct? And Mr. Delaney cut his hand upon a piece of glass, is that it?"

"That is correct, Constable," said Wells.

"Well, if you ask me, it's very fortunate indeed that no one was seriously injured," the policeman said. "You should always examine a firearm first to ensure that it's unloaded, Mr. Wells. It might stand you in good stead to remember an old adage, 'there is no such thing as an unloaded gun.' One can never be too careful.''

"Yes, I have certainly learned my lesson," Wells said, sounding sincerely contrite.

"Well, at least no one was injured. Things could have turned out much worse. From now on, Mr. Wells, you *will* be careful around firearms, I trust?''

"To be sure," said Wells. "This entire unfortunate episode has given me a frightful turn.''

No sooner had they gone than Delaney had unwrapped his hand and the ghostly figures of three men appeared out of thin air. Linda was astonished to see that one of them was General Forrester. Another was Colonel Steiger and the third, she realized, could only be the mysterious Dr. Darkness, the man who was faster than light. Darkness had an arm around each man's shoulder and as he released them, Steiger and Forrester stepped away from him and became substantial.

Darkness remained standing where he was, unable to move from the spot on which he had materialized, trapped by the immutable laws of the universe which his altered atomic structure violated. The only way Darkness could move from one spot to another was by translating into tachyons. He was incapable of taking even a single step.

"I *hate* it when you do that," Steiger said, rubbing himself as if to make certain he was solid once again.

"General Forrester!" said Linda. "What . . . what are *you* doing here? I don't understand, what's happened?''

"We were hit," said Steiger. He quickly told her what had happened. "The neighbors summoned the police when they heard all the commotion.''

"I am still amazed that they believed us," Wells said.

"Police are inherently suspicious," Steiger said. "You tell them something that sounds reasonable and they're liable to think you're lying. On the other hand, you tell them an outrageous lie that makes you out to be a fool at the same time and they'll figure you've got to be telling them the truth, because no one would make up something like that.''

"You have a fascinatingly devious mind, Colonel," Wells said.

"It comes of being a paranoid," said Darkness wryly.

"And you, sir!" Wells said. "Just when I believed that I could not be astonished any further, you come along, a man who can become *invisible!* How is it possible?"

"I am afraid the explanation would be beyond you, Mr. Wells," said Darkness. "Besides, you know too much already."

"We can worry about that later," Steiger said. "Right now, we've got a much bigger problem on our hands. Drakov was able to snatch Ransome and Rizzo, transform them into hominoids, then turn them against us. Andre is still out there somewhere, all alone." He turned and stared pointedly at Linda. "And you've been unaccounted for for several hours. Where were you? And where's Larson?"

"Larson's dead," she said flatly.

"How? What the hell happened?"

"We went back to the Metropole, looking for Scott. Scott didn't know that we had left the Metropole and I was afraid he might walk into a trap. So instead of Scott, we walked right into it. One of Drakov's creatures killed him. It was all my fault."

"I'm not interested in whose fault it was," Steiger said sharply. "I want to know what happened."

"I was hit with a stun dart. I didn't see what happened after that, but Dick must have shot him, only he survived long enough to throw Dick through the window before he collapsed trying to get to me. When I came to, the police were there. Inspector Grayson had me taken down to the Yard. The police took charge of the bodies. I guess they must have taken them to the crime lab, because while Grayson was questioning me, Dr. Holcombe came in. He told him the hair samples Conan Doyle took from one of the werewolf's victims matched the man who had attacked us."

"What did you tell Grayson?"

"I stuck to my cover story," she said. "I kept insisting I was a member of an academic research group from America, but he didn't buy any of it. He's thorough. He had checked everything out. He wired Boston and found out the foundation doesn't exist. He also checked with the American embassy and found out they didn't know anything about us, either. He established that our passports were forged or at least that mine was and he made the connection between our British cover identities and our American ones."

"What tipped him off?"

"He questioned the hotel staff and they identified Dick as one of the researchers, but he already knew him as a reporter. He followed it up and established that Tom and Scott were with the research group, as well, so now he knows the whole setup was a fake. He put me through a pretty good grilling, but I said I didn't know anything about it. I said I'd been hired through the mail and if my passport was a fake, I had nothing to do with it, because you had gotten it for me. He was already convinced the research group was a front for something, so I tried to convince him I was just part of that front, a victim who'd been conned."

"Did he buy it?"

She shook her head. "He let me go, but he had me followed. I ditched the tail and reported in. I'm sorry, sir, I—"

"Never mind that," Steiger said. "You're certain you weren't followed?"

"Yes, sir, I made sure."

"There's a chance Grayson might find out about what happened from those two policemen who were here and make the connection," said Forrester.

"I don't think that's likely," said Steiger. "It's a real long shot."

"I agree," Delaney said. "He'd have no reason to see their report and they'd have no reason to attach any significance to it."

"Neilson, how about the crime lab at Scotland Yard?" said Steiger. "It's closed now and there won't be anyone around, right?"

"I can give you the transition coordinates," said Neilson. "I computed them, just in case . . ."

"Well done," said Steiger. "All right, Neilson and Craven, you come with me. The rest of you stay here and touch base with Andre when she reports back in."

They quickly programmed the transition coordinates for the crime lab into their warp discs. Steiger gave Linda one of the two discs he had taken off Ransome and Rizzo, to replace the one Grayson had taken from her. Moments later, they were standing in the darkened laboratory at Scotland Yard.

"You're certain no one comes in here at night?" said Steiger.

"Yes, sir," said Neilson, speaking softly. "Dr. Holcombe always locks up when he leaves. He had me do all the cleaning up before we shut down for the night. He doesn't like to have people poking around his equipment when he's not here.''

"Where would the bodies be kept if they were brought here?'' said Steiger.

"They'd be stored in the next room, right through that door there,'' Neilson said.

Steiger handed him a disruptor pistol. "Go find them and get rid of them, right now.''

"Yes, sir.''

Steiger turned back to Linda. "Grayson has both warp discs, yours and Larson's?''

"Yes, but he tripped the failsafes and fused them,'' she said. "He also has the dart gun that was used on me.''

"Where did you see them?''

"In his office, where he questioned me.''

Neilson returned. "I found them,'' he said. "I destroyed both bodies.''

"Good,'' said Steiger. "Now—shhh!''

Nobody spoke or moved as someone walked past the lab in the corridor outside. They waited until the footsteps faded away.

"All right,'' said Steiger. "Neilson, I don't suppose you happened to compute the transition coordinates of Grayson's office when you went through his files before?''

"Yes, sir, I did,'' said Neilson. "I thought you might want me to break in there again, so I figured it would be a whole lot easier if I could just clock in there.''

Steiger grinned. "I'm putting you in for a promotion,'' he said. "Let's hope Grayson's not burning the midnight oil in his office. See if you can find those two warp discs and the dart gun Drakov's creature used. Destroy them and get right back here.''

"Yes, sir.'' He clocked out.

They waited tensely until Neilson returned.

"I took care of it,'' he said.

Steiger took a deep breath. "Okay, that leaves us with the question of what to do for our next move. Andre's still out there, tailing Conan Doyle. He may still be with Stoker, in which case she's got them both covered. I want to get back and see if she's touched base. If not, Darkness can home in on her symbiotracer and we can give her some back-up. Assuming her tracer's not gone out like mine has.''

He sighed and shook his head. "Damn it! We still have no

leads on Hesketh and we have no idea how many other people Drakov's creatures may have infected. Judging by what he did to Ransome and Rizzo, we can assume he's not only able to create more of them, but to control them, as well, undoubtedly through implant programming. We're down on manpower and we still have no idea where Drakov's new base is in this time period. And there's still Moreau.''

"Moreau may be our best chance," said Neilson. "If what Wells told me is true, Moreau can provide us with additional manpower through Lin Tao."

"I'll believe it when I see it," Steiger said. "I'm not taking anything on faith. Who is this Lin Tao?"

"The head of a secret organization known as the Green Dragon tong," said Neilson. "According to Wells, they're practically in control of Limehouse."

"I'm glad someone's in control of something," said Steiger wryly. "I think we'd better clock back and have a long talk with our friend Wells."

12 _____

Andre came to with a jerk, her body spasming as she regained consciousness. Whatever it was the Chinese man had done to her, he had reversed the effects with a sharp stab of his forefinger on a pressure point in her neck and she reacted as if electrically shocked. He stared expressionlessly into her eyes for a moment, then nodded once and moved back from her to sit on the opposite side of the coach.

Andre took quick stock of her surroundings. The windows of the coach were curtained off, so she could not tell where she was. The coach was not moving. She was not restrained in any way, but two young Chinese men sat on either side of her, both dressed all in black and wearing green headbands. The man who had rendered her unconscious and then revived her sat opposite her in the coach, dressed the same way as the two on either side of her. Next to him sat a withered old man, also Chinese, with long white hair and a long, wispy white beard. He, too, was dressed in black pajamas, but unlike the others, he was not wearing a green headband. Instead, he wore a small black skullcap.

"You are the temporal agent, Andre Cross?" he said, in excellent English, albeit with a Chinese accent.

Startled, Andre stared at him. "I don't know what you're talking about. Who are—*unhhhh!*"

The man sitting on her right touched her on the side, just

below her kidney, and she felt white fire lance up her spine like
an electric current.

"Please," said the old man. He held up her warp disc,
holding the bracelet gracefully and gently between his thumb
and middle finger. "You will be so kind as to reply, so that I
may be certain whom I am addressing."

"Yes," she said, seeing no point in denying it. "I am Andre
Cross."

The old man nodded once. "You need have no concern over
your warp disc, Miss Cross," he said. "It is undamaged. I have
removed it carefully, so as not to activate the device which
prevents its misuse. It shall be returned to you after we have
spoken."

"Who *are* you?"

"I am Lin Tao, master of the Green Dragon tong."

"You work for Drakov," she said bitterly.

"You are mistaken," Lin Tao said. "You were about to walk
into a trap, as Mr. Doyle and Mr. Stoker have already done.
They are in the hands of Count Dracula, the vampire Nikolai
Drakov has created."

"I don't know where you've been getting your information,"
Andre said, "or even where you stand, but Drakov didn't create
any vampires. A man named Moreau—"

Lin Tao held up his hand and she fell silent, fearing another
nerve pinch or whatever it was the man beside her had done.

"Have the goodness to hear me out, please," Lin Tao said.
"It is not Phillipe Moreau who has created this monstrosity, but
his pupil, Nikolai Drakov, who has taken his work and carried it
to a point beyond all sanity. However, Dr. Moreau does not
deny that the responsibility is his, which is why he has pursued
Nikolai Drakov to this timeline, to stop him even if it costs his
life. I have undertaken to assist him in this task, as has Mr. H.G.
Wells, who is at this very moment with your fellow temporal
agents, informing them of this."

"Why should I believe you?" she said.

The man beside her moved, but Lin Tao shook his head very
slightly and the finger withdrew from her side. Andre relaxed a
little.

"Ask yourself how else I could know these things," Lin Tao
said. "If I were not here to help you, what reason would there be
for my attempting to deceive you? You are powerless to do

anything against me and I could easily kill you. If Dr. Moreau and I were in league with Drakov, would you not now already be in Drakov's hands? Or dead? Or, perhaps, much worse than dead?''

He gave her back her warp disc.

''Go quickly and inform your fellow agents that Mr. Doyle and Mr. Stoker are in the gravest danger.''

He nodded and one of the men opened the door of the coach for her. She stepped out into the street, at the entrance to a small courtyard.

''When you return with your fellow agents,'' said Lin Tao, ''pay particular attention to the warehouse you will find at the far end of that courtyard.'' He pointed with a bony finger. ''Please do not delay. Time is of the essence.''

The driver whipped up the horses and the coach drove off into the fog.

There was a soft knock at the door.

''Yes, who is it?'' said Moreau.

''It is Madame Tchu, Dr. Morro,'' said the mistress of the bordello. ''Please to open door.''

Jasmine glanced at him with alarm. ''The old woman!'' she said. ''She must have told her about me!''

''It's all right, Jasmine,'' said Moreau. ''I won't let her send you away. But when your grandfather returns, remember your promise to abide by his decision.''

''He will be very angry,'' she said. ''He will send me home.''

''And with good reason,'' said Moreau. ''But remember that you promised.''

The knock was repeated. ''Dr. Morro!''

''I think we had better let her in,'' Moreau said. He got up and went over to the door. ''One moment, Madame Tchu,'' he said. He drew back the bolt and opened the door.

''You should have left well enough alone, Moreau,'' said Drakov, pushing the door open and shoving the woman in ahead of him.

''Forgive me, Dr. Morro!'' said the madame. ''Forgive me!''

Moreau bolted for his revolver on the nightstand by the bed, but Drakov was too quick for him. He shoved Madame Tchu hard into Moreau and they both tumbled to the floor. As Drakov reached inside his coat, Jasmine let out a ki-yai and came flying across the room, feet extended, and delivered a punishing kick to Drakov's chest. He staggered back, but managed to keep his balance. He blocked her next two kicks, which came like a blur in rapid succession, and deflected the third kick by turning it aside, adding his force to its momentum to spin her around, exposing her back to him. He moved in quickly and seized her from behind in a judo choke hold, jerking her up into the air, ready to snap her neck, when Moreau came up with his revolver.

"Nikolai, no!"

Drakov hesitated, maintaining the pressure, not allowing her to breathe. Jasmine thrashed in his grip and started making choking sounds.

"Put down the gun or else I'll kill her," Drakov said.

"If you kill her, Nikolai," Moreau said, "nothing will save you. I will shoot you where you stand."

"I have no doubt of that," said Drakov, "but she will be dead, too. If her life means anything to you, throw down the gun."

Moreau hesitated. His hand holding the gun started to shake. Drakov applied more pressure and Jasmine started to rattle in her throat.

"Damn you," said Moreau. He threw the gun down on the floor.

"And your warp disc, as well," said Drakov. "Take it off carefully and drop it on the floor."

Moreau complied.

Drakov dropped Jasmine and she fell to the floor in a heap, coughing and gasping for air. Drakov pulled out a laser pistol and trained it on Moreau.

"That is the difference between us, Phillipe," he said. "I would have fired."

Moreau got down on his knees beside Jasmine and held her in his arms. She started sobbing.

"That is a rather dangerous young woman you have there," Drakov said. "She was much quicker than the guards downstairs." He prodded Madame Tchu with his foot. "Get up, woman. Go tend to your whores. Tell them to keep quiet if they know what's good for them."

She got up slowly and looked to Moreau, shaking her head with tears in her eyes.

"Go on, Madame Tchu," Moreau said. "Please go. There is nothing you can do."

She ran out of the room.

"Somehow I never imagined I would find you in a whorehouse," Drakov said. "Really, Moreau. You disappoint me. Did you think I would fail to notice your Chinese thugs snooping about? Whom did you think you were dealing with? What did you hope to accomplish?"

"You know perfectly well," Moreau said.

"Why?" Drakov said. "What are these people to you? You are on opposing sides. Your superiors in the Special Operations Group would consider that I was doing them a favor."

"Perhaps they would condone what you have done," Moreau said, "but I cannot."

"I have only carried on your own work," said Drakov. "You should be proud. The pupil has surpassed his teacher."

"Yes, indeed you have," Moreau said, "and I will never forgive myself for the part that I have played in this. You may as well kill me now and get it over with. I no longer have any great desire to go on living. But if there is even one spark of human decency left in you, let her go. She is no threat to you."

"True," said Drakov, "but she seems to mean something to you, and I would hate to kill you now and deprive you of the opportunity to see just how far I have advanced your work. We will bring her with us."

"Nikolai, please . . ."

Drakov fired the laser and Moreau cried out as the beam grazed his shoulder, scorching the skin. Drakov grabbed Jasmine by the hair with his free hand and hauled her to her feet.

"I said, we will bring her with us. Pick up your warp disc and enter the coordinates I give you. Try any tricks and I will kill her."

With a sick feeling, Moreau reached for his warp disc. He had no thought for his own welfare anymore. He only prayed Lin Tao would reach the temporal agents in time.

"Where the devil *are* we?" Bram Stoker whispered. "What happened?"

"I am not certain, Stoker," Conan Doyle said, looking around, "but logic would seem to indicate that we have been drugged."

"Drugged!" said Stoker. "But I remember nothing!"

"Precisely," Conan Doyle said. "What is the last thing you remember clearly?"

"Being in Whitechapel, following Count Dracula into that courtyard . . ." Stoker frowned and pulled at his pointed red beard absently. "And then it is all a blank!"

"As it is with me," said Conan Doyle. "The only possible explanation is that a drug was somehow administered to us and we were brought here senseless. As we neither drank nor consumed anything since we left the pub, I can only surmise that the drug must have been introduced through our lungs, perhaps through an airborne agent of some sort, such as a gas or powder we might have inhaled. Or through our skin, most probably from a distance, possibly by a dart fired from an African blowgun or some similar instrument. I would think the latter method, since the breeze would have rendered the former uncertain."

He reached out and took Stoker's chin in his hand, turning his face to one side. "As I suspected," he said. "There is a tiny wound upon your neck, slightly inflamed, little more than a pinprick. I would venture to say that I have a similar wound upon my own neck."

"Yes, I see it," Stoker said. "Egad, Arthur, how do you know these things?"

"It is elementary, my dear Stoker," Conan Doyle said. "Observation, logic and a great deal of reading. I also perceive that we are not in England anymore."

"What!" Stoker exclaimed. "Impossible!"

"I assure you that it is so," said Conan Doyle. "You have but to take stock of our immediate surroundings to convince yourself that I am right. Observe this room, the obvious age of these stone walls, the dimensions of the blocks used in the construction. Where in Whitechapel could we find such an edifice? We are in a sort of keep, Stoker, or a castle—"

"That we are not in Whitechapel, that I can accept," said Stoker, "but we *must* still be in England, on the Cornish coast perhaps—"

"On the contrary, Stoker. The architecture is of a style such as that employed by the knights of the Holy Roman Empire. This is not an English castle. Besides, if you will take a moment to smell the breeze coming in through that open window, you will notice that there is no smell of the sea, so we can eliminate the Cornish coast. No, Stoker, what I smell is pure, clean, fresh mountain air. Air which is not laden with the damp of English breezes. Observe, moreover, the tapestries hanging on these walls. They are Turkish, unless I am mistaken, and quite old, dating back to medieval days.''

He walked over to the window, somewhat unsteadily, still feeling the aftereffects of the drug. Stoker sat up slowly, rubbing his head, and followed.

"Just as I thought," said Conan Doyle.

"Good God!" said Stoker.

They looked out upon a mountain view, with snowcapped peaks in the distance, covered by clouds. Below them was a sheer drop into an abyss. They were in a castle perched upon a cliff, overlooking a mountain pass.

"I must be dreaming!" Stoker said. "Where in heaven is this place?''

"Not in heaven, Stoker," said Conan Doyle, "but somewhere in the Alpine range, most likely one of the Balkan nations.''

"But . . . how is that possible? How did we *get* here? Who could have done this?" Stoker said.

"As to how we came here, that remains a mystery," said Conan Doyle. "But as to the identity of our abductor, there can be little doubt.''

They heard a key turn in the lock and the door slowly creaked open. Dracula entered, carrying a candelabrum.

"Count Dracula," said Conan Doyle.

"I see you gentlemen are awake," said Dracula. "How are you feeling? I trust there were no ill effects?''

"Beyond a slight dizziness and a lingering headache, no," said Doyle. "We are apparently little the worse for wear.''

"See here, Dracula!" said Stoker. "What is the meaning of this? What gives you the right to have us abducted in such a manner? What do you intend to do with us? I demand an explanation!''

"Calm yourself, Mr. Stoker," the vampire said. "You are in my home. Here, I am the master. I will insist that you address me in a civil tone. As to what gives me the right to bring you here, allow me to remind you that it was you who followed me, skulking in the night like a pair of common cutthroats.''

"Whereas you, Count Dracula, are a singularly uncommon one," said Conan Doyle. "It was you, was it not, who was responsible for the vicious murders in Whitechapel?"

"In part, yes."

"Then my suspicions were correct," said Doyle. "There was more than just one killer. You had an accomplice."

"In a manner of speaking, yes."

"Then you admit it!" said Stoker.

"Certainly," said Dracula.

"You are a monster, sir!"

The vampire smiled ruefully. "In more ways than you realize, Mr. Stoker. I am, indeed, a monster. I could no more help myself than you could contain your moral outrage upon hearing my confession. In order to survive, I must drink human blood and if I am to spare my victims the agony of an existence such as mine, it is necessary for me to kill them. I cannot always do so, but when I do, believe me, I am doing them a kindness."

Stoker stared at him, appalled. "You are insane!"

"I shall not debate the point with you," said Dracula. "Insanity, you might say, runs in my family. The very idea of a creature such as I am is insanity itself."

"Then you truly believe that you are a vampire?" said Doyle.

In response, Dracula bared his teeth, exposing his fangs.

Stoker gasped and recoiled, but Doyle stood firm.

"Merely a malformation of the canines," he said. "An unfortunate defect, but not even all that uncommon. Certainly no proof of a supernatural existence."

"How very curious that you should use that word," said Dracula. "Ironic. Mine is indeed a 'super-natural' existence, although not quite in the sense you mean. Come, allow me to show you something."

"The man is a raving lunatic!" whispered Stoker as Dracula led them out of the room, lighting their way down a long flight of stone stairs which followed the curvature of the castle wall.

"Unquestionably," said Doyle, "and highly dangerous, but he is nevertheless a man and not some reincarnated demon."

"He is only one and we are two," whispered Stoker. "We can easily overpower him—"

"Perhaps not so easily," said Doyle. "Lunacy often lends extraordinary strength. I have seen grisly evidence of what this man can do in the bodies of his victims. Let us not be hasty. He has not acted alone in this. We must learn what we can and wait for a moment that is opportune, then we must make our move. But we must do it quickly. We can take no chances with this madman.''

He led them down the stairs to the great hall of the castle and they saw that part of the huge structure was in ruins. Piles of rubble were on the floor where old mortar had given way and stones had fallen down, leaving large holes in the high ceiling. There was a gaping fissure in one wall and bats flew in and out of it, screeching, the echoes of their cries reverberating throughout the great hall. Huge cobwebs hung in the corners and rats scurried across the floor. Everything looked as if it had been abandoned for centuries. They continued downward, through a great wooden, iron-reinforced door and down another long, steep flight of stone steps, the light from the candelabrum throwing huge, garish shadows on the walls.

''Where are you taking us?'' said Stoker fearfully. He stopped on the stone steps. ''These stairs lead down to the dungeons, don't they?''

''Yes, Mr. Stoker, they do,'' the vampire said.

''In that case, I refuse to go another step!''

''I have no objection,'' Dracula said. ''You may remain here if you wish and wait for us. Mr. Doyle, I think, would be interested in seeing what I have to show him.''

''Very well, lead on,'' said Conan Doyle.

''Wait!'' said Stoker, hurrying after them. He caught up to Doyle and whispered, ''Forgive me, Arthur. I am ashamed of myself. Whatever happens from here on, we shall face it together!''

''There is no shame in being afraid,'' said Doyle. ''I can feel my own knees shaking, but we must screw our courage to the sticking point and see this thing through, come what may.''

''Listen!'' Stoker whispered harshly. ''What in heaven's name is that?''

From below, as if from a great distance, came a keening wail, an inhuman chorus of animal shrieks that grew louder as they descended.

''My God, Arthur,'' Stoker said hoarsely, ''what on earth have we gotten ourselves into?''

''Steady, Stoker,'' Doyle said. ''Whatever it is, we shall find out soon enough. Be prepared for anything.''

They reached the bottom of the steps and followed Dracula down a damp, narrow stone corridor with a low ceiling. Stoker uttered a sound of disgust as huge rats scurried past their feet. Soon they reached another large wooden door. The screams were louder now. Dracula drew back a huge iron bolt and opened it. The chorus of screams rose suddenly in volume, almost deafening them.

They were on a stone landing high above a large, underground chamber lit by torches set into sconces in the walls. In front of them was a steep flight of stone steps, leading down to the dungeon floor. There was no wall or railing, nothing to stop them from falling to the stone floor thirty feet below should they lose their footing and slip.

"May the saints preserve us!" Stoker said. "We have descended into hell!"

Below them in the dungeon, behind thick iron bars set into the stone, were scores of creatures bearing only a passing resemblance to men and women. Their clothes were torn and filthy, stained with blood. Some were completely covered with hair, looking like rabid, snarling beasts. They hurled themselves against the iron bars and howled like wolves. Some attacked each other, jaws snapping, claws slashing, and a few had fallen and were being greedily devoured by others in their cells. Still others looked almost normal, except for their emaciated appearance, their hollow, staring eyes devoid of any sanity, and their abnormally long and pointed canine teeth, visible as they opened their mouths to emit throat-rending screams and thrust their hands out through the bars.

There were manacles set into the walls and, in the center of the chamber, there was a smaller room partitioned off by steel-framed glass, inside of which they could see a bizarre array of laboratory equipment, among which were a number of large standing lamps, metal cabinets with trays holding surgical implements and a long operating table with strong restraining straps.

"Here is the solution to your case, gentlemen!" Dracula shouted over the uproar. "The dawn of a new race! The new breed brought forth by my creator!"

Both men stood frozen on the steps as Dracula descended to the floor of the chamber. He looked up at them, eyes blazing.

"Here is *true* insanity for you!" he shouted over the din.

"You wanted to learn the truth? Well, gaze upon it! Allow me to introduce you to my family! My brothers and my sisters! My creator's legacy!"

He hurled the candelabrum at the iron bars with all his might, sending some of the creatures scampering back.

"Shut up!" he screamed. *"Shut up, damn you all, SHUT UP!"*

As Conan Doyle and Stoker stood motionless, staring in stunned disbelief, the vampire slumped down, brought his hands up to his face and wept.

"For God's sake, Arthur!" Stoker said, grabbing Doyle's arm and spinning him around. "This is madness! Hurry, we must get out of here before—"

He saw the expression on Doyle's face as Doyle looked past him and quickly turned around, expecting some new horror. Standing on the landing behind them was a beautiful young woman dressed all in white, with long black hair hanging loose down around her shoulders.

"My God!" said Stoker, *"Violet!"*

"Mr. Stoker!" she said, coming down towards them and holding out her arms. "Help me! Please! Take me away from this dreadful place!"

Stoker started towards her, but Doyle suddenly grabbed him and pulled him back. *"Look out, Stoker!"*

She snarled as Stoker was yanked out of her reach, revealing sharp, elongated canine teeth. She lunged at Doyle, but he twisted away from her and she screamed as her momentum carried her over the side of the long stairway. The scream was cut off abruptly as she struck the stone floor below, breaking her neck.

Dracula stood over the creature that had once been Violet Anderson, staring down at her broken body. "Forgive me, Violet," he said softly. "I could not help myself."

Slowly, he raised his head to look up at the two men above him on the stairway, his eyes glittering. Then he turned and walked over to the wall, taking a ring of keys down from a hook.

"Run, Stoker!" Doyle shouted.

As they sprinted back the way they came, the vampire threw open the first of the cell doors.

• • •

The lock on the warehouse door yielded to the laser easily. Steiger slowly pushed the door open while the others covered him.

"I think it would be best if you were to remain out here, Mr. Wells," said Forrester.

"Absolutely not," said Wells. "I will ask you to remember our agreement, General."

"I do remember it," said Forrester, "and I appreciate your cooperation more than I can say, but my concern is for your safety."

"So long as Jane remains safe with your people at the Charing Cross Hotel, that is all that matters," Wells said.

"Mr. Neilson and Miss Craven will take good care of her," said Forrester, "and with Dr. Darkness there as well, she will be more than adequately protected. I'd feel much better if you were with them. If anything should happen to you—"

"You need have no fears on my account," said Wells. "I have no intention of indulging in any foolhardy heroics. But you will need me to deal with Lin Tao and Moreau. They trust me, whereas, I am sorry to say, they do not trust you people at all."

"I guess that makes us even," Steiger said. "I don't trust Moreau. And I don't know anything about this Lin Tao character."

"What is it you wish to know, Colonel Steiger?" said a voice from directly behind them.

They turned quickly to see the old Chinaman come walking towards them slowly out of the mist. He stopped a short distance away from them.

"It's him," said Andre.

The old man bowed. "I am Lin Tao."

"Stay right where you are," said Steiger, covering the old man with his disruptor, but Wells immediately stepped in front of him.

"Put that away!" he said. "Is that any way to treat a man who's trying to help you?"

"Stand aside, Wells," Steiger said, reaching out to shove Wells to one side, but Wells batted his arm away.

"General," he said, "I insist that you honor the terms of our agreement!"

"Steiger . . ." Forrester said.

"Sir, I really don't think—"

"Put it away," said Forrester.

Reluctantly, Steiger holstered his disruptor.

"A wise decision, Colonel," Lin Tao said.

"Never mind that," Steiger said. "Where's Moreau?"

"Regrettably, I have just now learned that he has fallen into the hands of Nikolai Drakov," Lin Tao said.

"How convenient. More likely they've been in this together from the start," Steiger said.

"It's a trap," said Delaney.

"No!" said Wells. He turned to Forrester. "General, you must believe me—"

"Take it easy, Mr. Wells," said Forrester.

"If I had truly led you all into a trap," Lin Tao said, "then it would already have been sprung. Observe."

He clapped his hands once, sharply, and dark figures seemed to materialize out of the fog all around them. They moved noiselessly, carrying clubs and hatchets and various other weapons. They were all Chinese, wearing loose black pajamas and green headbands. There were at least fifty of them.

"*Damn!*" said Steiger, quickly unholstering his sidearm. Andre and Finn already had theirs out.

"Wait!" said Wells.

"Steady, people," Forrester said. "There's too many of them. We could never get them all. Besides, they could have nailed us as we clocked in."

"Quite so," Lin Tao said, nodding slightly.

"Why?" said Steiger. "What's your interest in this?"

"Phillipe Moreau is my friend," Lin Tao said, "and Nikolai Drakov poses a danger to us all. And now there is a still more personal reason. Drakov has abducted my granddaughter, Ming Li. I am anxious for her safety. And I am concerned that we are wasting time." He spoke quickly in Chinese and the men who had appeared in answer to his summons moved quickly past them through the warehouse doors.

"This is crazy," Steiger said. "These people aren't trained troops. And we've got no idea what we're going into."

"There's only one way we're going to find out," said Andre.

"Hell, don't look a gift horse in the mouth," Delaney said, clapping Steiger on the shoulder. "We wanted reinforcements, now we've got 'em."

It was almost pitch black inside the warehouse. They moved slowly, waiting for their eyes to become accustomed to the darkness. The men of the Green Dragon tong had fanned out once they entered and now they moved like wraiths among the stacks of dusty wooden crates. Suddenly someone screamed.

There were shouts and more screams and over them, the sounds of bestial growling. A werewolf had dropped down from a stack of crates on one of the Chinese men and the victim had time for just one scream before his throat was torn out by the beast. Several of Lin Tao's men brought the creature down, only to be thrown violently aside as if they didn't weigh a thing. Three more men leaped upon the werewolf, brandishing their tong hatchets, and the creature howled as the sharp blades sank home, but even though mortally wounded, it continued fighting, killing all three of them before others jumped in to take their place.

Another creature had been spotted crouching atop a stack of crates and as it leaped, a dozen lethal throwing stars went spinning through the air, striking it in the chest, face, and head. With a doglike squeal of pain, it fell to the floor of the warehouse and died, but there were still others.

Hatchets rose and fell as the men of the Green Dragon fought with Drakov's creatures and human screams mixed with animal roars as both men and hominoids died. Delaney brought one down with his disruptor and the werewolf fell howling through the air, wreathed in a blue glow. It disintegrated before it hit the floor.

Andre stayed close to Wells, protecting him, firing at the creatures as they rushed at them out of the darkness. One landed on Forrester's back, but Forrester dislodged the creature and threw it into a stack of crates, then shot it as it came charging back at him. Lin Tao avoided a rush by one with a movement that was almost imperceptible. He seemed to lean to one side slightly at the very last moment and then his hands shot out in a blur of motion and the beast flew past him, its own momentum added to the force of Lin Tao's throw, so that it landed in just the right manner to break its neck.

It was over quickly. There had been about a dozen of the creatures, but their assault had been so furious that nineteen of Lin Tao's men had died. They stood over the corpse of one of the creatures, watching in mute fascination as, in death, it slowly reverted to its human form. Moments later, instead of a fearsome man-beast, they were looking down at the crumpled, bleeding body of a teenaged boy, not yet even old enough to shave.

"What manner of man could do such an awful thing?" said Wells hoarsely.

Forrester looked away.

"This warehouse can't be Drakov's base of operations," said Delaney, "but those creatures were here protecting something."

There was a cry from the other end of the warehouse, someone shouting in Chinese. They rushed in the direction of the shout and found several of Lin Tao's men gathered around a large, glowing circle on the warehouse floor. The men of the tong drew back from it fearfully, pointing at it and talking excitedly among themselves in Chinese. The man who had first discovered it had stepped within the peculiar-looking borders of the ring; it had started to glow brightly and he had disappeared. Now, as they watched, its glow slowly faded once again.

"And that's what they were guarding," said Delaney, staring at the border circuits laid out in a circle on the floor.

"What *is* it?" said Wells.

"A chronoplate," said Andre. "Sort of an earlier version of the warp disc, obsolete now, but nevertheless, quite functional."

"Set in the active mode," said Steiger. "No wonder we were never able to find any trace of the creatures. They were clocking in, killing, and then escaping through time, using this place as a transition point. There's got to be another plate mated to it on the other side . . . wherever in hell the other side is."

"And that is where Count Dracula has gone," Lin Tao said, "along with Mr. Conan Doyle and Mr. Stoker."

Forrester glanced at Lin Tao and spoke to the old man in rapid Chinese. Lin Tao raised his eyebrows, surprised to hear such fluency, then nodded once and bowed. He gave a quick, soft-spoken command and two of his men came up to stand on either side of Wells, taking him firmly by the arms.

"What?" said Wells. "Lin Tao, what is this?" Then realization dawned and he started to struggle, but it was useless. "No, wait!" he shouted. "Let me go!"

But it was already too late. He stood watching helplessly, unable to follow as the others stepped into the glowing circle and disappeared from view.

"Show me exactly where it happened," Grayson said.

Inspector Tremayne walked forward several yards, then backed up four paces and stood looking at the ground uncertainly. "Right here, I think," he said. "I had just turned the corner there and the blighter coshed me from behind, neat as you please. My head is still ringing like a bloody bell."

"And you saw nothing?"

"Not a blessed thing until I woke up just now and ran into you just down the street. How on earth did you know where to find me?"

"I received an urgent message at my home, delivered by a Chinaman," said Grayson. "He ran off before I had the chance to question him. It was a note directing me to find you here and with it was a ribbon of green cloth, a head scarf such as those worn by the members of the Green Dragon tong. Would you believe it, he even brought a coach for me to use."

"Then the Green Dragon is behind these murders!" said Tremayne.

"No," said Grayson. "Strange as it may seem, it would appear that they are trying to aid us."

"Well, they've got a damn peculiar way of going about it!" Tremayne said, rubbing his head.

"You still have your revolver?"

"Blimey, I didn't even think to check!" He slapped the pocket of his coat. "No, it wasn't taken," he said, pulling it out and checking it to make sure it was loaded.

Grayson pulled out his own revolver, a Webley, and looked around at the fog-shrouded street. "You say both Doyle and Stoker were following the Count as well?"

"All the way from the Lyceum," said Tremayne. "Left their coach when he did and followed him on foot. Damnedest thing, I thought at first they were together and merely traveling by separate coaches, but it soon became clear that they were dogging him just the same as I was."

"Which way did you last see them go?"

"Straight down that street there, into that courtyard."

"A cul-de-sac," said Grayson. "Nothing down there but an old warehouse. Hmmm . . . strange. How long would you say you were unconscious?"

"Damned if I know," Tremayne said. "Why? Does it make a difference?"

"It does if you were struck over the head *after* I was informed of it," Grayson said. "It took me perhaps half an hour to drive here by coach. If we assume that your assailant coshed you, then immediately took a coach straight to my lodgings to inform me of it, and allowing for the time it took me to arrive here, then we would have to be dealing with a time span of something over an hour at the very least and one has to wonder how they knew you would remain unconscious for so long. No, Tremayne, I do not think it could possibly have happened that way. Our friends in the Green Dragon are orchestrating these events in a most singular and peculiar manner, a manner that suggests complex organization."

"I don't understand," Tremayne said.

"Don't you?" said Grayson. "It seems obvious to me. They *knew* that you were following the Count because they were shadowing him themselves. You must have been spotted following him from the Lyceum, whereupon our friends in the Green Dragon sent word to me that you could be found unconscious here, long *before* you were actually assaulted. They planned to take you down right here, on this very spot, and they must have used some means to do it whereby they would know with some certainty how long you would remain unconscious— undoubtedly one of those strange Oriental fighting tricks of theirs—which can only mean that they *knew* Dracula would come here because they had trailed him to this place before. But why did they knock you out and then make certain I would be present on the scene a short while later? Because they wanted us here, but only at a specific time."

Tremayne stared at him, utterly confused. "I can make no sense of that, sir."

"Can't you? There is only one possible answer to it all. The Green Dragon has been deeply involved in these events, possibly since their very beginning, and they have known far more than we have all along."

"What does it all mean?" Tremayne said.

"I wish to God I knew," said Grayson, frustrated. "Almost

from the beginning, I have had the certain feeling that there was a great deal more to this case than met the eye. I continually had a sense that there were other presences involved. First these American scholars, who are clearly not involved in scholarship, but something far more complex and mysterious, to the extent that at least three of them were posing as British subjects—two as newspaper reporters and one right under our very noses in the crime lab! And now we learn that the Green Dragon is involved! *Why?* We have stumbled onto some sort of fantastically complicated plot, Tremayne, but *to what end?"*

"Perhaps we need more men," Tremayne said nervously.

"I wish I had an entire regiment with me," said Grayson, "but I fear there is no time to summon any reinforcements. Clearly, it was intended that I should be here now, in this precise place and at this very moment, but for what reason has yet to become apparent."

He looked around uneasily.

"The streets appear unusually deserted," he said, "even for this desolate part of town and for this late hour. Yet, I have the strongest intuition that we are not alone. There are unseen forces all around us. I can almost *feel* it, as a palpable tension in the very air!"

Tremayne glanced at him fearfully. "What are we to do, then?"

"You have your watch?" said Grayson.

"Right here."

"Good. Wait here for me. And watch yourself. If you hear me blow my whistle, you had best come running. Otherwise, if I have not returned within ten minutes, go for help."

"Where are you going?"

"Where it is apparently intended I should go," said Grayson. "To have a look around inside that warehouse."

13 _____

They ran through the narrow subterranean corridor, stumbling in the dark over soft, furry shapes that squealed in protest and snapped at their shoes, but neither man gave any thought to the rats as they fled. They ran blindly in the dark, their hands held out before them, hearing behind them the howling of the creatures released from their dungeon cells and the crashing of glass and equipment as they destroyed the underground laboratory.

Stoker grunted with pain as he fell forward onto the stairs leading up to the great hall of the castle and Conan Doyle dragged him to his feet, hooking his arm around him.

"Hurry, man! We must flee for our very lives!"

They half ran, half stumbled up the damp stone steps, feeling their way along the slimy wall in the darkness. Behind them, the inhuman screaming sounded terrifyingly closer. At last, they reached the door at the top of the steps and threw it open. Gasping for breath, they lunged through it and then slammed it shut, throwing their weight against it.

"The bolt!" said Doyle. "Quickly, throw the bolt!"

"It's stuck!" said Stoker.

Doyle added his strength to that of Stoker's and the iron bolt shot home.

"That should hold them!" Stoker said.

"I would not wish to stake my life on it," said Doyle,

breathing hard. "I shall not feel safe until we're gone from this accursed place!"

"But how?" said Stoker. "How do we get back home?"

"Steady, old friend," said Doyle. "One problem at a time. We are not safe yet. Quickly, we must find our way out of this place."

They started to run across the great hall when a deep, reverberant voice cried out, *"Stand where you are!"*

Startled, both men stopped in the center of the great hall. Drakov stood above them on the curved stairway, with Jasmine and Moreau.

"Who are you?" said Conan Doyle.

"The question, sir, is who are *you*," said Drakov, "and how did you get here?"

Before they could reply, the door to the stairway leading down to the dungeon splintered and broke and the hall became filled with the howling screams of the creatures from the dungeons. Drakov's head jerked towards them as they streamed out into the great hall and in that moment, Jasmine's foot whipped out and kicked the laser from his hand. They grappled for a moment and then Drakov shoved her away from him. She fell into Moreau and they both tumbled down the stairs.

"STOP!" shouted Drakov.

The creatures all fell silent instantly and stopped where they were, staring up at him fearfully.

"My God, Arthur," Stoker said, as they backed slowly away from the suddenly immobile creatures. "Look how they watch him!"

"With the manner of whipped dogs," said Doyle. "Whoever this man is, he is obviously their master. And our fate is entirely in his hands."

"Dear God, Nikolai," Moreau said, staring at the creatures who cowered before Drakov. "What have you done?"

"I would not advise anyone to move," said Drakov. "Moreau, I will thank you to retrieve my laser and return it to me, otherwise I will have them tear those men to pieces right before your eyes. Remember, I am all that protects you from them now. One word from me and they will attack without mercy."

"Arthur, what do we *do*?" said Stoker.

"For the moment, it appears that we must stand very still and do whatever that man tells us," Conan Doyle said. "If we tried to run now, they would bring us down before we had run twenty feet.''

"The laser, Moreau," said Drakov. "Now!"

Moreau felt Jasmine tense and he took hold of her firmly. "We must do as he says," he told her.

Together, they went over to where the laser pistol had fallen and Moreau bent down to pick it up. Drakov remained where he was, on the long stairway leading down from the upper floor. Doyle and Stoker stood close to one another in the center of the great hall, between Drakov and his creatures.

"Look at them!" said Stoker, his voice scarcely above a whisper. "They cannot possibly be human!"

"No, Stoker," Doyle said, staring at the creatures, "I am afraid they are. Only something terrible has been done to them, something beyond all reason. Their minds have snapped, poor devils, and yet this man controls them with a word. He has them mesmerized. It appears that we have found the guiding intelligence behind these awful crimes and he is without a doubt a madman."

"And who are *you*, sir, to call me mad?" said Drakov. "I repeat my question. What are you doing here and *how* did you get here?"

"My name is Arthur Conan Doyle and this is Mr. Bram Stoker. As to how we came here, we were rendered unconscious and abducted, brought here against our will by Count Dracula. And now you have the advantage of me, sir."

"Indeed I do," said Drakov with a smile. "I admire your composure, Dr. Doyle, but then I would expect no less from the distinguished creator of Sherlock Holmes. My name is Nikolai Drakov. Forgive me for not having recognized you, but I hardly expected to find you here, of all places. I had heard that you were working with Scotland Yard. Allow me to congratulate you for having come so far. And as for you, Mr. Stoker, your presence here is an exquisite irony. Where is Dracula?"

"It was he who released these wretches from their dungeon cells," said Stoker.

"And has doubtless been torn to pieces for his trouble, the sentimental fool," said Drakov. "What a pity. What a criminal waste. He was my prize, my greatest achievement! You should have *seen* him, Moreau!"

Moreau raised the laser pistol, but Conan Doyle shouted,

"Don't do it, man! Don't be a fool! He is all that holds these murderous creatures in check!"

Moreau hesitated.

"Well, Moreau," said Drakov, smiling down at him, "go on, shoot. You wanted to kill me. You will never get another chance. But kill me and you condemn yourself and the others to a decidedly unpleasant death."

With an air of helpless resignation, Moreau started to lower the weapon.

"Wait, Mr. Moreau!" said Doyle, his voice ringing out in the great hall, echoing off the ancient walls. "So long as you possess that weapon, we still have a chance. Kill him, and the creatures will be freed from his will, released to butcher every one of us. But so long as you possess that weapon, you still have the threat of death over him. And that, I assure you, is undoubtedly all that is keeping us alive! We are at a stalemate."

Jasmine ran to Moreau's side and clutched his arm. Moreau raised the laser once again and pointed it at Drakov.

"Very good, Dr. Doyle," said Drakov. "Moreau was always spineless, but I had not counted on you to bolster him up. Between you, the girl, and his newly awakened sense of morality, he is becoming a veritable pillar of masculine vigor."

"Don't let him rattle you, Moreau," said Doyle. "He wants to make you angry. Anger makes people's hands shake, their aim becomes unsteady."

"Time does much the same thing, Dr. Doyle," said Drakov. "How long do you think we can all stand here before his arm starts to become tired?"

"However long it takes for us to resolve this stalemate and leave here safely," Doyle said. "If his arm should become tired, he can pass the pistol to the girl. She seems capable enough."

"As are you, apparently," said Drakov. "What happens now? Even if I were to let you leave, under the threat of being shot, how far do you think you would get before they ran you down? Look at them. They need but one word from me and they will tear you apart. They have been down in the dungeons for a long time. And they are hungry."

"We could take you with us as our hostage," Stoker said.

"I do not think so, Mr. Stoker. I have no intention of moving from this spot. Perhaps you would try taking me by force?"

"Stay away from him!" Moreau said. "He has at least three

times your strength and he is an expert in the art of unarmed combat. You would have no chance against him.''

"At the risk of sounding immodest," Drakov said, "he is quite correct. Your position is untenable, Dr. Doyle. I am not sure how long I can hold them back. They are quite difficult to control, sometimes. Personally, I do not wish either you or Mr. Stoker any harm. I never intended that you should become involved in this."

"Precisely what *did* you intend?" said Doyle. "These poor creatures have obviously been the victims of some sort of brutal and perverse medical experimentation. Leaving aside the despicable act itself and the question of morality, it took the skills and knowledge of a genius to accomplish this. How could a man of such obvious intelligence do such a horrifying thing? What possible reason could there be to justify such cruelty?''

"Cruelty, Dr. Doyle?" said Drakov. "You speak to *me* of cruelty? What do you know of cruelty, you who have enjoyed a life of pampered indolence and taken it for granted, your facility with words netting you sums of money that would feed entire families for months? Your trade is that of obfuscator! You weave pretty little spells to entertain the masses, or at least those privileged enough to have one shilling to spend for a copy of *Lippincott's Monthly Magazine*. Spells meant to distract them from the squalor of reality; stories meant to entertain them so there will be no necessity to think! Lord forbid that they should think, for thinking is dangerous and most of them do not do it very well! Let them think and they will devise new ways to further degrade themselves and despoil the world, a world they look upon as nothing more than property to be used, bartered and developed!

"The beasts of the jungle have more ethics than they do," Drakov continued. "When the tiger makes a kill, it consumes enough to satisfy itself, but it leaves something behind for the hyena and the hyena in turn leaves something for the rodents and the insects, each—by instinct—taking only what is needed to survive, each leaving something for the others. And what does *your* noble species do, Dr. Doyle? They kill for the sake of pleasure and they consume for the sake of greed, leaving nothing behind for anyone! Their instinct is only for rape and domination, their drive towards self-destruction!

"I have had generations in which to study cruelty, Dr. Doyle, to experience it firsthand! I have seen humanity spread out over the world like maggots on a carcass, breeding on it, choking it, all in the name of progress, when their true motives were gluttony for wealth and lust for power and their only progress was the progress of decay! You call what I've done cruelty? No, Dr. Doyle, it is a kindness, the last kindness that anyone can give to a beast in its dying agonies, the kindness of the *coup de grace!*''

''The man is hopelessly insane!'' said Stoker.

''He is worse than insane,'' said Doyle. ''He is a cynic. For a madman, it is at least possible to feel pity. For a cynic, one can feel nothing, because the cynic does not suffer. He does not feel. He has enclosed himself within his armor of disdain; his buckler is contempt and his shield is bitterness. His lance is sarcasm and his sword is pessimism, but they are blunted weapons, dulled by hopelessness. Yes, Mr. Drakov, I do have a facility for words, as you put it, not unlike yourself, yet the words I live by do more than merely entertain. They set forth the principles by which I believe we can avoid those dying agonies you speak of. There are things worth living for, worth dying for, and it is that which separates us from the jungle beasts, that the best of us will live for honor and die for an idea. If I die here today, I die knowing that I have done my best and that even if I ultimately failed, the struggle was worth it even so. I will have died for something. You, on the other hand, seem to have nothing left to live for and your death, when it comes, will have no meaning. In these poor, tortured creatures, you have not recreated humanity stripped of its pretensions, as you might believe. Rather, you have made them living mirrors of yourself. I shall pity them, even as they kill me, but I shall never pity you, because you are not deserving of it.''

''I could not have said it better,'' Forrester said.

Drakov spun around. *''You!''*

Forrester fired.

The plasma blast took Drakov in the chest and blew him back against the wall as he exploded in a ball of fire. The creatures howled and surged forward, but the time commandos opened up with their disruptors on a wide spray pattern, laying down a deadly stream of neutrons. Moreau tackled Doyle and Stoker, knocking them off their feet and shielding them with his body as he yelled at Jasmine to get down. Creatures wreathed in a blue aura of Cherenkov radiation staggered forward for a step or two before their atoms were disintegrated. Forrester added the firepower of his plasma pistol to the disruptors of the commandos and creatures erupted into flames, flames which consumed them before they even had the time to scream. With all of them bunched up the way they were, there was no chance for any of them to escape. It took less than a minute.

"All right, Moreau," said Steiger, aiming his weapon down at him. "Get up and stand away from them."

"No!" said Jasmine, throwing herself in front of Moreau.

Doyle and Stoker slowly got back up to their feet, stunned by what they had just seen.

"You made an agreement, Colonel Steiger," said Lin Tao from behind them. "I will expect you to honor it."

He stood just behind Andre, pinching her with his thumb and forefinger at the base of the skull, exerting tremendous pressure. She stood stiffened, paralyzed, trembling slightly. With his other hand, he plucked the disruptor from her grip, then released her. She collapsed to her knees with a gasp of pain.

"Rest assured, she has not been seriously injured," said Lin Tao, aiming the disruptor at Steiger. "However, I perceive that the extent of injury given by this device cannot be controlled quite so precisely. I have closely observed its use. It does not seem to require much skill. Please lower your weapons."

As they complied, Delaney, who stood closest, launched a kick, but Lin Tao's aim didn't even waver. In one smooth motion, he stepped back and used his free hand to impel more motion to Delaney's foot, so that Delaney was carried off balance by the force of his own kick and straight up into the air. For a fraction of a second, he seemed to hang horizontal in midair, then he crashed to the floor, flat on his back.

Moreau took advantage of the distraction to grab Jasmine and quickly activate his warp disc. Doyle and Stoker stared in disbelief as Moreau and Jasmine disappeared.

"Did you *see* it?" Stoker said. "I cannot believe my eyes! They simply vanished! How . . ." He shook his head, unable to go on.

"I do not know how, old friend," said Doyle, "but wherever that man has gone, he could have escaped in such a manner at any time. It seems he stayed for us. Whoever he was, we owe him our lives."

"We promised not to kill him, Lin Tao," said Forrester, "but we can't let him go free. We're grateful for your help, but you know we'll have to hunt him down. He's a dangerous man."

"Perhaps General, in an earlier life, he was," Lin Tao said, "but he is no longer. He has left behind his work, his world, indeed, everything he knows. I understand how he must feel. I know what it means to become cast adrift in a new world. All he wants is to find a small, insignificant place for himself in it. He may have nothing left of his old world, but in this new one, he has at least found friends and that, I have learned over my long years, is priceless and most valuable. He has suffered more from his own conscience than from any punishment you could inflict upon him. Have you never made a mistake, General, for which you could not forgive yourself?"

Forrester held the old man's gaze for a long moment, then he looked away.

"You will have much to do here," Lin Tao said. "And you have your warp discs to take you back to where you came from. The passage through time which leads here from the warehouse shall be destroyed. And this weapon I have taken shall be delivered to your friends at the Charing Cross Hotel. I give you my word that you have nothing to fear from myself or Phillipe Moreau. I have fulfilled my part of the bargain. All I ask is that you honor yours. I do not think that we shall meet again. Goodbye."

He bowed very slightly, never taking his eyes off them, and backed away towards the room at the far end of the corridor on the upper floor, which contained the mate to the chronoplate back in the warehouse. The moment he was out of sight, Steiger lunged after him.

"*Steiger!*" said Forrester.

"Sir, if we hurry, he won't have time to—"

"As you were."

Steiger looked as if he were about to say something, but he clenched his fists and took a deep breath, let it out slowly and said, "Yes, sir."

Forrester glanced at Finn and Andre.

"You think I'm making a mistake?" he said.

Delaney shrugged. "If you did, we'll probably find out about it sooner or later. I do know we never would've gotten here without their help."

"I don't know if I could ever trust Moreau," said Andre. "But I think I can trust that strange old man."

"He does put that out, doesn't he?" said Forrester.

Steiger shook his head. "If you ask me, I think you're all crazy," he said. He glanced down at Doyle and Stoker, who stood looking up at them like two lost little boys. "And I'd hate to ask them what *they* think."

Andre looked at Doyle and Stoker, then turned back to Forrester. "I think we've got a problem, sir."

Delaney snorted. "So what else is new?"

Grayson smelled the smoke as he came into the courtyard. He blew several sharp blasts on his whistle, then broke into a run as he saw the flames start to lick up from the warehouse roof. In a moment, he saw that putting out the fire would be impossible. By the time the fire department arrived, it would be all that they could do to save the neighboring buildings. And then he froze when he saw what was nailed to the warehouse door.

Smoke streamed from the cracks around the wooden warehouse door, framing the body of Tony Hesketh, which was nailed to the door by an iron railroad spike driven through its chest. The corpse's head lolled grotesquely on its neck, blood ran from the corner of its mouth, open to reveal long, protruding canine teeth.

Tremayne came running up to stand beside him. "Jesus, Mary and Joseph!" he said. And then words failed him.

Sparks shot high into the air, swirling like swarms of fireflies. The building groaned as the flames destroyed it and wood cracked as the roof started to fall in. The door started to burn and as the flames licked at the body, Grayson stood and stared at the dark green ribbon tied around the end of the iron spike.

EPILOGUE

They sat around the table in the dining room of Number 7 Mornington Place. Amy Robbins, soon to be Mrs. Wells, brought in the coffee and biscuits.

"And so that is where we stand, gentlemen," Forrester was saying. "And, of course, Miss Robbins. I have the means to compel you to forget the parts you played in this incredible experience, but there are certain complications associated with the process—think of it as a sort of hypnotism, if you will—risks I would prefer not to incur or even to discuss with you at length. Such a radical . . . 'enforced forgetfulness,' for lack of a simpler way of describing it to you, could have certain unforeseen effects upon the personality. Since you are all highly creative individuals, that is a chance I would not wish to take. However, I hope I have made you see the importance of never revealing what you know to anyone, not under any circumstances."

"I quite understand, General," said Doyle, "and you have my word. Even if we were to tell anyone about what we have seen, who in their right mind would believe it? Although, I must admit, the idea of pitting Holmes against a vampire has a certain charm to it."

"I thought you had grown tired of him?" Stoker said. "Don't tell me you now plan to resurrect him from the dead?" he added with a grin.

Doyle cleared his throat. "Well, who knows?" he said. "Perhaps the old chap never really died. Watson was never the keenest of observers, after all. And even if I were to write such a story, it would necessarily stress the rational over the supernatural, the truth over the fanciful. And as I knew right from the beginning, there was a *rational* answer to this perplexing case. An answer, perhaps, that is impossible for those of us in this time to fully comprehend, but a rational answer nonetheless. We were *not* confronted with the walking dead. There was a scientific explanation."

"Still," said Stoker, "there is something compelling about the notion of a dark, Satanic afterlife, a living hell on earth."

"I will leave such musings to your somewhat overly romantic soul," said Doyle dryly. "For my part, I am content to have seen this nightmare brought to a conclusion. Grayson believes that he has found his killers with the help of the Green Dragon tong and if he is puzzled by the riddle of the mysterious American scholars who have disappeared without a trace, then it will give him something to dwell upon in his retirement someday. The one mystery which he could never solve."

"Unlike Holmes, who solved them all, is that it?" Stoker said.

"Well . . . perhaps that yet remains to be seen. And as for Moreau, well, good luck to him, I say."

"You've been very quiet, Wells," said Stoker. "You've hardly said a word all evening. I don't know about you, but for my part, I do not know if I would object greatly to this process of 'enforced forgetfulness' the general has spoken of. I will have nightmares about this experience for years to come."

"I suspect I will have dreams, as well," said Wells, "but of a rather different sort."

"Will we see any of you again?" said Amy Robbins.

"I trust that you will not misunderstand and take offense, Miss Robbins, if I say that I sincerely hope not?" Forrester said.

She smiled. "No offense taken, General," she said. "Thank you all for all that you have done. Especially you, Miss Craven, and Mr. Neilson, for looking after me."

"It was our pleasure, Miss Robbins," said Neilson.

"And please give my thanks and my regards to that strange, invisible man," she said.

Wells frowned slightly and looked thoughtful.

"There yet remains one final question to which we do not have an answer," Doyle said. "We know about the poor creatures who were killed back at the castle and we know about their victims who had died, but what of their victims who survived? If they had attacked people and failed to kill them, will they not also develop the same blood-craving disease?"

"We will remain on the alert for any further murders of this nature, Dr. Doyle," said Forrester, "as, I trust, shall you. You could be of invaluable continued service to us in this regard. We will not rest until we have established to our satisfaction that this threat has been eliminated once and for all."

"I will, of course, be glad to help in any way I can," said Doyle. "I will never forget the sight that greeted us when we descended once again into those dungeons. The way those creatures tore several of their own number apart in their frenzy of destruction, it was like a slaughterhouse!"

"Parts of bodies scattered everywhere," said Stoker, "the remains unrecognizable. I cannot help but wonder, how can we be certain that among them were Count Dracula's remains? The idea haunts me. He could be there still, somewhere in those labyrinthine dungeons, still alive and waiting."

They all stared at him uneasily.

"I just cannot help but wonder," Stoker said, "if we have truly seen the last of him."

The bell rang over the door and a sallow, thin-featured, clean-shaven man dressed in a dark tweed overcoat and bowler hat entered the apothecary shop. He smiled at the young woman behind the counter. She was several months pregnant and just beginning to show.

"Good afternoon, sir," Jasmine said.

"Good afternoon, Madame," Grayson said. "I wonder, might I speak with your husband?"

"Certainly, sir," said Jasmine, not thinking that there was anything odd about the man's request. There were many times when gentlemen had problems of a very private nature that they were reluctant to discuss with a woman. "One moment please and I will bring him."

She stepped through the curtains leading to the back rooms and a moment later, a slightly built man with prematurely grey hair came out, wiping his hands on a leather apron. Grayson was surprised to see that he was not an Oriental.

"Yes, sir," said Moreau. "My wife said you wished to see me? How may I assist you?"

Grayson frowned. "Perhaps I have made some sort of mistake," he said. "I was expecting someone else, an older gentleman, a . . . that is, well . . . excuse me, you are the proprietor here?"

"Ah," said Moreau, "you must mean my wife's grandfather, Lin Tao. One moment, I will ask him to come in."

Moreau disappeared behind the curtains and came back a moment later with Lin Tao.

The old man gave him a slight bow. "Good afternoon," he said. "Excuse me, perhaps my memory fails me, but I do not recall that we have met before."

"No, we have never actually met," said Grayson. "But you might say that our paths have crossed on numerous occasions."

He reached into his pocket and took out a length of singed, dark green ribbon. He held it out across the counter to Lin Tao.

"I am Chief Inspector William Grayson of Scotland Yard," he said.

Lin Tao regarded him steadily. "Yes," he said. "I know."

"It took me a very long time to find you," Grayson said, putting the ribbon down on the wooden countertop. "I did not come here in an official capacity. I believe I owe you a great debt of gratitude and I have come to thank you. And also to ask a favor. I have had difficulty sleeping these past few months."

"Perhaps a preparation of tincture of opium and belladonna would be the solution to your problem," Lin Tao said.

Grayson smiled. "No, I do not think so. However, I think the answers to some puzzling questions which have kept me up at night for weeks on end might do the trick."

The two men held each other's gaze for a long time. Then the ghost of a smile appeared on Lin Tao's face and he gave a slight nod.

"In that case, Inspector Grayson, perhaps you would like to join us for tea?"